The Crimson Portrait

A Novel

Jody Shields

W F HOWES LTD

This large print edition published in 2007 by
W F Howes Ltd
Unit 4, Rearsby Business Park, Gaddesby Lane,
Rearsby, Leicester LE7 4YH

1 3 5 7 9 10 8 6 4 2

First published in the United Kingdom in 2007
by Doubleday

A CIP catalogue record for this book is available
from the British Library

ISBN 978 1 40740 204 8

Typeset by Palimpsest Book Production Limited,
Grangemouth, Stirlingshire
Printed and bound in Great Britain
by Antony Rowe Ltd, Chippenham, Wilts.

For Jane Wildgoose

The eye is traitor of the heart.
—Thomas Wyatt (1503–1543)

CHAPTER 1

A man in uniform sat across from her. It was a hot afternoon, and the sunlight in the drawing room turned the metal buckle at his waist into a sharp bright square and made the gold buttons on his jacket perfect as coins. A stiff collar surrounded his soft neck. His face was indistinct, unaccustomed to giving orders. She guessed he had been called into the military from a minor profession in the city.

'It will be a great adjustment to have the men occupy your house, ma'am.'

'Yes, it will be strange.' She attempted a smile.

'Had you thought of relocating for the duration of the war? Staying with family?'

'I have no other family. My late husband arranged for the hospital to be set up here before he enlisted. I encouraged his plan. I've never considered leaving. It's my duty to stay.'

'You'll find the patients are a quiet group.'

'I'm certain they will be.' Her dress was thin, loose over her body, only its dark color gave it weight. She leaned forward. 'Tell me, did you give the order to remove the mirrors from the house?'

'No. The head surgeon, Dr McCleary, gave the orders. Best to have precious things out of harm's way when the patients arrive.'

'Yes. There has been enough destruction.'

The major's hands opened, a gesture of apology. 'We'll leave what we can in place. The lighting fixtures. Some of the draperies. By the way, your chandelier is quite remarkable.'

They simultaneously looked up at the ceiling. The chandelier was immense and unlit, its prisms dulled by fine dust, as if a flood of dirty water had risen through the room. When her husband was alive, two servants'-hall boys had tended the chandeliers, slowly lowering the tinkling, transparent tiers on ropes once a month to be cleaned with feather brushes.

The major's lips moved, but the young woman couldn't hear him, as if he spoke from a great distance. He had come to cast a spell over the house. A spell of urgent purpose, the soldiers' mission to spread disruption. She imagined men's shadows moving through the rooms, swift, black, gigantic, altering each space with the brutality of an eclipse. Others would follow and together they would rob the library of its stillness, strip the dining room of pleasure, disturb the cold core of the well and the lakes. It was 1915, the first spring since the war started, and her home was being transformed into a military hospital.

She sensed the major had asked a question and

was waiting for an answer. Yes. She nodded. Yes. Yes.

He gently coughed to break the silence.

'The weather. Unusual for this time of year.'

'It's a pity, but the rooms may become quite warm when they are fully occupied by soldiers. They weren't designed for such a purpose.' She stood up, forcing him to follow. 'I will have someone show you out.'

'I'll find my way. Thank you, ma'am.'

From the library window she watched the stout figure in a brown uniform walk straight down the drive without looking at the landscape or the house. She realized that he had no need to observe his surroundings, since everything was already in his possession. The estate had been conquered. Was he carrying a weapon? Had she seen the curved handle of a pistol? A sword?

She opened the door to the powder room. There was a small mirror on the wall, and as she adjusted its angle, her reflected hand seemed disconnected from her body. She smudged her initial on the mirror's dusty surface, C for Catherine. No last name. She was a widow. She stepped aside and her image slipped out of the mirror cleanly, as if she'd passed through water. An odorless, bodiless thing.

The mirrors were the lakes in the landscape of this house, she thought. Somehow they were linked to one another, as all glass and water were related. The immense mirror in the ballroom, a triptych positioned at the heart of the house, was a great pool, a place of transfer, and the other mirrors magically flowed into it, tributaries of silver.

When the last mirror was taken down, it would mark a turning point in the fortunes of the house, a darkening of the places formerly stung by light.

Official papers from the military listed the rooms that would be requisitioned to accommodate the wounded soldiers and the hospital staff. All the reflective objects in the public spaces were to be put in storage.

The military would take away the mirrors: perhaps they would also demand clocks, watches, other witnesses and timekeepers. Sundials. Calendars. Everyone was concerned with time. How slowly it passed. How long it would be until the war was over. The names of the dead wound through the *Times* like an immeasurable gray ribbon, filling page after page in small type. How could faith work against this?

Followed by the elderly head gardener and two silent boys, Catherine quickly walked through the Long Gallery into the Pink Drawing Room, stopping before a mirror in a lacquered chinoiserie frame. Held in the unforgiving slant of its rectangular surface, they appeared ill at ease, their faces dilated, her somber crepe dress and the servants' rough work clothing clumsily shrouding their thickened bodies.

'Take this mirror down first.' Catherine struggled to compress her bitter feeling of loss, afraid that the mirror would exaggerate her expression.

'As you wish, ma'am.'

The mirrors in the next room had even greater age, set in cracked gilt frames, darkened with a lichen-like black growth on their back sides, evidence of time's poisonous breath. At the corners of the frames hung tiny golden bells that remained silent, poised to delicately protest their descent from the wall.

'Remove everything in the room that has a shine or reflection. The clock, the silver bowl, and the vases on the mantel.' A moment later she said, 'No. Leave the bowl there. Let it tarnish. But take this away too.' She pointed to the mirror set in the door of a cabinet and left them to work.

The three servants cleared the mantelpiece, emptied the bureau, secretaire, and kneehole desk. A letter opener, a picture frame, and a compass plated with bright silver were discovered inside a desk compartment lined with scratched green leather. The older boy wrapped them in a flannel cloth and laid them in a box. He picked up a paperweight, a smooth dome of colored glass irresistible as candy. The gardener wasn't accustomed to working in the house, and his voice was too loud as he told the boy to put the thing down and fetch a ladder.

The boy raced across the bare wood floor, his footsteps shaking the chandelier, jarring its prisms into quivering motion, creating sharp-angled patterns that swept across the walls and ceiling around them, transforming the room into a giant kaleidoscope.

Returning with the ladder, he set it in a timorous balance against the wall. The smaller mirrors were slowly lifted free from the walls, and the boys carried them to the attic one at a time, where they were laid in rows on the floor.

The gardener waited, casting a nervous eye over the huge central mirror hanging in the Pink Drawing Room. When the boys returned, he made them study the mirror on the wall for a full three minutes to familiarize themselves with its weight and fragility.

The mirror was more than six feet long and it wobbled and flashed in their hands, as if with its removal from the wall a spell had been broken and it might suddenly become less reliably physical and flow out over the frame. The boys whispered to each other, soft speech a charm against dropping it.

Bundled in blankets, the mirror was carried horizontally, the boys as careful as pallbearers maneuvering it through the enormous house, up the front staircase, then to a narrower flight of stairs. Under their sweating hands the blanket around the mirror released a pronounced odor of raw wool.

They reached the attic, and without setting down the unwieldy burden, one of them kicked the attic door. It swung violently open, and they stopped, dazzled by the reflection from the mirrors covering the floor. As they entered the room, a hot line of sunlight leaked through a window, magnifying the mirrors into brilliance so the floor appeared to be flooded with silver water, and they marveled like explorers encountering a strange, unexpected sea.

Early in the eighteenth century, the owner of the estate had paced the grounds and ordered a number of small ornamental pavilions, follies, and grottos built in the most picturesque locations. Seemingly made for temporary pleasure, some of the structures were as fragile as theatrical scenery, fabricated from porous rock, plaster, limestone, and ancient bricks scavenged from ruins on the property. The walls and ceilings glittered with stalactites, crystal spars, molten glass, or were roughly patterned with fossils, shells, pebbles. The sawed leg bones of oxen had been painstakingly set into one still-intact floor.

The structures had long been undefended against time, weather, the purposeful stones of vandals, and since the gardening staff had volunteered for military service, they had been untended for two seasons. Stone walls and glass had cracked; streams had clouded with silt. The Chinese temple was near collapse; the extravagant gilt on the carved, finned fish at the top of its pointed roof had faded to coarse scales. Inside, the painted figures on the walls were

7

clothed in shabby fragments of color that had once been lavish Oriental dress. A temple dedicated to an unknown nymph had lost its faux limestone base, and a mock Gothic tower had a broken parapet.

One of the smaller follies had been captured by nets of vines, and the walls of another were half submerged by the lake. Entire buildings and statuaries had been stitched over by threads of grass and weeds, lost to memory. Recently, Catherine had been startled by a sudden gurgle of water, a captive noise below her feet as she stood on a hidden drain near the vinery.

The under-butler had pointed out the icehouse to Catherine, a sandstone vault surmounting a conical brick well nearly twenty-three feet deep. His father had been born on the estate and passed on the living knowledge of a time when this well was filled with ice layered with salt and straw to keep it frozen through the summer months. Now it was empty and echoing, and the spidery steps that clung to its sides were so steeply angled that they induced vertigo in the few who had risked a descent.

Months after her husband's death, Catherine had met a friend at the Carlton Hotel and announced she intended to raze all the ornamental buildings on the estate. 'The buildings have no purpose. There is no question that since the war, I have simply lost tolerance for damaged things. I only want to keep what's worth keeping.'

'Oh, leave them be. It's not as if you need the land,' her friend had answered, bored with the discussion.

But Catherine had been insistent. 'I want to pull down the buildings and use the materials for something else.' She had longed to sweep everything away. She waited for the flat landscape of winter, the oblivion of snow, to erase her choices. Making choices wearied her.

It became Catherine's habit to listen, convinced she heard the sound of destruction, the wrenching of brick and stone as the ornamental buildings were forced from shape, exposing bare earth underneath to light for the first time in one hundred and forty-nine years.

At a shattering noise, crisp as china breaking, Catherine looked up from the letter she was writing. Curious, she put down her fountain pen and left the house. Walking past the lake, she composed a picture of the mirrors as they had been taken down in the house behind her, their brilliant, sharp-angled reflections sweeping across the rooms, passing over silk draperies and painted surfaces without a mark, altering nothing with the cold blankness of their light.

The entrance to the grotto was hidden by marsh grass, its door a rounded opening between rough stones. Inside, her eyes adjusted to the taper of light created by a hole in the roof, and gradually the dimness lifted, revealing an intricate pattern on the walls, thousands and thousands of shells, a surface softly lustrous as a fruit stripped of its skin and fragile as porcelain. Catherine stepped forward, her boot blindly crushing the fallen shells into powder.

I intend to join my regiment in two weeks' time,' Catherine's husband had told her in the Pink Drawing Room. Catherine remembered that as Charles had spoken, a maid approached and the silver tray in the girl's hands reflected a zigzag of glare into her eyes. Now she understood it had been a warning that a bullet or the flash of an explosion in a field would take his life, destroy their future.

Charles had died and she remained in the huge house, surrounded by a constellation of objects collected by generations of his family. Catherine had also been born into a house filled with valuables and was conscious of their inviolability, like a walking stick that was always the correct length for the reach of the arm. When she married Charles, one set of objects had replaced another. Wood. Stone. Iron. Clay. Gold.

Charles's possessions had been left untouched in his dressing room adjoining the master bedroom, and only two open trunks betrayed his absence. Nearly a year ago, the trunks had been packed according to his list sent from the front: inflatable air cushion, luminous compass, chocolate bars, twill breeches from Sandon, tobacco, tinned paté, scarves, gloves, a heavy wool blanket, and a copy of *The Oxford Book of English Verse*. Handkerchiefs doused with Catherine's perfume, Jicky, were tucked into the corners of the trunks.

Catherine had imagined him opening a trunk in his tent and, genie-like, the familiar scent of lemon, orris, and bergamot rising, eliminating the elastic distance between them. The news that Charles had been killed on the battlefield arrived before the trunks were shipped.

During her earliest stage of mourning, Catherine was pinched with the desire for destruction and had furiously circled the rooms, searching for evidence of tarnish, rotted wood, cracked plaster. The rich colors of the upholstery, draperies, and carpets had faded as if they had ripened backward. Charles's death had revealed the truth of the house's fragility.

This house contained many beautiful objects, but she wanted only what Charles had touched. A shagreen box that held his stationery. His fountain pen, his paperweight, the silver bibelots on his desk. A piece of sea glass discovered in a trunk. An umbrella with a mahogany handle his fingers had gripped. The sound of a cup against a saucer when he had set it down. The span his eyes had traveled to a clock. The suspense of waiting as his hand reached to caress her.

In the wardrobe, Charles's jackets retained the shape of his body, fit twelve times by his exacting cutter at Poole & Co. on Savile Row, so that the lapels unfurled over his clavicle, the shoulder pads defined a handsome curve, the pockets slanted at the angles his hands would enter.

Catherine found a camphor-wood box filled with his gloves and pulled one over her own hand, certain that the soft leather interior held an impression of his fingers, the lines on his palm, the thick horizontal welt of his wedding ring. She knew his skin intimately. Once, after a quarrel, Charles had gently placed his hand on her bare neck, his touch as familiar as stone. When they were first married, she had opened her eyes to find him studying her face. She had slipped from the bed, pressed her hand against the freezing windowpane – snow swirled wildly outside – and then laid her cold palm against his cheek. Her gesture had amused him, but she had made her mark. He was hers.

She now tried to restore this encounter, lengthen it, fasten it to words, to their conversation. What had they said to each other? What was his expression as their eyes met? Her memory wouldn't expand. It evaporated, elusive as a taste or scent, trackless as a wave. What she wanted was to be surprised by him again.

She craved the image of her husband. Each day she selected a room in the house and forced her memory to place Charles there, reclaiming him, little by little, from the past. But these glimpses could be created only indirectly. If she studied a chair in the library he appeared at the fireplace.

Or if her eyes followed a pattern in the carpet, she could visualize him at the window. He couldn't escape her, but she was unable to command him to move, cross the room, walk through the door. He was always a static figure. Why should this be so? She had believed memory was constant in its appearance, as a fire was always hot.

Surely she could be granted one wish, just his shadow, a flat and valueless thing. The outline of a man that blocked the sun, without breath, color, dimension. Like death filling a body. She searched her memory for Charles's face but was granted only details – his profile, his lips, the lines at the side of his mouth, the familiar lengthy scar on his hand – as if viewing a portrait from different angles. Perhaps these fragmentary images were related to his wounds.

She had squandered the time she had been granted to study him. Now she would exchange the hours she'd spent before a mirror, her own chronicle of vanity, for a single glance at him. Her thoughts fused into a circle of regret. *If only I had . . . I wish I had . . . If you were yet . . . Even though you are . . .* If only she had been more observant.

Two months after Charles's death was reported, she had received a photograph of him standing with several other soldiers before a wall of sandbags. The image had been badly developed, or the light on the battlefield had harshly affected the men, because their eyes had faded into halos and their faces were drained and ghostly, too weak to hold the film's sensitivity. Or perhaps the photographer had captured them as they were in the process of dissolving, dying. Metamorphosis. It was magical that Charles hadn't returned from war. Death was an envelope, a letter, words. Not a body.

Catherine lost the grace of sleep. A widow's burden, to be awake. In darkness, she had no edges, she contained a stain, a vapor that would dissolve her from inside. Charles had been the weight that kept her from floating away.

Catherine's father had forbidden his daughter the use of his library, although its books were never read and haphazardly organized, having been inherited from his own father. When she was barely sixteen and had outgrown lessons with her governess, her father had insisted the elderly woman remain in residence at their home, his strategy to discourage Catherine from attending college, Newnham or Somerville, as some families in society had permitted their daughters. The governess stayed on, a hostile, fretting reminder of her pupil's abbreviated education. Catherine was launched into society, too young to be regretful.

During the season she was presented at court, Catherine had worn dresses by Lucille and Redfern, a tiara and shoe buckles set with diamonds. She enjoyed the sleight of courtship

14

with several suitors, the speculation, the whispered confidences, the careful cursive of her misspelled entries scrawled in a journal bound in mauve silk, later burned.

As a farewell to summer, the Chetwodes had held a ball at Market Drayton on the last day of August. Mrs Chetwode – Maudie – was Catherine's dearest friend. The dancing ended at sunrise, when Catherine and Maudie mischievously tossed garlands of wilted flowers at guests from a balcony and fled the house, laughing. Outside, they discovered the deserted tennis court. Without exchanging a word, they picked up two rackets and daringly played a fast game, the diaphanous flounces of their ball gowns rippling around their ankles.

Years later, Charles confessed he'd secretly watched the young women play and immediately determined to marry Catherine. He had suddenly appeared on the tennis court, a mysterious man in an evening coat, holding an errant chalk white ball as if tempting her with a forbidden fruit.

Charles had wooed Catherine, sending half a dozen telegrams every day and armloads of Madonna lilies. They were a popular married couple, seldom separated, invited everywhere. There were hunt balls, teas, card games, dinners followed by charades, weekend parties at Lansdowne, Bridgewater, and Londonderry House. Catherine relied entirely on Charles to interpret their social life. By the second year of their marriage, neither of them had close living relations.

What had Charles said on the tennis court, the first day of September years ago? What was the first sentence he had written to her? How many telegrams had he sent?

In the first month of the war, Maudie's husband had been fatally injured, and Catherine was unable to comfort her. She'd grown distant from her friend, and Charles securely ruled the place Maudie had occupied. Now she bitterly regretted Maudie's absence.

Catherine's grandfather had died when she was a child, and though she had attended the funeral, she had no memory of the service. She did remember watching her widowed grandmother while she cut roses in the garden of her house a few months later. 'The sound of your grandfather's voice has faded for me,' the elderly woman had said. 'I command his voice to return, but my ear has no memory. No one will ever speak my name as he did.'

When she had seen the dismay on Catherine's childish face, she quickly added that it wasn't important. Not at all. Then Catherine's frail grandmother had looked away, the pruning shears forgotten in her hand, as the silver arrows of her tears plunged into the grass at her feet.

Two stable boys carried the chairs, tables, and the writing desk from the library, freeing the carpet from the pointed legs that had pinned it to the floor. The boys stripped the shelves, loosely wrapping the books in sheets, newspapers, lengths of burlap and linen found in one of the storage rooms. Although they worked very slowly, Catherine didn't criticize but studied them from the doorway. She was in no hurry to follow the major's orders.

She was at the window as the boys stacked the books in wheelbarrows and pushed them to the stable, each jolt sliding the books out of line. In the afternoon, the boys grew careless, and books fell from the wheelbarrow, splitting their bindings, losing their pages. The younger boy looked up to see whether she'd noticed the papers blowing over the lawn. Catherine dropped the curtain back over the window, couldn't be bothered to reprimand them.

Later, Catherine stood in the library and closed her eyes, imagining that nothing had changed, since the scent of the books – ancient paper and leather – still lingered, as the odor of honey is inseparable from its comb. She blinked. Light from the tall windows slanted across the rows of empty shelves, transforming the room into an immense hive. She had a brief sense of peace, a humming contentment.

In the weeks since Catherine had announced the arrival of the doctors and hospital support staff was imminent, the servants had quietly rebelled. Catherine noticed that they were neglecting their work. No one wound the clocks.

Silver was unpolished, the lamps unlit. The map of conduct that overlaid the house was torn. One morning, Catherine and the youngest housemaid approached each other in the corridor, and she saw that the girl's cap was crooked. The housemaid had boldly met her stare, and they passed each other without speaking. Catherine had walked five paces before she allowed herself to recognize the girl's insolence.

The household staff dwindled as the coachman, butler, footmen, and grooms, the odd men, hall boys, steward's-room and servants'-hall boys enlisted in a local battalion. All the able-bodied men. Although Catherine barely knew their names, she ceremoniously gave each man a watch in the music room and shook his hand. Godspeed.

Most of the maids went to work in a munitions factory, where wages were higher and their reddened hands would gradually acquire a yellow tint from the poisonous TNT.

The four remaining housemaids nestled the china with straw in wooden barrels and packed smaller items from desks, cupboards, and armoires into boxes and trunks. As a farewell gift, the women received new lisle stockings and one of Catherine's Callot Soeurs hats from last season.

Only the youngest servant boy and the elderly gardener stayed to attend Catherine and the estate.

★　　★　　★

On the afternoon of a beautiful day, strangers in uniform entered the house, walked the corridors, gazed at the paintings, commanded the views from the windows. When Catherine encountered these strangers, she acknowledged them with a curt nod, her eyes registering surprise, as if she were unaware that the house was occupied. She fled to her suite of rooms on the third floor.

With the butler and the first footman gone to war, the gardener had taken it upon himself to act as *majordomo*, and Catherine asked him to identify the newcomers. He testily replied that they hadn't properly introduced themselves. In his worn jacket, his gnarled hand guarding the doorknob, the gardener was helpless against these efficient invaders. The men in uniform mockingly called him 'the shepherd' and brushed him aside.

Outside, there was an atmosphere of feverish preparation as carriages, wagonettes, broughams, motorcars, and half a dozen other unfamiliar vehicles lined the back entrance road, their errant wheels immediately tearing up the lawn. Without anyone requesting permission, huge packing crates and boxes were stacked into a shoulder-high wedge along the kitchen corridor. The cellar was completely filled with supplies. Signs were affixed to interior walls and posts outside, providing directions to unfamiliar destinations: *emergency, dry store, orderly station, stockroom, wards, receiving hall*. A larger sign, *Military Hospital*, was secured over the scrolling black iron gate at the entrance to the estate.

Catherine's attention was caught by a distinguished older man who gently, tirelessly conducted this campaign. His name – Dr McCleary – was called from early in the morning until lights-out, but the doctor seldom raised his voice. He apparently had little regard for military protocol, since he casually layered a tweed jacket over his medical garb.

The jagged hours passed, broken, snared by lines on the face of the clock. Catherine sullenly watched the workmen as they moved boxes, trod the gravel drive, smoked, talked – utterly commonplace activities that occupied a familiar realm and now excluded her. Everything was stubbornly set against her wishes.

Each morning required greater effort for her to rise from bed, sit in a chair. Each mouthful of food was as tasteless as paper. This gave her a bitter satisfaction as the true nature of another pleasure was revealed. The burden of photographs on the dresser, the ormolu clock and porcelain figures on the mantelpiece, a feathered hat on its stand, were flimsy reminders of her place in the world.

She numbly picked up her clothes in the order they had been dropped the previous evening. She struggled to dress herself, the tiny pearl buttons on the blouse awkward as pebbles, the jacket and riding trousers cumbersome, unyielding. A maid's clever fingers had always fastened hooks and eyes, tightened the laces of her clothing, retrieved the dresses abandoned on the floor, collapsed circles of silk.

Catherine emptied her jewel casket, winding lavalieres and pearl necklaces around her throat, hiding them under a high collar. Platinum and gold stickpins were secured inside her lapel, and brooches from Cartier and a hair ornament in the shape of a butterfly weighed the pockets. Rings on every finger. If she must flee, these valuables were safe on her body. She wore a dead man's jacket for luck. It had belonged to her husband.

She became a secret nomad in the house. At night, she slipped down one of the three servants' staircases, confident she would encounter no one, as they were too curved and narrow for the hospital staff. She memorized the treacherous labyrinth of sound, the scrape of board against board on the steps and uneven floors, avoiding spaces with the presence of murmuring voices and cigarette smoke.

Anchored only by memory, Catherine drifted quickly through the rooms, finding that objects and furniture had been relocated without regard for their value or usefulness. A fine satinwood sideboard had been moved to the medical-supply room and covered with rolled towels. A secretaire from the library had lost its top and now held transparent jars of sterile cotton wool. In the east wing, a heavy crystal bowl on a mantelpiece contained flowers a nurse had surreptitiously picked in the greenhouse. In the top-floor nursery, a valuable portrait had been shoved behind a daybed.

Metal supply cabinets with glass doors lined the corridors, and nurse stations were set up outside the dining room and ballroom. Glazed white linen screens hid the fine handiwork on the walls, the grissailles, carved detailing, and plasterwork. The grand piano remained in the Blue Drawing Room, its silhouette enlarged by a clumsy canvas cover. The gramophone had been carried to Catherine's room.

Linoleum or coarse runners covered the floors, leaving only shining strips of polished wood along the sides. An Aubusson carpet padded the space under the night wardmaster's desk in the vestibule, the threads of its pattern already distorted by his boots. A mantelpiece carved by Gibbons had been painted over in an attempt to sanitize the room with whitewash.

In the morning room, orderlies had propped ladders next to the windows, released the draperies from their rods, and the stiff fabric slowly crumpled into sharp-angled, mountainous folds surrounded by storms of dust. Without draperies, the bare rooms became boxes – painted, gilded, or polished – stacked one on top of another, with stairs mounted between them.

Iron beds were moved into the largest rooms on the ground floor, and there – bored and immobilized – the patients would study the ovolo molding and wreaths on the ceiling, marred by a blurry bloom of rust, as hidden nails slowly oxidized beneath the stucco.

At night, when the warm air propelled the noise, the determined pulse of hammering sounded from deep in the house. There were odors of sawed wood, of acrid paint. Thin black wires harnessed the house to telephone poles, installed by men who squinted into telescopic devices and then pushed a huge roll of wire like an outsized toy over the fields.

Catherine left no trace of her passage through the rooms, touching none of the few familiar objects. Only her eye was entitled to possession. She imagined that the furniture and objects had been turned out of the house into water, a stream. Immersed, everything was of equal value. All that mattered was whether these things would break, sink, or float in the water. Or save a life.

There was a rumble in the distance. Catherine angled her chair near the window as the headlights of the first vehicle jerked down the drive, revealing its bumpy relief and the narrow ribbons of grass along its sides. Several ambulances stopped under the stark light of flares, and a strange ceremony commenced as men quickly surrounded them, swung open the back doors, and clambered inside. The stretchers – each burdened with a single body – were handled so swiftly they seemed to levitate horizontally from the ambulances and vanish into the house, exactly like a magician's act. Less severely injured men moved at a measured pace up the steps, heedless as kings to the frantic activity around them.

A harsh ringing startled Catherine, and the thread of noise pulled her to the telephone. The official's words were rapid, soothing. 'I saw the light in your room,' he said. 'The first wounded soldiers have arrived from the battlefield. I hope you weren't disturbed.'

'There is no need to notify me. The house is yours.' The receiver loudly struck the telephone as she slammed it into place.

She woke in a chair turned away from the window with no memory of the previous evening. Outside, the lawn was scattered with objects – crumpled jackets and shirts, a single boot, towels, papers, rags, and a knapsack – discarded as if unnecessary for the next stage of a journey. Who had left these worthless things?

Catherine listed the occupiers of her house:

Nurses. White peaked caps with string ties. Dark capes. Nurses have two stripes on their blouse cuffs.

V.A.D. Volunteer Aid Detachment women. Mauve-and-white pinstripe dresses. Starched collars, and cuffs. Flat black shoes and black stockings. White bib aprons. Caps pinned to heads.

Doctors. Operating jackets. Rubber gloves.

Patients. Loose blue suits. Red neckties. Bathrobes worn outdoors.

Officers. Long jackets. Trouser legs tucked into boots. Suits color of sand. Gold buttons.

Orderlies. Tunics with four pockets, five buttons. Caps with badges.

After the arrival of the wounded soldiers, night separated itself from day by sounds that ran through the rooms like water, passing doors, windows, walls, a thick tide that carried footsteps, rattling trolleys, the dry click of instruments discarded in metal pans, drawers closing, the whispers of the nurses.

The clock in the second-floor corridor had been allowed to remain in place. Catherine could hear its sonorous chimes over the constant vibration throughout the house, orchestrating a memory of this place when she had been happy, a married woman. She switched on the light and picked up a book. It was a clumsy object in her hand, papers sewn together, sentences organized into gray shapes on the page, indecipherable, as if fused.

As Catherine watched from her window, the landscape told the hour. At first horizontal, the rising sun struck the greenhouse, appearing to transform it into a solid shape, silver replacing its glass. She was certain of what followed as the light gracefully rose, extending its familiar pattern across the distant fields, transforming a stream into a white line connected to the circle of a pool.

The day was mild, and a number of patients, some in wheelchairs or beds, were steered through the double doors, an armada launched upon the lawn. Other patients made halting progress on crutches to chairs arranged on the grass, where the nurses, distinct in enormous starched caps, stiff white wings around their heads, swooped over them. One woman must have recently returned from the front, since a large Red Cross insignia was sewn on her apron.

There was a space of silence between Catherine in her room and the patients below, mute men in identical robes or hospital suits of blue, their bandages a tie that bound them together. She watched them for hours, the scene so strangely unreal that only the pressure of her hands gripping the windowsill convinced her that this vision wasn't unwinding before her in a dream.

A young nurse in a dark cape leaned close to listen to a man in a wheelchair, her hand on his shoulder. She threw back her head, laughing at his comment, and he turned to her, his body radiating joy from her reaction. Catherine looked away, stricken by their intimacy. No one in the house knew Catherine well enough to please her. Or cared to please her. But wasn't it better to be alone than to be joined by illness to a stranger, the most unequal relationship? The wounded men who occupied her home were proof of the way luck was distributed. Their misfortune would spread to everyone around them, the rooms they lived in, the objects they touched. The estate was quarantined, unholy, accursed, its purpose to shield the rest of the world from their ruined bodies.

This must be interrupted.

She started up the gramophone, leaning on the windowsill as music from *The Mikado* arranged its gaiety around her, conducting her grief into waves.

The wind came up, and as if on cue, the nurses clutched their unwieldy caps and moved in the same direction, their long skirts tangling wildly around their legs. It suddenly began to rain, and they moved slowly toward the house, the men stoically lowering their heads or holding a hand over their faces to protect their white bandages, fragile as sugar. The men who were immobilized waited patiently, rain streaming over their bodies, until nurses ran back with armloads of blankets to cover their heads and guide them to their rooms. It rained the rest of the day, then darkness hardened the vast lawn into black stone carved by the hieroglyphic of the drive, a pale and curved line.

After midnight, there was shouting directly below Catherine's window, and she leaned out to watch two men hop and spin, arms extended and faces upturned, gleeful at the downpour. The light from a lower window struck the rain into brilliance, so the men appeared to be held upright by thousands of moving strings.

She slept. Suddenly she was jarred awake, aware that the mirrors in the attic were absorbing light from the landscape – the minute reflections of water on grass and leaves, puddles, the faint gleam of gray gravel in the drive – and redirecting it as a beacon for enemy aircraft. Their bombs would find their target, would shatter the mirrors in the attic, sending shards of glass – certain as daggers – straight to her heart.

Under the tight bedsheets, her legs were pinned in a ballet dancer's position, making her helpless. Her legs were stilts. The immense glittering weight of the mirrors pressed down on her. Terrified, she waited, unable to move, listening for the droning of the aircraft she was certain would come.

CHAPTER 2

D r McCleary had ceremoniously placed the lid on an empty sterilizing jar, and this delicate click had signaled the end of forty-one years as a practicing surgeon. He had driven to Bruisyard in east Suffolk and settled in a ramshackle country house, formerly a nunnery of the Order of Saint Clare. He fished, organized his classics library, spoiled his dogs. Although he had never married, the solitude of retirement didn't suit him. Fifteen months later, the war found him.

He had packed scores of Hagedorn's half- and full-curved needles and holders, rongeurs, wireworking pliers, sets of mouth retractors, extracting forceps and knives, an assortment of hemostats, a tracheotomy kit, and a sharpening stone of Carborundum into his medical bag and joined Dr Cole, the chief surgeon of the Maxillofacial Department at King George Hospital. There, colleagues had affectionately called McCleary 'the grand old man,' acknowledging his age and formal character. 'Don't go showing off or they'll send you to the front,' the youngest resident had teased.

'We can't do without you, Doctor.' It was September, and everyone was confident the war would be over in a few months. Surely by Christmas.

Since injuries to the face were uncommon during peacetime, surgeons were woefully unprepared for the severity of the wounds caused by bombs and shell fragments. McCleary had limited surgical experience with facial injuries, but what knowledge he possessed was enough to make him a specialist.

At a medical conference held at the hospital the week after his arrival, there had been no speaker on jaw grafts because none of the surgeons had ever performed the procedure. In fact, the majority of current papers on facial surgery had been published in foreign journals.

As required by his early medical training, McCleary had memorized the skin's topography as an aid to diagnosis. The skin was rich with infoldings, outfoldings, multiple layers, stoppered orifices (the ear), and open orifices (the nose). The slightest invaginations were foveas, a term applying to dimples and the tongue, its macroscopically pitted surface dense with foveas identified as 'follicular crypts.' Skin made invaginated folds around a flexed limb; smaller creases formed around these folds; wrinkles and macroscopic lines, including the whorls and ridges on the fingers and palms, extended their nearly invisible pattern over the entire body, binding it with a pattern, the finest of skeins. The largest folds of skin outside the body were mostly sexual: the penis, prepuce, scrotum, labia, and clitoris.

However, McCleary had known nothing about the development of facial surgery, and the scant and haphazard information in the Royal College of Physicians library astonished him. There was little evidence of systematic progress in the history of maxillofacial surgery, which bore out Hippocrates' observation that 'war is the only proper school of surgeons.' McCleary had realized that he had the peculiar privilege of witnessing the establishment of a corpus of knowledge, as surgeons were now compelled to consult forgotten or rejected documents to aid the wounded.

During his weeks of research, McCleary discovered that the first book about skin, *De Morbis Cutaneis*, appeared in 1572, and it was another two hundred years before the second book on the subject was published. During much of this time, it was strictly taboo to cut or violate the surface of the body for anatomical dissection.

The words used to describe skin were dense, unexpectedly multifarious. In Greek, *derma* for 'hide' was familiar, and it was only one of the many subtle aspects of skin the language defined. There were also multiple words in Latin, including *cutis* for living skin and *pellis* for skin that was sloughed, dead. *Horror* was traced to the *horrilation*, or 'lifting,' of the skin.

Plato believed skin was 'a canopy of flesh,' merely 'felting' laid over the interior organs as protection.

31

Aristotle claimed skin had been formed by 'drying of flesh, like the scum upon boiled substances.' These dismissive attitudes – skin as crust, a curdled material, congealed fluid, a temporary substance, a jelly-like covering – lasted for centuries. By the eighteenth century, skin was finally recognized as a permeable membrane, a threshold for exchange of fluids and air with the exterior world.

Curiously, the actual color of skin was rarely described, but McCleary had found a beautiful citation in the *Mishneh Torah*, a fourteen-volume work by Moses Maimonides dating from the twelfth century. Skin could have degrees of whiteness, like 'snow in wine' or 'blood in milk.' It could be white as lime or 'the skin in an egg.' The Hebrew words for 'light' and 'skin' were closely related. One text stated that skin affected by leprosy had thirty-six distinct colors; another author claimed seventy-two. There were limited choices for the appearance of damaged skin; scars were 'livid' or 'angry.'

Early accounts of facial surgery were as fantastical as mythological tales. In India, around the sixth century BC, the renowned Hindu surgeon Susruta wrote the first treatise on facial surgery, *Salya-tantra*, which instructed how to transplant skin, suture muscle, tie veins, and monitor a patient's dreams for healing, finally translated into English in 1794. Many of Susruta's patients were adulterers who had been punished by amputation of their nose. McCleary had discovered a

32

passage he admired from Susruta's work and copied it into his commonplace book: 'Those diseases which medicine does not cure, the knife cures; those which iron cannot cure, fire cures; and those which fire cannot cure, are to be reckoned wholly incurable.'

In the ancient world, it was believed to be impossible to graft skin between individuals, as there was a 'mystic sympathy' between skin and its owner. McCleary had diligently tracked down fragmented accounts, written hundreds of years ago, of a nose grafted from a slave onto a wealthy man. The donor nose had failed along with its original human source.

In the early fifteenth century, the Branca family of Sicily were renowned for their secret facial-reconstruction techniques, learned from the Greeks or Arabs. A professor at the University of Bologna, Gaspare Tagliacozzi, became the first European to illustrate and describe the reconstruction of the nose, ears, and lips with the publication of *De Curtorum Chirurgia* in 1597. However, Tagliacozzi was accused of practicing magic; Paré and Fallopius, the most famous surgeons of the time, denounced him; and the Church prohibited his surgical techniques. Years after his death, a voice told the nuns in the convent of San Giacomo that Tagliacozzi was damned and must be disinterred from their burial ground. The nuns exhumed his body. Though Tagliacozzi was cleared by the Tribunal of the Inquisition and reburied, his techniques were lost. Surgical advances languished.

In 1743, Henri François Le Drean repaired the lower lid of a fourteen-year-old boy with a flap of skin moved from his nose. Nearly fifty years later, François Chopart reconstructed a lower lip with skin obtained from the patient's neck. By the nineteenth century, pioneering developments in soft-tissue repair were published in *Handbuch der operativen Chirurgie* by J. von Szymanowski. *La Rhinoplastic* by Nélaton and Ombrédanne also offered a wealth of information on skin flaps.

In 1869, Jacques-Louis Reverdin grafted a millimeter of skin onto a patient's wound. Although the transplant flourished and successfully healed, Reverdin's discovery was dismissed and he was ridiculed. However, Louis Ollier and Carl Thiersch persevered, developing a razor-cutting technique to obtain thinner areas of skin. The Ollier-Thiersch graft laid the foundation for plastic surgery.

McCleary had been oddly comforted by this disjointed history, as if in the last chapter of his working life he had joined an exalted but little-understood and secretive brotherhood.

When he had read that the word *flesh* in Sanskrit was from the prefix *pluta*, meaning 'floating,' it was a revelation. He then understood the skin was neither liquid nor solid, but a curtain of sensation. Mutable, pliable, and unstable, its boundaries were undefinable, uncertain as smoke. Skin was simultaneously a canvas and the paint on its surface.

McCleary had also been jolted into recognizing a simple truth: by changing color, the skin communicated an expression while remaining absolutely still. An involuntary system. The face represented both the skin and the mind.

McCleary was rotated to different hospitals, from a forty-bed unit established by the Red Cross at Brook Street to a larger facility at 24 Norfolk Street, then Roehampton and the majestic General Hospital, which had been converted from a former orphanage. He was also assigned to evacuate men with face wounds as they arrived at Waterloo Station, a cavernous structure that echoed with shouts and the whistled blasts of the ambulance trains.

The fighting intensified and casualties mounted while McCleary was posted at King George Hospital. The medical staff worked with a raw energy. No one slept. The situation was intense, fluid, and the disorganization was shocking, as hospitals were never notified until the last minute about the number of incoming wounded. This was done deliberately, to confuse enemy spies and avoid alarming civilians.

McCleary had been on duty when one of the first groups of face-injured soldiers arrived. He waited as the canvas flap at the rear of the Commer ambulance was thrown back and thin torchlight hesitantly intruded into the dim interior of the vehicle, faintly illuminating six seated men, their heads misshapen by enormous bandages, their bodies strapped to chairs against the walls. They were unmoving, still as rocks or guardian figures at the entrance to a sacred cave. Because they were absolutely silent, McCleary momentarily thought their mouths were sealed by thin, dark bandages until he saw that their jaws were wired shut. They had been transported sitting upright – never prone on a stretcher – because they could choke to death lying on their backs.

Some of the men were conscious, and McCleary tried to catch their eyes to reassure them. One man, his face heavily bandaged, signaled weakly with his good hand and struggled to speak with his damaged lips. McCleary couldn't understand his words and leaned closer, his nostrils filling with the terrible smell of infection that carried the man's whisper, *'Kill me. Kill me.'*

The face-injured men who had been sent to regular hospitals in error were immediately isolated or transferred to special maxillofacial units. Other patients refused to share a ward with the disfigured men, as they were a depressing influence. Some men with shattered faces had been shuttled to eight different hospitals within a few months, paper tags scrawled with their names and terse descriptions of their injuries tied to their toes if they were unable to speak.

Months later, after spending fifteen hours in the operating theater, McCleary had stripped off his jacket and moved in a daze of fatigue down an empty corridor, the sunlight spread in dazzling stripes under his feet. From the window overlooking the hospital garden he watched two patients – slightly hobbled by the casts on their legs – use bayonets to attack a cloth dummy in enemy uniform swinging from a tree.

He closed his eyes, unable to bear witness.

That afternoon, he requested transfer to a hospital outside the city.

Even before McCleary had toured the estate, he'd ordered the mirrors removed from the house. No patient was allowed to use or own a mirror. He controlled their images, protecting them from their own faces.

'Truth won't heal these men,' McCleary had later told the medical staff assembled in the ballroom. 'The sight of their damaged faces will hinder recovery. Better to keep their hope alive.'

If anyone in the room disagreed with McCleary, they left it unspoken.

It became policy that the orderlies would search each man admitted to the hospital and confiscate anything with a reflective, shining surface: shaving mirrors, flasks, cigarette cases, compasses, scissors, bottles of spirits, letter openers and penknives with gleaming blades. Even an ink bottle with a flat gold cap, a framed photograph, and a polished watchcase were forbidden and locked up in the supply room. They were as dangerous as weapons.

★   ★   ★

37

When McCleary first evaluated a patient, he spoke briefly and used Latin terminology for the muscles and bones of the face, since elevated language strangely comforted the men. He'd tell them that the Greek word for skin, *thumos*, had two interpretations, 'anger' and 'spirit.'

'Your skin is a live, constantly changing thing, and healing is a process,' he'd explain. 'New surgical techniques are always being discovered. I will do everything in my power for you.'

McCleary had always been able to anticipate the progression of healing the way other men could predict time, weather, the risk of a bet. But there was no such certainty here. Some of the patients' faces were so cruelly damaged he couldn't reassure them that his work would be successful. He couldn't promise that their faces would become whole again or even passable enough to join their families, earn a living, simply walk down a street without drawing stares. No explanation of why they weren't allowed a mirror was offered unless a patient asked. He struggled to evade his patients, to give them an honest but indirect diagnosis in order to extend a green branch of hope.

Hearing their fate, few men wept. Few asked questions other than *When can I go home? When will my bandage be removed?* This scene was repeated over and over.

A great number of patients were fixated on time and constantly spoke of exactly when they had been wounded. The moment, the hour, day, month when it happened was observed as an anniversary. *It has been a week since I was injured, Nurse. It has been forty-seven days since I was injured, Doctor.*

Most men were proudly self-reliant and grateful for McCleary's attention, but a few reacted violently to the doctor, misinterpreting his expression, becoming hurt, and raging against him. Their gaze was barbed, heightened, as if the expression that injury had taken from their faces had magnified their ability to decipher expressions on others'. McCleary was conscious that the patients waited to ambush the slightest sign of uncertainty, pity, or disgust in his eyes, watched for the delicate, telltale tremor of his *zygomaticus major*, pulling the left corner of his upper lip into a false smile, marked by its asymmetry. He directed compassion to flow through his hands while his eyes remained firm, clear, neutral. A rock in a pool.

It was far easier for McCleary to examine an unconscious patient, since a neutral expression required a discipline of deceit that was almost impossible to maintain. At times, he felt himself lose control, transformed from a neutral doctor into an observer who judged a man's maimed face.

Plato believed there must be a bond between doctor and patient, a profound understanding. This would be created by 'a beautiful discourse,' a charm, the *epôdê*. The patient must relinquish himself, offer his soul to the doctor, or the medicine would not work and no cure could take place. Why did the men need mirrors when he offered his compassion and learned interpretation? McCleary reasoned.

Some men under McCleary's care didn't seek intimacy or comfort from their doctors and fellow patients. They needed distance – or a state of willful ignorance – to heal. They were the worst patients. Difficult to treat. Slow to mend. Impossible to console.

But a pair of unasked questions was always suspended between McCleary and his patients. *How can I bear this? How can I live in the world again?*

Hands aching after hours of surgery, McCleary returned to his quarters in the former coachman's house near the stables. His room was austerely furnished with an iron bed, a nightstand, a worn high-backed chair retrieved from the main house. A collection of books, finely bound in full Morocco and inelegantly shelved in boxes, was the only personal memento.

The lamp propped next to the bed barely illuminated the room or the book in his hands, but he found the soft light comforting after the exacting glare of the operating theater. When he puzzled over a certain procedure or a patient's healing, he shared his thoughts with no one but turned to the works of Henri de Mondeville, a fourteenth-century physician-surgeon and demiurge who had attended King Philip the Good and his son.

His discovery of Mondeville's *Chirurgie* while still a student had been an inspiration, as the author was a renegade who had harnessed the patient's own belief to his cure, certain this was equally as effective as medical treatment. When all other measures failed, Mondeville recommended a practice called *pious frauds*, telling lies to the gravely ill, bringing a patient 'false letters telling of the death or downfall of his enemies, if he expects some promotion after their death. His visions and dreams must be given a favorable interpretation.'

Mondeville also urged the healer to be silently present for the patient, secretly directing positive thoughts toward him, binding them together in a web that only one of them had spun. This gift of imagination was as potent as the promise of relief in a sleeping draft.

CHAPTER 3

At the crest of the hill, McCleary leaned against a stone wall to rest. The hour was ill suited for walking, as the light had begun to shift and deepen, darkening the tall grass and his white jacket to bluish bronze, the color claimed by twilight. He gazed back at the enormous house, and only from this distance was it clear how the landscape had been designed around the structure at a later date, to provide a panoramic view from the windows. The road had been moved, the faint line of a sunk fence was still visible, and perhaps the clump of dark cedars were descendants of the original planting. During the following hundred-odd years, the landscape had exuberantly reverted, and now the grounds were marred by the tracks of vehicles and lights that bleached the fields.

McCleary watched a young man make his way toward him, wearing a blue hospital suit loose as a child's clothing, unshaped by masculine padding or a lining. He moved stiffly, holding his shoulder at a protective angle, as if his gait were affected by the thick bandage slanting across his face.

Slightly breathless from the climb, Julian gave McCleary a lopsided grin of relief and eased himself against the wall next to the doctor. He had been injured by shrapnel, and layers of gauze hid the wrecked symmetry of his face as neatly as a cocoon. His right eye had been only slightly injured and was uncovered to aid healing. Julian was the sole patient who gave McCleary a degree of comfort, and they had occasionally explored the grounds together, companionable acquaintances.

McCleary pointed out the anomaly of a curiously peaked gray roof, too small for a house, barely visible in the trees. 'It must be an ornamental structure. A folly. A pleasure pavilion.'

Julian followed the direction of his hand. 'Pleasure? Imagine.'

McCleary noticed that Julian scanned the landscape with a practiced eye, even with his limited vision. 'You're an artist, aren't you? There was a sketch pad by your bed.'

'An artist with limits. I'm a mapmaker. I calculate and record perspective from one point to another. I can't draw a face or figure. Terra incognita.'

On the horizon, ribbons of color – a secretive violet – had been arranged against a pale yellow background. McCleary hadn't seen such a display in weeks. The burning circle of the silver lamp over the operating table marked his dawn and dusk, bestowing a sense of timelessness.

'I always seek true north. For luck,' said Julian.

'It's the holy grail for mapmakers. Even if every landmark were obliterated, true north could still be found, since it's unanchored to any physical object.'

'Tell me how it works.'

'I'll demonstrate. First you must loan me your wristwatch. Now the hour hand of the watch is pointed at the sun. Imagine a line midway between the hour hand and twelve o'clock. It will point south. An imaginary line in the opposite direction from this point is north. See?' He stood a little straighter. 'I always showed this to the new recruits. Some of them thought it was hocus-pocus.'

'Some of my patients believe their treatment is hocus-pocus.'

'That's not quite true. Some believe it's closer to black magic.'

McCleary caught Julian's smile, and the gathering of lines around his eye, the *orbicularis oculi*. With a shock of wonder, he realized he might not recognize Julian without his bandage. 'I noticed a statue when I was here earlier. Just ahead. You might find it interesting.'

The men walked at an angle across a cropped pasture, and two stone figures were gradually revealed against a background of trees. The flowering gentian around its base, barely visible in shadow, provided delicate support for the statue's somber weight.

A woman carved of marble, clad in a short draped tunic, held a bow in one hand, a triumphant, scornful expression still unmistakable on what remained of her white face, missing a crucial fraction of nose and cheekbone. Her eyes were directed down at a stooped man suffering a transformation, his mouth distorted in a howl of fear and astonishment, his lower body replaced by the legs and flanks of a stag. Snarling, fierce dogs crouched around him.

'We've intruded on a tragic couple,' Julian said quietly.

McCleary reverently touched the woman's sandaled foot. 'She's Diana the huntress. The goddess has punished Actaeon by turning him into a stag. He had secretly watched her bathing. Actaeon's hunting dogs didn't recognize their master the stag and furiously tore him apart.' He walked around the statue, evaluating Diana's anatomy. The curve of the *superficial cervical plexus* on the woman's neck was correct. Accurate angle of jaw to ear. The *risorius* muscle lifted her lips into a sardonic grin. The sculptor had graced the goddess with a generous mouth.

'So poor Actaeon experienced the same pain as the animals he hunted.'

'Yes. But Diana's enchantment was even more diabolically cruel. Actaeon's body was transformed, but his mind was unchanged. He recognized his fate. He knew that he was a prisoner in his own body.' Too late, McCleary caught the significance of what he'd said. Grieving for his blunder, he wished his words could be transformed into stones and thrown away.

'I thank the gods that I wasn't pursued by a vengeful woman.'

'Yes indeed.' Embarrassed, McCleary sat down in the grass and felt a hard small object beneath his palm. He turned it over in his fingers for a moment before he recognized it. 'If I'm not mistaken, here is the missing bit of the goddess. Her profile.'

'Your work has followed you here, Doctor. Even those who aren't living require your skill.' Julian squatted down, careful not to lean too far forward, as his balance was unsteady, and gently parted the tangled grasses, searching for more fragments from the statue. 'It's a wonder I have any sensation left in my fingers. In the trenches, the steel knives and forks were so cold they burned bare skin. Many times I buttered bread wearing gloves.'

McCleary was content to have the younger man conduct a search, as he was very careful with his own hands, convinced even after years of surgery that his sensitivity was a conditional gift.

'Found something.' Julian extended his hand with a flourish that McCleary could only half appreciate in the dimming light. He delicately took the fragment, a bit of gravel, unshaped by a tool. He didn't want to disappoint Julian, so he pocketed the stone and promised to examine it again under a lamp.

McCleary began to stiffly clamber to his feet, but Julian was quicker and offered a hand of support.

'After you, Doctor.'

'Thank you. My old bones. I forget how easily the young can move. When I was your age, I was practicing the fine points of swordsmanship in Heidelberg. And studying medicine in my spare time.'

'Heidelberg? I imagine you've lost touch with your fellow students over there.'

'Yes. The war has seen to that. But this was forty-odd years ago. I was taught very little about facial surgery. It wasn't considered important. I could recite everything I learned about faces over two pots of tea.'

Lost in thought, McCleary veered slightly from the path. 'Students fought with sabers in those days. It was a point of honor to have a slash on your face. There was even a special medical attendant, the *Paudoktor*, who attended the duelists. He re-attached the students' amputated noses and ears with applications of red wine, the yolk of a hen's egg, balsam, and gauze. And some stitching. The procedure was occasionally successful. The *Paudoktor* claimed he attended ten thousand saber duels in twenty-four years and salvaged an uncounted number of noses.'

'This piqued your interest in medicine?'

'Actually, I found the duels more fascinating. It was a civilized ritual. Before the match, all the dogs would be chased out of the park.'

After a moment, Julian chuckled. 'Scavengers. Of course.'

47

McCleary sensed the slope of the hill, but his mind focused on another image. Smooth snow and bare trees in a dim quadrangle, and two students struggling to walk with a figure slumped between them, his shirtfront darkened with a bloodstain, jagged and irregular as a broken stick.

'My good sir, regard the apparatus that removes the subtlety of consciousness.'

McCleary smiled as the anesthetist, Brownlow, gestured at his battery of equipment arranged on the table. Glass beakers, transparent vessels marked with horizontal ribs of measurement. Gauze. Scissors. An efferent tube, a syringe, an eyedropper, a pipette, an inhaler. A Riva-Rocci sphygmomanometer with a stethoscope. A foot bellows that controlled anesthesia vapor. A thermos flask to warm the anesthesia gas. Gauze pads to place over the patients' eyes, a mask to fit over the nose and mouth. Flannelette wrist and leg straps used for restraint.

'This is the masterpiece.' Brownlow held an oval-shaped wire mesh contraption, constructed like a dog muzzle, over his face, and it fit like a mask. A 'cage' over his mouth held a light blue feather.

'Could there be a more primitive implement? A bird's feather to monitor the patient's breath?' Brownlow spoke from behind the mask, and the feather wavered with the hiss of his words. 'Preposterous. Clumsy tools betray my skills. My equipment should be fine as the devices of jewelers.'

Ether could free the mind from all constraints, and it was never predictable which men would react to the anesthesia in the operating room, summon superhuman strength, and struggle with the doctors, believing they were still on the battle-field, pursued by the enemy or their own private demons. Some men had to be restrained with straps until the drug took effect. Even the most self-contained had been known to betray them-selves and cry for a woman, gibber intimate detail. Rumor enriched the anesthetist with enough secrets to support himself with blackmail.

Moody, often sullen, Brownlow seemed to welcome these violent encounters, as if they confirmed his power to subdue and control a body.

'I covet each breath a man takes,' Brownlow had told McCleary. 'No, I don't covet the breath; I grant each breath. Like a god.'

The patients feared Brownlow as a bitter reminder of their helplessness before pain, the ritual of anesthesia and the blank black passage that followed. Many were convinced that during surgery he somehow magically threaded his pres-ence into their consciousness. If they displeased him, he might use his power over them, as a witch commands her familiars. Some patients compulsively fingered good-luck talismans – their *gris-gris* – when they saw the anesthetist approach, carrying the tools of his trade – a black rubber mask and a small glass bottle of ether – like a shaman.

A gaunt figure, Brownlow stalked the corridors and the area around the operating theater, where the strong odor of ether lingered, his eyes unfocused like the numbed survivor of a catastrophe, his thin, lined face revealing little, as closed as the secretive nature of his equipment.

A reckless young orderly had once dared to wrinkle his nose behind Browlow's back, pretending to inhale the telltale odor. 'Here's the Grim Reaper,' he whispered as the patients watched, uneasy with his mockery. 'Brownlow hates the sunlight for no good reason,' the patients gossiped, critical of the dark round spectacles that he sometimes wore indoors, reportedly stolen from a blinded officer.

During surgery, Brownlow's eyes were luminous, dark, and focused with concern, the tender gate that opened for each man before the spike of anesthesia took his ticking brain. He could put a man under ether in less than five minutes and suspend him there during surgery, hovering over the prone body, monitoring his blood pressure, timing the rise and fall of his chest, regular as music. An interruption in this pattern had terrible significance.

McCleary was mildly jealous of Brownlow, who could leave after an operation or simply turn to the next patient. His work allowed him the luxury of distance from the wounded, and he rarely entered the wards.

With his knowledge of the classics, McCleary identified Brownlow with an emissary from the underworld, Charon the ferryman, as he steered the feather weight of the men's consciousness, a cargo more precarious than the balance of a vessel upon water.

Brownlow was another vessel that he prayed would balance, stay afloat.

The dense sound of colliding ivory balls rose from the billiard table. Brownlow grimaced with satisfaction at the young redheaded medical officer's clumsy shot and made a pretense of casually circling the billiard room, a cue stick swinging in his hand.

The young officer avoided him and addressed McCleary. 'So you've quarantined the mirrors in the house, Doctor?'

'Yes, I did. Best for the patients to see themselves after their surgery is completed.' McCleary's voice came from the deep shelter of an armchair by the fireplace.

The young officer absently considered his next shot. 'They're hardly unprepared for a shock. They've been in battle. Men have died next to them. Let them get on with it.'

His words made McCleary feel ill at ease, as the officer conducted himself with the self-confidence of a military man, not a fellow doctor. *This young man is inexperienced and too literal*, thought McCleary, needing to grasp something for comfort, a walking stick, a dog's warm muzzle. He squinted at the billiard table, a brilliant green island. 'I wonder at your quick judgment, sir.'

Brownlow smacked the edge of the billiard table. 'Some poor blighter will see his noseless reflection in a puddle and die of fright. Or he'll shoot himself. Or shoot you. What about Ward, who talks constantly about his fiancée, wondering when they'll marry? Let him look at his own face, see the hideous truth.'

McCleary found his voice. 'The patients' lives will be worse when they leave here. Why rob them of their last illusion? Give them this frail time to mend.'

'Yes, let the patients pass their time here in a delusional dream. It's our duty to provide comfort,' said Brownlow, and it was unclear from his expression whether he was joking.

The young officer took his time lighting a cigar, its smoke magically blue where it strayed under the light from the lamp shade. 'We'll take your decision, Dr McCleary. But we can't be sentimental and mollycoddle the patients.'

'No danger of that,' muttered Brownlow.

'Gentlemen, if the practice of medicine has one certainty, it is that nothing concerning the body is permanent.' McCleary took the last sentence for himself, for the sake of the men he would heal.

There was shouting outside, and as the admitting clerk raced across the room, the doors slammed open for four bellowing orderlies with a shaking, blanketed figure on a stretcher. The clerk's frantic gesture directed them down the corridor. The stretcher tilted dangerously around the corners, the nurses stepping back against the walls, eyes on their clipboards, barely taking notice as they already anticipated the next crisis, the next arrival.

An orderly stumbled, losing his grip on the stretcher, and at McCleary's warning cry, a boy darted forward and grabbed its edge as the helpless patient rolled to one side.

McCleary and an orderly gently lifted the patient to the examining table, keeping him upright, for his mandible was fractured and edema of the palate was so severe that he was unable to close his mouth. The patient's eyes were pinched red folds lost in his swollen, contorted face, making it impossible to guess his age.

'Easy there.' McCleary held the patient's thin arm, stroking his hand until he was calm and his forehead relaxed. The comfort of skin on skin. After a brief examination, McCleary was saddened to realize that the patient was perhaps seventeen years old. Must have lied about his age to enlist.

'You're very young, soldier. Good for you,' McCleary managed to say. The patient's eyes flickered briefly, registering his pride, and then he noticed Brownlow dangling the black rubber mask.

The alarmed patient pushed McCleary aside, scrambling to jump from the table. Brownlow gripped the patient's gown, trying to hold him down, and they struggled.

'Damned fool.' McCleary shoved their flailing bodies apart. Brownlow was needlessly aggressive.

The young patient clung to McCleary as Brownlow stealthily edged around them, then swiftly pressed the mask packed with ethyl chloride-saturated gauze over the patient's nose, holding it there as the young soldier jerked and went limp. There was a loud wail, and McCleary turned to see the boy who had held the stretcher clapping his hand over his mouth.

'He'll be well looked after,' he said kindly, addressing the dismayed boy.

During the operation, McCleary remained tight with anger as Brownlow hovered over the young man, lavishing him with a tenderness he would never show while a patient was conscious. He minded his every breath, as two lovers will wait face-to-face with lips parted, the teasing delay of a kiss.

Suddenly, quicker than a brushstroke, the young man's lips turned lilac, his respiration became shallow, and he went into shock on the operating table. Brownlow's hands shook; he glared at the fractional slip of the colorless ether in the jar as the patient's breath grew softer and his blood pressure dropped. Then the liquid was still.

After all hope of recovery was abandoned, Brownlow swiftly left the room.

Outside, dew had turned the grass into unmarked silver, and in his white uniform, Brownlow seemed barely to touch the ground as he strode away. McCleary shouted his name. Brownlow whirled around and lifted his arms in utter defeat, then his faint figure was lost in the landscape.

Later, McCleary sought out the boy who had helped with the patient and found him cautiously drying a syringe in the pantry. When he noticed McCleary observing him, the boy started but didn't drop the syringe.

'I won't break it, sir. Doctor. The assistant matron asked me to clean the syringe.'

McCleary introduced himself and asked the boy about his background.

The boy, Artis, and his father had both been born on the estate. When the house steward went to war, Artis had taken over some of his duties. As the hospital staff had filled the house, he had lost certain places that had been his alone – the oriel window at the top of the front staircase, a stool next to a cupboard in the larder, a low shelf in the storeroom where he kept a few prized possessions: books, a brass spyglass, a pipette, a wooden box with a broken lock. He was seventeen, tall for his age, distinguishable from the youngest orderlies by his shabby jacket and long hair, infrequently trimmed by a scullery maid. Catherine still paid his wages, although he spent all his time in the patients' wards. He was no longer beholden to her, could walk away without waiting for orders. Because of the war.

Recognizing Artis's deftness, McCleary assigned him small tasks to perform. The boy became a committed hunter of wayward surgical instruments in the rooms where he had once lit lamps and carried serving dishes. The nurses treated Artis kindly, and the doctors accepted him more easily than did the orderlies, an unruly group of men who were jealously conscious of their inferior position.

A few days later, following a successful round of operations, McCleary found Brownlow alone in the supply room and expressed his sympathy for the young soldier's death in surgery.

Brownlow wouldn't meet his eyes. 'I miscalculated his weight. The anesthesia was too strong. He survived the battlefield to die on an operating table in his own country.'

'I can't allow you to take all the blame.'

Brownlow's voice was slow and thick. 'When a man is under my care during surgery, he's filled with my air, my anesthesia. I'm settled inside his body, under his ribs, in his lungs. I calculate everything, even the fear that quickens his pulse and his breath. I'm exacting. But I failed.'

McCleary noticed that the anesthetist's shoulders were drawn up in distress, and he spoke from fatigue and the fumes threaded into him during hours of surgery. His own light-headedness echoed

Brownlow's condition, as they had both worked without protection from leaking anesthetics. 'The body is utterly unpredictable. Even pain is difficult to locate.'

CHAPTER 4

T hree crouching workmen deftly unrolled gray linoleum over the parquet floor in the dining room.

'What are you doing?' Catherine stood in the doorway.

A workman leaned back and squinted up at her. 'Ask him. He's a doctor.'

She turned to face a tall man in a uniform. 'Dr McCleary.'

They gravely shook hands.

'Since you're in charge, tell me why they're covering the floor.'

'This will be the new operating theater.'

'Please, you must use a different room.'

'The dining room was selected because of the light. The north-facing windows.'

McCleary read her face. Her blue eyes narrowed, the muscles at the corners of her mouth, *triangularis menti*, moved downward, indicating distaste. Not hostility. Possibly she remained civil only because of his age. He straightened his back. 'After we leave your home, this room will appear exactly as it was before we arrived.

58

Even the floor will be restored to its original state.'

'But men could die on the operating table. In my dining room. How could I invite . . .' She let her question trail off.

McCleary was touched by her concern – no, optimism – about a future dinner in this room. One day, God willing, there would be guests here. A table set with china and silver. Faces flattered by candlelight. 'Ma'am, the house must date from the sixteenth century. Over the years, the rooms have certainly been the setting for many unpleasant events.'

Her expression didn't change.

'I am an excellent surgeon. I swear I will leave no ghosts.'

As she abruptly left him, McCleary noticed sawdust around the hem of her skirt, pointed shapes like flames.

With a single swift motion, a workman drew a blade down the thick roll of linoleum, and it neatly fell in two.

In a box of papers salvaged from the library, Catherine had found a map of the estate, a bird's-eye view inked as fine as a feather by a draftsman in 1721. The main house was a rectangle surrounded by formal gardens, the trees drawn as circles, a code, dot-dot-dot, as if the paper had been punctured. The pleasure garden was divided by serpentine walks, which began at the house and led down to the smallest pond. The draftsman had filled the interior of the lakes and larger ponds with wavy lines, the irregular evidence of water, and his unerring quill had laid down the carriage drive to scale in a gentle five-mile curve, east to north, through oak and wynch elm to the stables.

The border of the map held chevaux-de-frise and a stream with artificial cascades, just as they determined the actual boundaries of the estate. The severely trimmed hedges and the ha-ha, a trench running for miles across the pasture, no longer existed, commanding space only on the map. But the ancient brick walls guarding the two kitchen gardens still stood, gently crumbling, and the coach houses and the lodges were recognizable, although rebuilt and expanded past their original outlines. A number of the later structures not featured on the map – the conservatory, the three-division vinery, the cold greenhouse, the span-roof flower and mushroom houses – had fared less well; few of their glass panes remained intact, and rust bloomed inside and outside.

On a morning of light rain, Catherine walked around the sentries and orderlies at ease on the steps. They barely moved aside, their focus on their cigarettes, the parallel motions of their arms as they smoked. She was nameless, unconnected to official business. Not wounded. A woman.

Under an open umbrella, she paced out the dimensions of the vanished garden she had calculated from the draftsman's map, seeking the huge fountain that had been its hub, a circle besieged by radiating lines. Forty steps. Here. The fountain must have been here. She pressed her fingers into the sod, searching for a subtle shift of depth, a rupture, a hard line where the subterranean lead pipes had directed water to its transformation, the joyful release of spray. Perhaps there would be fragments of stone, marble, broken evidence of the fountain. She found nothing.

She tilted her umbrella for an unobstructed view of the vast lawn. Charles could have deciphered the plan of this landscape. Why had she never asked him? She studied the grass, a crosshatch of colored lines hiding the lost garden and its fountain. After a time, a barely perceptible pattern of squares and circles emerged in the grass – wan green – where the urns, statuary, and herms had once stood. It was as if they had been sunk but their shapes radiated up through the earth, as an object is visible in a depth of water.

Catherine imagined her former life restored, the house wavering, its walls fluid, shimmering free from the moment it had stopped when Charles died. She was the beloved mistress, and he would reappear, a dim figure in a familiar tweed jacket, whistling 'Barbara Allen' over and over, making his way to her on a path since made insignificant by weeds.

McCleary had solemnly paced through the house and was surprised to find that some of the grandest spaces had been haphazardly converted to storage. On the second floor, the Green Bedroom had been stripped of carpeting and draperies, and was empty except for a massive dining table. The floorboards had protested as he circled the table, then stooped over, conscious of his stiffening back, to examine it more closely. A thin, errant stripe of sunlight revealed the reddish tone of its dark-grained wood, secret as a glimpse through a keyhole. The table must have been more than two hundred years old, the style of its tapered legs indicating its age. What feasts had been set here? he had wondered aloud.

An orderly had delivered McCleary's note to Catherine, forgetting to place it on a tray as ordered. The next day, she slipped into McCleary's office. After talk about the weather – neither mentioned the occupants of her home – he moved from the desk to the armchair next to her.

'It has been a difficult fortnight for the staff,' he said. 'Perhaps it's a fanciful notion, but would you agree to hold a dinner? You can be properly introduced to everyone.' As she hesitated, he quickly added, 'Our cooks will prepare the meal. The orderlies will deliver it on trolleys and do the serving. This exercise of etiquette will do them good.'

'I'm willing to be your hostess, but please don't bring the patients to my table.'

'You don't need to be concerned. It isn't correct protocol for doctors to dine with patients. We'll be a small group. Brownlow, our anesthetist; Dr Pickerill, one of our young surgeons; and Hunt, our head orderly, will be invited.'

They agreed the dinner would be held in the Green Bedroom, where the table was located, since it could not be easily moved.

Two days later, Catherine dressed in black for their dinner. A widow's armor. Her wardrobe contained infinite degrees of black, transparent silk, crepe, opaque wool, and weightless taffeta, veils of such matte, uncompromising pitch they could have been powdered with charcoal, kidskin gloves so precisely fitted that her hands appeared to be oiled. Nothing, nothing was black enough to ease her heart.

Burdened with its candelabra, the table was a white raft that held Catherine and the four men together against the darkness that submerged the room. *Now I can rest*, thought McCleary, his eyes passing over the flushed faces around him. Just for an hour. Or an evening. Conversation, meals, sleep, a book, everything was interrupted by the patients' needs. Several bottles of wine had been brought up from the cellar, and he savored a glass of Château Latour, 1871, heavy and fragrant, before he surfaced back into the conversation.

'We were able to locate the enemy by sound,' a voice repeated from the end of the table.

'How could that be possible?' Surprised, Catherine put down her glass and stared at Pickerill.

'The radiographs were set up at three different points in the field.' Pickerill gestured with a spoon. 'Each recoil of enemy artillery created a wave of sound that was timed and charted by the radiograph machines. The engineers were then able to locate the position of the guns. I saw this demonstrated countless times.'

'Miraculous. To pull something invisible from the air and make it visible.'

'No more miraculous than a machine flying in the air.'

Brownlow's sarcasm was ignored by everyone but Hunt, eager to prove himself to this company. 'True miracles aren't made by man. Dr Pickerill, were you near the battlefield when the angels appeared?'

'The angels of Mons? No. They were sighted quite a distance from the base hospital where I was stationed.'

'But do you believe they really appeared?'

'All the newspapers reported it was so.'

'They said the angels were thirty feet tall and hovered over the battlefield like pillars of fire. They held the enemy back with flaming swords. The angels prove that we have God's blessing and will triumph.' Hunt's defiant gaze traversed the table.

'Many men take good-luck charms into combat,' McCleary pointed out. 'Italians carry crosses. Strangely, some put three peas in a pocket. I've never deciphered this particular symbolism.'

'Perhaps the Holy Trinity?'

'Heathens,' Brownlow muttered.

'Who can say? A Bible in a pocket can stop a bullet. So can a medallion of the evil eye.'

'Yes, that's the trouble with religion, sir.'

'Well said, Brownlow.'

Hunt's voice sputtered against the laughter around the table. 'But the newspapers' account of the angels must be accepted as truth.'

'The papers? They don't even print all the names of those who died,' Brownlow declared. 'I knew someone killed by a zeppelin bomb in the city. His name never appeared in the newspaper. I checked every day. That's your truth.'

'The papers probably have their secret orders,' whispered Hunt.

Two gangly young orderlies angled trays of thickly sliced beef and potatoes around the table, their utensils clattering, as they had no skill at serving. There was fresh bread and last year's root vegetables, retrieved from barrels in the cellar. Catherine drank but didn't eat so the wine would quickly release her, make her careless. Her fingers were light around the wineglass; it seemed to float from the table to her lips. She leaned back, fully accepting the disaster she imagined for herself, welcoming the lacy plasterwork that would drop from the ceiling over her face and neck like a net, white dust and red blood.

She remembered a dinner at Rufford Abbey, when Charles had been seated across the table. He had glanced at her; she had blushed and looked away, pierced by what his eyes had revealed, as if he had fashioned arrows from their intimate secrets and struck her heart. Everything else – the brilliant prickling of the women's diamonds, the reflected silver and crystal, the murmured conversation, the figures around the table – was less real than his knowledge of her. His private arsenal.

Brownlow drunkenly motioned for more wine and stared at Catherine. 'Sometimes the patients can hear your music, ma'am. When you play the gramophone. Thought you should know.'

'I didn't know. I apologize.'

He laughed. 'No, no. The men enjoy it. Someone is always awake in the wards. No matter how small the hour.'

'Brownlow is our god of sleep.' McCleary acknowledged his colleague with a gesture.

With an effort, Brownlow rose from his chair, waving his wineglass over their heads. 'My lady and gentlemen, here's to Morphia. My muse.'

They drained their glasses to humor him, the men's tired faces softened by the candle flames.

'With morphia, I can make men babble and cry for their lost companions.' Brownlow continued his spoken skirmish. 'Betray their own confidences. Free their body from care. Give a man morphia and you can take off his arm neat as a door from its hinges and he feels nothing.'

'Until he sees his empty sleeve when he's conscious.'

'The patients hate Brownlow more than the

enemy.' Hunt resolutely crossed his arms, perhaps needing protection to continue. 'Just watch them before an operation. When Brownlow walks in, you'd think the devil had arrived to collect his due. Although judging by their faces, the devil has already done his damage.'

'What's wrong with their faces?' Catherine's voice interrupted.

The men shifted uneasily in their chairs and looked expectantly at McCleary, waiting for his answer. Pickerill made a motion as if he would answer, then thought better of it.

Betrayed by fatigue, McCleary was at a loss for words and felt the pressure of tears behind his eyes, spreading like a stain.

'Perhaps our hostess should meet the patients. The nurses could conduct her through the wards during a quiet time,' Brownlow said.

'You haven't answered my question.'

Everything was suddenly sharpened, as if a lens had refocused the room. McCleary broke the silence, his words selected as carefully as beads. 'All the men here – the patients – have face wounds,' he said slowly. 'It is extraordinarily diffi-cult for the men and those who care for them. But I can assure you that after a time, their faces lose the power to shock.'

'I don't wish to see these men. They're at liberty to wander through the house?'

McCleary shook his head. 'I know you wouldn't want to isolate them, ma'am. They don't carry the plague. Their faces have been destroyed, but many men still have sound, healthy bodies.'

'It won't help if she treats the men like monsters,' Brownlow added loudly. He always sought contact with a surface and he leaned against the mantel-piece, arm stretched out along its edge.

'Remember we are here because of the generosity of our hostess,' McCleary said. 'Gentlemen, more wine?' He carefully filled their glasses, their servers having long since left the room.

The conversation changed as immediately as a pulled curtain obliterates an unwelcome view. Pickerill related an anecdote about the château of Pronleroy, where he had once been quartered. The owner of the château, a widow, had stubbornly remained in the house even as battle uncoiled closer and closer. She never spoke of the conflict, and anyone who mentioned it during a meal was obligated to forfeit a coin into a small box on the table.

McCleary thoughtfully took a coin from his pocket, and it made a clean, brittle sound as it dropped into a porcelain dish. 'I suggest we follow the widow's discipline. Here is my contribution. Now, will you please excuse me? I go to my evening rounds.'

Expressionless, Catherine followed McCleary to the door, and he bent his head in acknowledgment as she walked by without a word.

Why hadn't the doctor warned her? He'd brought the injured men here to haunt her house.

He had mentioned the plague. Wasn't misfortune equally infectious? Catherine imagined a line of men, their faces wrapped in bandages, walking through dry woods and the trees alongside spontaneously bursting into flames as they passed, like water churned by a boat.

She was dizzied as the angles of the walls seemed to solidify, the windows settled into mercilessly clear shapes, preparing for the moment when she would encounter a man with a ravaged face in the corridor or unexpectedly on the stairs, behind a door, turning a corner. This was as inevitable as the slam of a clock's black hands around a dial.

Another night marked by sleeplessness. Catherine silently peered into the open doors along the corridor, discovering that the lights recently installed by workmen had transformed the still pools of the rooms, creating unfamiliar depths and shadows. The Pink Drawing Room had been entirely rearranged; its new furnishings – tables, cabinets, lamps with glass shades – possessed a clean and unadorned inevitability that she now recognized as a function of service. On a trolley, white enamel containers held medical instruments upright, like jagged, leafless metal bouquets. With each footstep, the instruments betrayed her with a rattling sound, cold as chimes. She stopped. Silence. The rattling waited until she stepped forward, then spread throughout the house, a signal for a weapon or a watchman.

She escaped this trap through the door into the corridor, and disoriented by the sudden brightness, she didn't notice a man silently approaching until he was fifteen paces away. Brownlow abruptly slowed down, his eyes scanning the corridor, encountering no recognizable object. Behind him, the light from a sconce erupted around his head, a halo.

'Have you been working?'

He nodded absently, spreading one hand against the wall to steady himself, and his eyes trailed over Catherine as if she were painted on the wall. Was he drunk? Sleepwalking? Suffering from nerve strain? Some soldiers had returned from battle mute, unable to speak. Then Catherine noticed the man reeked of anesthetic and realized their conversation would waver from Brownlow's mind. She was a wraith, an invisible woman, free to ask any question.

'Tell me about the men with injured faces.'

'Ah. The patients.' The word was mockingly drawn out. 'Do you dream, ma'am? Because the men could be in your nightmares.'

'Aren't you afraid of them?'

'No.'

'Why?'

'I only fear for them. Some men can't breathe through their noses. Or talk with their lips. Some are blind too.'

Her hands gestured her dismay. 'How can you bear to see them?'

He spoke more gently. 'When I administer anesthesia, no matter how many times I've witnessed it, a man's last look is a weight thrown at me. I carry their trust. They are bare men.'

'Are the wounded men recognizable as men?'

Brownlow laughed. 'They look like the damned.'

As if from a distance, he focused on her, then turned and walked away. Catherine was angry, not so much at his lack of courtesy but because she hadn't finished questioning him.

At the east wing of the house she slipped behind the japonica shrubs, their skeletal branches ornamented with blunt buds, and peered through the window into the patients' ward. The red-shaded lamps on the night tables spread a hot crimson glow over the furniture and the motionless figures swaddled in blankets and bandages on the beds. Above their heads the chandelier prisms were aimed downward like daggers of glass, luridly stained red by the lamplight. Invisible air forced the prisms into motion, blurring their sharpness. A nurse suddenly jerked upright in her chair, startled from her doze, and stared directly at Catherine.

Catherine shoved her way through the branches and stumbled onto the lawn. Red light was impressed on the radius of her eye, and wherever she turned, a film of red was suspended over the landscape.

Anger at the men's dumb presence in the house, their terrible vulnerability, rippled into a sensation that shook her weightless. Behind her, the windows of their rooms were crimson rectangles, as if the house were a burning ship, sinking into the dark swell of the landscape. Fire would find these wounded men who were never at peace – the sleeping hollows of their eyes, empty mouths, combustible bandages – waiting for the lick of flames.

CHAPTER 5

Catherine stood at her bedroom window watching the patients – figures uniformed in hospital blues – as they sat in canvas chairs or slowly wandered without purpose over the grass. It was a strange ballet, the nurses in identical costumes the only rapidly moving figures, hurrying to a patient with a blanket against the wind, retrieving a dropped newspaper, a hot-water bottle, a fallen crutch, their performance by turns harried and gently solicitous.

Two patients spoke animatedly together, and at the taller man's gesture, her breath stopped as she recognized Charles. No, not Charles himself, but his presence, as he animated this stranger to signal her. He occupied this man like a glove, a suit of armor, a waiting emptiness that he filled. She recognized her husband among these men whose appearance was constantly changing, their identity fluid, impermanent, unstable.

Someone stepped in front of the tall man and he was lost to view.

She raced downstairs, stopping at a back

entrance. She imagined approaching the silent patients as they waited for her horrified reaction to their damaged faces. They were the audience, the watchers, and she was the performer. She returned to her room.

That night, the stream of Catherine's sleep was interrupted by the soft sound of Charles's hat and gloves tossed onto the chair in his dressing room.

'Catherine?' His voice.

Half asleep, she blindly stumbled into Charles's bedroom. Her foot stubbed against an open trunk; a compass fell out and rolled across the floor, the luminous blur of its progress halted by a chair leg. Its glowing, circular green heart waited, the black numerals pulsing like writing against fire, the needle positioned at eleven o'clock. It was a sign. The eleventh day of the month was Charles's birthday. He was here.

This was proof that the presence of the dead could be summoned by the fierce possessiveness of the living. The force of her memory had called her husband, would keep him with her.

The next day before sunrise, Catherine was at the window, craving the sight of the patients as they assembled on the lawn, confident that Charles would send her another sign. A man could be recognized by his mannerisms as easily as by his robe of skin. Occasionally one of the men's gestures or a movement caught her eye and then he would be submerged into the crowd.

Suddenly, as easily as wind moves leaves, a tall

stranger assumed her husband's identity. See how his hand smoothed his hair back from his forehead? This was Charles's habit. See how he walked? A fragment of Charles had struck this stranger as sparks fly from fire. She didn't need her husband's body or voice to divine his presence. All the men sang of him. This vision abruptly vanished, and she stared at the patients, protected by their bandages.

But she would wait for her husband. Waiting was familiar; it was constructed around an empty center, secure as stones around the hollow center of a well.

A jeweler at Cartier had once told her that some diamond cutters could recognize one another by the way a diamond had been cut. She had asked how a cold stone could retain the mark of an individual hand. *Identity isn't permanent as a sum of figures*, the jeweler had answered.

She could peer into the dazzling heart of light and read what other eyes would miss.

Charles began to appear in Catherine's dreams and seemed about to speak, but his mouth was still, his eyes anguished. He was always empty-handed. For three days, she waited for him in the places that had been significant for her husband. The Pink Drawing Room. The morning room. The tapestry corridor. Footsteps approached, then paced away outside the rooms without stopping. It was unbearable. But in the corridor, she noticed the unmistakable scent of his cigarettes, a blend of Havana and Latakia tobaccos.

Perhaps Charles could no longer recognize his home, the rooms occupied by strangers and hospital equipment. He must be insensible, drugged into forgetfulness. Or wounded, unable to speak, his mouth sealed, bandaged. She must find Charles, help him. She would seek him outside the house, find her way among these terrible men, carrying the memory of her husband like a thread. Perhaps the bold touch of her hand on a stranger's shoulder, a kiss, or a tear would be enough to break this stalemate, this spell.

Sheltered by the allée of linden trees, Catherine nervously twisted a leaf, thinner than glass, and it snapped, leaving a faint, bitter scent on her fingers. She watched the patients on the lawn, their movements seeming to unwind from a slower sense of time, as if they waited for clarity of what had befallen them, the common catastrophe of their injuries.

At a costume ball, she'd once marveled at a guest who had dressed as half man, half beast. The Minotaur. Didn't the patients resemble the Minotaur, with their monstrous faces masked by bandages and the bodies of normal men?

Frightened, she saw that the figures in blue suits made a spectacle of feints, hidden exchanges, and maneuvering, sending messages she couldn't interpret, meant only for one another and their caretakers.

Charles had returned, but she must earn his appearance with faith and patience. She was equal to the task.

Catherine began to listen more carefully to the workmen's shouts, the whispering of the nurses and V.A.D. women passing by the window. *Will you wait for me? What about it?* a tenor's voice wavered in song from the staff quarters. Other voices, those of the orderlies outside, did not carry with enough clarity to tell her anything. But when they worked in the house, she stood by the door and heard words and phrases that her husband had routinely used. She overheard a conversation about a *garden near Naples*, which Charles had insisted they visit on their honeymoon. She heard *Cobham*, the name of Charles's best horse.

She jealously guarded every precious moment, since watchfulness would bring Charles back. Insomnia elongated her waking hours until the sense of the day's progression was lost, marked only by the changing light on the walls, from palest yellow white to brilliant sunlight, lamplight, and darkness.

Downstairs in the wards, the patients were also awake at night, lacking the pollen of sleep, of forgetfulness. Light from their windows striped the black lawn, and the pattern of voices and footsteps made by the orderlies and nurses were faintly audible at all hours.

Over a period of weeks, the signs from Charles multiplied. His calling card slipped from between two books she moved on a shelf. It was Wednesday, the same day of the week he had left to join his regiment. Only Charles would have known the significance of this day.

He spoke to her through music. Two of Charles's favorite songs were played one after the other on the gramophone set up near a fountain, his spirit guiding someone's hand to place the needle. She clearly heard the music, but it was an indecipherable code.

Once after a hunt, Charles had entered the house through a back entrance, tossed his hat onto a chair, turned, and smiled at her over his shoulder, revealing black mud from the horses' hooves spattered up the back of his pink riding jacket. He was a man who filled a room, and his presence was expanded by the frigid air and the fresh odor that surrounded him that afternoon.

Catherine whispered her husband's name out loud, and at that instant, a lark sang outside, creating a fissure in time, and there was a sudden flash of pink in the distant field, the exact color of Charles's riding jacket.

Another day, Catherine saw Charles outside, walking past the drawing-room window. He stopped to stare at his reflection and was transformed into Artis, wearing an old jacket that had belonged to her husband. She ran outside, grabbed the surprised boy's shoulders, and shook him.

A man leaned over the red bridge on the lake, looking into the water. Was he Charles? She willed the man not to move, not to shatter into a stranger. But he shifted his shoulder, and casually, as if he'd thrown down a newspaper, he was revealed as an orderly.

Tomorrow marked the anniversary of when Charles had proposed marriage. It would be the day he would return to her. She must be ready. She quickly packed a satchel with precious rationed goods: sugar, butter, silk stockings, matches, and a dozen candles she'd hoarded. She would never be without light.

Catherine laid Charles's clothing on the bed in his room. A fine wool suit and a starched shirt from Budd. Cuff links in gold, once warmed by his wrists. His pocket watch. An antique tobacco caddy of gold-washed silver.

It was evening. She could hardly dress; her blunt fingers fumbled against her clothing. She lay on the bed in an elaborate gown, bound by the silk wrapped around her, secure as carving. When she had been intimate with Charles, there was no sound but his sound, no blood but his blood; his body had absorbed all her senses.

The bedroom door was open so Charles could enter, as he had on other evenings. Other lovers had come to her like this, materializing from darkness into two hands, a mouth, breath. The surprise of pleasure.

The tension of waiting wounded her, as if a vibration, needle fine and sharp, were drawn to the wedding ring on her finger, made a crack in the diamonds finer than the eye could register, and then moved up to pierce her heart.

Catherine jolted awake in the morning. She had slept without disturbing her clothes. Dreams, had there been dreams? Had she missed Charles? Panicked, she raced into Charles's room. Everything was exactly as she'd left it.

Someone was keeping Charles from her. The doctors and the nurses conspired against them.

The door to the morning room swung shut behind her, and Catherine waited to be certain she was alone. Moonlight leveled itself across the furniture – the curved seats of the chairs, a smooth metal table, a tray top – irregular shapes floating in darkness, as if the room were filled with black water. She stepped forward slowly, uncertainly, anticipating furniture that had been removed from the room.

Outside, the thick grass of the lawn formed into lines of combed silver, black on the sides hidden from the moonlight. Near a fringe of trees, an unmoving figure – a man in light-colored garments – was intently focused on the window where she stood. He cupped his hands to light a cigarette, and at that moment she recognized Charles.

Catherine didn't realize she'd cried out, but his head jerked up, and with two strides he vanished into the trees. She pounded her fist against the window. He must hear her.

She ran outside to the place where Charles had lit the cigarette. The trees were an impenetrable screen; the landscape gave her nothing back. Had he made no mark? No footprint on the grass? She spun around.

There. By the trees in the distance. A pale figure. He was waiting for her.

She moved blindly forward, the wind striking the blades of grass together, sharpening them to cut her. The pump of her heart magnified until it sounded over the field like an echo, pushed by the explosion of her breath. Someone would hear her, sense her fear. Her perspective became distorted; her shadow reversed itself and soared up from the ground. Wasn't that how soldiers tracked the enemy? She was a target. She stumbled to her knees and the world spun around her. When it was quiet, she stood up unsteadily. She was isolated, as if everything in the landscape were suddenly color- less and she stood out, the sole living figure, her flesh vibrant, alive, pink with racing blood.

Arched branches, set with thorns like the punctu- ation of stars in a constellation, guarded a passage between the trees. He couldn't have passed here.

Hands gripped her arm and jerked her around.

Who are you? A mouth moved in a man's dim face.

'Charles? Are you Charles?' She fell into the full scent of dry grass, felt its spikes under her hands, then this pressure dissolved.

CHAPTER 6

Anna Coleman had sailed from Boston harbor with her husband, a doctor, disembarking in a port filled with hospital ships. He continued on to join other volunteers in a war casualties hospital funded by the Vanderbilt and Morgan families. They had agreed she would join him at some point in the future, which would be determined by the course of battle. Until that time, the military was entrusted with their communication.

Two hours after arriving at Base Hospital No. 22, Anna was asleep alone in a camion parked in a field. The hospital was one-quarter mile from the Dannes-Camiers railroad depot, a main line that was a target for enemy aeroplanes. The locomotives were painted gray to make them less visible, but the pale tents were visible in sunlight. 'No, we certainly aren't in any danger,' said an officer, gesturing at the red cross painted across the roof of a tent. 'The cross is clearly visible, even from a thousand feet up. There can be no mistake.'

'What if the aeroplane's visibility is limited?'

He had shrugged off Anna's question. A hospital would never be bombed. It was sacred ground.

During the first weeks there had been few patients and little for Anna to do, so she wrote lengthy letters to her husband and a few of her patrons. When the hospital was expanded, railroad engineers and a construction regiment erected additional tents for surgery, supplies, disinfection, recreation, a chapel, a kitchen, and quarters for the officers, doctors, and nurses. Anna had been puzzled by the 'Glory' sign on the largest tent near the morgue until a nurse explained that the wounded who weren't expected to live would be sheltered there. It was April, and the weather was already hot.

Accustomed to the quiet isolation of her studio, Anna had been unnerved by the constant noise and activity. As a defense against this chaos, she had unpacked her supplies and begun to sketch the surrounding landscape, but it seemed as insubstantial as the canvas tents.

Weeks later, a small group of physicians, surgeons, dentists, and several nurses from Harvard University arrived at the base hospital. The doctors were distinguished by their loose white infirmary coats decorated with gold embroidered Harvard patches on the shoulders.

Anna noticed one of the doctors, a sturdy, dark-haired man with thick spectacles, because of his habit of sketching in a small notebook during meals. This was also her practice. The others usually took their enamel mugs of tea outside, leaving him alone in the dining tent. When she heard him speak, his heavy accent didn't surprise her. Dr Kazanjian was a foreigner.

Anna realized his sketching was a way to extend his work. Fill every hour. Did he ever sleep? Kazanjian would hurry into the surgical tent before noon and emerge very late at night. His constant activity ensured that nothing – the isolation, the lack of supplies, the approaching threat of battle – would catch up with him.

She asked the chief matron, a plainspoken woman, whether Dr Kazanjian was a surgeon.

'Not likely,' she answered, indicating that Anna should help refold the blanket draped over her arm. 'Mr Kazanjian is a dentist. I'm not even certain he can properly be called doctor. You're not a trained nurse?'

'I have no training.' She didn't mention that her husband was a doctor, which might have changed the matron's sour expression, her dismissal of Anna's usefulness at the hospital. She was an artist and didn't need to be yoked to the rules of aid.

Regiments of engineers laid down miles of new railroad track, and supplies and ammunition could rapidly be delivered directly to the front and the base hospital, sometimes arriving within days after leaving Southampton.

This morning, fresh butter and bread were available in the mess tent, and cut flowers in tin cups had been placed on the long tables. Anna sat down next to Kazanjian, and her eye noticed a face drawn with a hatch of lines, its muscles exposed, before his hand covered his sketchbook.

'At last we meet each other properly.'

She gave him her hand. 'Anna Coleman.'

'Varaztad Kazanjian.'

'I see you also sketch, madam.'

He indicated her faintly blue thumb and index finger, proof she'd handled a stick of chalk. She laughed.

They discovered they had no friends or acquaintances in common, although they'd both resided in Boston. Anna left it unspoken that her husband was a prominent physician in the city and her family had lived there for generations.

Kazanjian was smuggled out of Turkey as a teenager after protesting the massacres of Armenians put him in danger. He worked in a factory near Boston and learned English from coworkers and later tutors. He was thirty years old when he passed an admission examination and enrolled at Harvard, the oldest student in the dental college. Now he was one of the oldest members of the Harvard Surgical Unit, a group of volunteer medical personnel.

The Unit had come resolutely prepared for war, but even with the enormous crates of supplies they brought to the base hospital, the medical supplies were wholly inadequate for the anticipated number of wounded. Kazanjian despaired when

86

it was reported that there were only fifteen dentists to serve the entire army. 'We must rely on our wits,' he said.

Early in the morning before the day became too hot, the artist and the dentist walked through camp together, scavenging. 'I will make splints from stray telephone wire, flattened coins, paper clips, bits of leather and rope,' he explained. Pieces of discarded equipment, packing material, even empty condensed-milk and meat tins would be cut into pieces for jaw splints. When he expressed a wish that kindling could be transformed into metal, she declared he was a hoarder of metals, a modern Midas.

'A sniper's bullet typically tears a three-by-five-inch hole in flesh,' Kazanjian told her. 'The jawbone is hard as ivory and it fractures. A man can live without arms and legs, with a severe face wound, but not without his mouth.' A man's life could be saved by saving his jaw. An intact body was already an anomaly for Kazanjian.

Anna and Kazanjian were constantly together. During one scavenging expedition, she picked great armfuls of wildflowers and presented him with a single flower, which he kept in a bully beef tin next to his cot.

Anna ignored the critical eyes that watched her, a married woman without her husband. Having found an accepted place in the midst of war, she put aside her own work.

For one week, Anna observed Kazanjian as he

performed dental surgery on the staff. She was dexterous and quickly learned the vocabulary of his shorthand gestures – sometimes just a glance – indicating certain requests or instruments. Since his heavy spectacles concealed his eyes, she preferred to read his expression up close, as his forehead and his lips were more revealing. His words were always carefully considered, and he was wholly present to everyone who spoke to him, his concentration a gift from translating a second language and his natural reserve.

After she officially became his assistant, she committed all his supplies to memory: saline solution. Higginson's enema syringe to cleanse wounds. Provocaine and novocaine. Modeling compound, Vulcanite and gutta-percha to hold damaged jaws in place. A Brophy gasoline-powered blowpipe for soldering. Orthodontic wire, forceps, pliers, tongue and extracting forceps, cleft palate instruments, mouth gags. She completed the first difficult extraction of a soldier's blackened teeth before becoming ill.

'It's good you learn the work now,' Kazanjian told her. 'Everything will change when battle shifts in our direction. Once the wounded arrive, time is our intractable enemy.'

The long scar dug in the earth that the soldiers occupied was only fifteen miles away. There were wild rumors of battle, of enemy sightings and atrocities. Pervasive as sunlight or heat, fear of the impending battle seized words in conversation, interrupted appetites and dreams. The situation slowly became claustrophobic. Everything was stasis.

Weeks passed and Anna had received only a single letter from her husband. He sounded remote, harried, and there were few words of affection or regret. She was surprised only by her anger. She glued the letter to the back page of her sketchbook, flap side down, so it was safe but couldn't be opened.

One afternoon Anna and Iris, a V.A.D. girl from Mayfair, ducked into a marquee tent to watch a cinematograph show. There was no piano accompaniment, and Anna was unable to focus on the silent, jerkily moving figures; the characters and the story held no interest for her. A melodrama filmed before the war.

Afterward, Kazanjian accompanied the two women into the woods nearby, where Anna had noticed a patch of wildflowers. Deep under the sheltering trees, the muted sound of the supply vehicles had the gentle regularity of surf, so their surroundings seemed enchanted, artificial, remote as an island. They found the lilies, pale gold flowers, their sharp star shapes puncturing a luxuriant bank of foliage.

Kazanjian wandered off and the women gathered flowers, their hands sticky from the broken stems, brilliant orange pollen streaking their white-and-gray uniforms.

Without a sound, three dark, bearded men in uniform suddenly emerged from the underbrush. Anna stood stiffly in place, but Iris waved at them.

'*Bonjour, bonjour. Ça va?*' She turned to Anna. 'They're foreign soldiers. Turcos. From Algeria.'

Iris had been looking after the man with the bandaged arm. He grinned in recognition, bowed, and presented her with a roughly bundled handkerchief. She thanked him profusely.

Kazanjian returned and offered the men cigarettes, which they solemnly tucked into the breast pockets of their uniforms. He managed a few words in Arabic, which delighted the Turcos, respectfully shook their hands, and wished them luck.

After the men had left, Iris untied the handkerchief and found a handful of wilted rosebuds. 'I can't very well keep this, can I? Not from their dirty hands.' The handkerchief unfolded as she tossed it in the air, scattering the pink buds over the ferns. She was willing to nurse the Turcos but scorned them outside the hospital setting. After all, she was of her class.

Kazanjian said nothing, but by now Anna knew him well enough to catch the contemptuous look he gave Iris before he turned and a dense green reflection masked his spectacles.

Since only a handful of soldiers were currently being treated at the base hospital, the staff focused on one another as distraction from the medical supplies laid in rows on towels, the sharpened surgical tools, the rolls of white cotton wool bandages. Everything was uncannily quiet.

A wag on the hospital staff announced it was Midsummer's Eve, and it became an excuse for a celebration. Freshly laundered sheets were draped over the long tables in the mess tent. A selection of wines and champagne, dishes of pickled quail eggs, foie gras, ham, and cheeses appeared, all of it mailed from home or donated by new recruits or staff returning from leave. A doctor had smuggled back a haunch of wild boar, and the slices – the red black of garnets – were arranged on huge platters. The buzz of flies sounded the depth of the tent as the women went around pouring champagne into mugs.

A majestic rumble of gunfire echoed across the distant fields, penetrating the tent as easily as an odor. An instant later, an echo repeated the noise. The battle had begun. One of the nurses wailed, then stretched her hand over her mouth.

A drunken lieutenant threw himself on the ground and motioned for quiet before pressing his ear against the thin grass. Those who had served time at the front continued to eat and drink, accustomed to battle and this type of behavior. The others, half drowsy from the wine, nervously waited.

'I can hear the movement of great vehicles,' he whispered. 'It won't be long. Won't be long.'

★   ★   ★

As the fighting raged five miles away, the ground trembled, the vibration and the sound indistinguishable from each other. Anna felt it through her feet and legs, her bones a conductor of this telepathy, impossible to disconnect, linking her to battle. It possessed her as if she were under water. Anxiety constricted her shoulders, dried her throat, and she wished for Kazanjian's comforting presence. In that instant, she recognized the first betrayal of her husband.

Messages pulsed along the miles of telegraphic wires from the front to the hospital, and everyone worked frantically, preparing for the imminent arrival of wounded soldiers. The wave of noise in the distance grew louder, and late in the afternoon a convoy of ambulances, camions, and horse-drawn wagons bearing the injured swept onto the grounds. After all the cots had been filled, the wounded were laid on straw in the chapel and under nearby trees by the light of hurricane lanterns. There was scarcely room to walk around the prone bodies. Some soldiers had to be cut free from their clothing and their stretchers, since blood had dried during the time it had taken to evacuate them from the battlefield. Some men had waited several days. Gas gangrene was common, and the stench from the wounded bodies was so terrible that the tent with the most gravely wounded men could be distinguished by smell alone. Anna's skin and clothing reeked of pus, and the odor persisted even after cleaning.

Anna was astonished that there were so many ways a body could be damaged. She stared as a nurse used an indelible pencil on a man's naked torso, drawing circle after circle on his skin. 'It's the quickest way for the surgeons to find the shrapnel,' the nurse muttered, already studying the next quiet man on a stretcher.

In the operating tent, the five surgical tables were staffed by an anesthetist, a surgeon, a nurse, and an orderly. No one rested, and an entire day would pass without a meal or an opportunity to sit down. Constant motion was hypnotic, an incantation, a way to keep the mind occupied. Anna knew this from her own work. Her eyes sought blankness, staring at the army blankets, a strangely brilliant crimson, thrown over each cot.

A few trees shaded the compound, and as the heat grew stifling, the tent flaps were roped back to allow a breeze to pass through. This had little effect, since the canvas was still warm to the touch at eleven o'clock at night. The women were miserable in their long, thick skirts and their caps.

Anna shared a single tent with the other women, and when there were a few hours to sleep, they collapsed – without a greeting or a good-night – fully clothed onto their cots, unable to soothe themselves or one another. Occasionally, a groggy nurse would hold up a torch from her nest of sheets so another woman could undress illuminated by its weak light. When there were fewer casualties, their shifts were shortened to twelve hours.

At first, stress and the constant noise made sleep impossible. Then one type of sleeplessness was replaced by another, a state of dazed wakefulness, dreaming disbelief. Anna wasn't certain if she was awake or asleep or drifting in a third, unknown condition.

Sitting by a patient's bedside, Anna read a feverish, recently blinded man a letter from his wife. Careful of his privacy, she didn't look at him as his wife's news of their garden, the weather, their youngest son, was shaped by her voice.

'Show me where she made the marks,' he murmured, holding out his hand. 'Show me the exact place my Susan signed her letter.'

She slipped the paper into his hand, guided it to his lips so he could kiss his wife's bold, private XXX of love, too intimate for another woman to read aloud.

At four o'clock in the morning, Anna struggled alone to help a choking man. Kazanjian's hard shoulder suddenly pushed her aside, and he pulled the man into a seated position. He swiftly inserted his fingers into the soldier's throat.

'Secure his tongue,' Kazanjian gasped as a nurse ran over, his eyes never leaving the man's face. Or what was left of it.

Anna stumbled outside and bent over her knees on a crate. Oblivious to her distress, figures hurried along the paths of pocked sand, stopping to jerk aside a tent flap and expose a harsh triangle of light from the interior.

Anna's shoes were wet, and when she slipped them off, she realized they were filled with dark blood from the wounded men.

The doctors at the base hospital were never quite comfortable with Kazanjian. He was a foreigner, a dentist. But he proved to have an uncanny gift for improvisation – which was necessary given the shortage of supplies – that they lacked.

Soldiers with jaw injuries were routinely sent across the channel with closed-bite splints. Many died of lockjaw. Kazanjian solved this by creating a device fashioned from two tapered wooden sticks, a small block of wood, and a piece of elastic that kept the patient's mouth open until arrival at a permanent hospital.

Nothing Kazanjian did could be imitated or anticipated. The doctors took note of his expertise and addressed him with new respect. They began to seek Kazanjian out at mealtimes and invited him to the officers' mess for card games, their acknowledgment of his superior skill. Once they shared a bottle of fine wine found in an abandoned rucksack, as Kazanjian had a reputation as a man with sophisticated taste. However, he maintained a space of solitude around himself.

Kazanjian stopped Anna outside the mess tent. They were both late for the meal.

'I've volunteered to serve at another hospital. I will be leaving the country.'

The wind lifted Anna's thin apron, and she smoothed it down against her skirt.

He held up a strip of rubber. 'This was cut from a hot-water bottle. I'll use it to splint a jaw.' He shrugged in exasperation. 'I'm a scrap man. I don't mind. I'm here to serve. But my abilities will be better used in a proper hospital.'

'When will you leave?' Her question was automatic, her voice flat.

'After the next military push. Every pair of hands will be needed.'

The sun was hot on her bare neck. She squinted against the light reflected from the canvas tent, trying to read Kazanjian's eyes through his thick spectacles.

'Mrs Coleman, are you comfortable with the wounded men?'

'Yes.'

'Can you depict a grotesque face with a neutral eye, without judgment?'

'I can draw anything set before me.' Sensing this was an audition, she tried to calculate the response he wanted. 'The skill of the drawings is for another to judge, of course.' She rarely apologized for her work and was irritated at her own criticism. Irritation to cover her dismay at his leaving.

'No debate about your skill. But these portraits would require physical detail, not the psychology of character. They are a record of medical treatment.'

'I believe I have that ability.'

'Good. A drawing can be crueler than any photograph.' He indicated she should precede him into the tent. The interview was finished. Kazanjian had enlisted her.

Without an official title, Anna could slip into another role, another establishment or country. She wrote to her husband explaining that she would be leaving the base hospital. There was no reply, and a second letter was forwarded to the hospital where he was working, a few miles from the front. Communications were erratic. The *Times* arrived across the channel the day after it was published, but letters sent fifty miles were delivered weeks late. It was a paradox. Decisions made during wartime were sometimes equally paradoxical.

She fit chalks, pencils, paints, brushes, and India rubber erasers back into their original wooden boxes, and brushes into leather cases. The three legs of the stout sketching stool were refolded under the pigskin seat. The enormous rolls of Arche, Whatman, and watercolor papers from Messrs. Dixon of Liverpool had never been unpacked. Before the last trunk of her personal effects was locked, she removed her wedding ring, knotted it into a rag, and hid it in a paint box.

The Wolseley staff motorcar delivered Kazanjian and Anna to the coast, where they boarded a hospital ship, the *Guildford Castle*. They disembarked at three o'clock in the morning, and it seemed the hour had been reversed, as military and hospital personnel bustled around the platform as if it were afternoon. An enormous heated shed was filled with rows of War Department ambulance trains. The coaches were thirty-one feet long with the Royal Arms and a Geneva cross painted on the sides, crimson against khaki gray. The interiors had white enamel walls, mahogany fittings, maroon leather seats, spotless enamel basins, and could accommodate up to five hundred men slung in hammocks from floor to ceiling, swaying with the rhythm of the train. There were separate coaches for the pharmacy, kitchen, and mess room, and a sitting room for the staff.

During the journey to the new hospital, Anna studied the face under Kazanjian's tutelage, learning different details of physiognomy than the drawing masters in Rome had presented. She enjoyed her role as pupil, appearing more obedient than she believed herself to be.

'A single nerve commands the face. Here.' He touched her cheek directly in front of her ear. 'This is the root of sensation. The nerve branches again and again into upper and lower branches like a tree, spreading sensation over the face.' She had once fitted her thumbs into a dry skull's empty sockets and marveled at the minute span of the eyes' connection to the brain. Close as two lips.

Twenty-two muscles on each side of the face, most of them longitudinal, created an infinite constellation of expressions, pulled into place by the emotions just as planets obey the sun. The Latin names for the muscles were as exotic as locations on a map: *mylopharyngeus*, *levator palpebrae*, and the *buccinator*. To express happiness, the mouth curved upward with the *zygomaticus major*, the cheeks lifted, and the muscle around the eyes, *pars orbitalis*, contracted into a gentle squint. Fear was complicated, involving the inner and outer brow and the mouth. The eyes widened, the lips were stretched back by the *risorius* and the *masseter*, and the jaw might drop. He solemnly demonstrated this.

Kazanjian also explained that shrapnel caused more severe facial injuries than bullets, as the jagged pieces tore the skin. These types of wounds usually went septic because debris was forced into the body along with the fragments. Gas was worse. It burned away skin and eyes.

When Kazanjian put away his diagrams and turned to gaze out the train window, Anna secretly studied him, the light pouring over his face, the green landscape that filled his eyes, returned by its image across his spectacles. She regretted the lack of paper and chalk to create a memento of him at this moment.

'When will we arrive?' she asked, purely to give herself distance from him.

'Half an afternoon.'

The view through the window was a moving channel, a distraction that allowed him to speak more freely than usual. 'I hope I've acted correctly, persuading you to work at a new hospital in another country.'

His apologetic tone surprised her. 'It was my choice.'

'I'm very grateful for your company.' He still didn't look at her.

He could concentrate anywhere, had tolerated the grim conditions at the base hospital without complaint. In the time they'd worked together, she had seen his breaking point only once.

Kazanjian had lost a patient, a very young man. The funeral service was held on a raw day, and the wind tore at the chapel tent, shaking the ropes and canvas. Even the primitive white-painted wooden cross over the rough altar trembled. Afterward, Anna had found Kazanjian behind the tent, and the face he turned to her was naked with grief. He quickly put on his spectacles, and she walked away, leaving him alone.

'Only the wounded truly suffer,' he'd once told Anna. Simple words that she kept like a talisman, uncertain she understood them as he had intended.

It was dark when they arrived at the estate, and as their motorcar smoothly curved up the long drive, the huge silhouette of the house swung into sight, all the windows heavy with light, as if guests attended a fete inside.

CHAPTER 7

Two dozen squat-legged chairs, their backs the exact height of the bolection molding, had once stood below rows of double-hung paintings in the Picture Gallery, leaving the center of the vast room empty. The chandeliers remained in place, illuminating the newly installed hospital beds in irregular patches, as if still bound by the ghostly imprint of the original furnishings.

The lather boys progressed from bed to bed, sitting by each patient with a basin of warm water, a beaver bristle shaving brush, a wooden bowl of hard soap, and a straight razor. Some patients' faces were so fragile and contorted by their injuries that the operation of shaving could take more than an hour. Artis excelled at this task, interpreting the slightest shift of the men's eyes to gauge their comfort or distress as he wielded the razor.

Patients with severe mouth injuries required a painstaking system of care, as they were troubled by a constant flow of saliva, which wet the cloth bibs draped around their necks. Every hour, the nurses irrigated their mouths with a warm salt solution, 5 percent Eusol, or dichloramine-T disinfectant, prized because its slight oiliness adhered to damaged tissues. At night, the men were awakened every two hours for the same treatment.

Delivering nourishment by syringe and tube into the body was another process that required constant supervision from the nurses. The men's diet was entirely liquid, based on scarce, costly raw eggs and cream, and supplemented with purees. When ground meat was added, their mood was considerably improved.

Many men managed to continue smoking, dampening their lips with water or coffee to secure the cigarette in place. More grievously wounded smokers stuck the cigarette in a wetted nostril. At night, those who couldn't sleep revealed themselves by the ruby-tipped glow of their cigarettes. McCleary never considered depriving them of this pleasure, as their mouths were the center of their existence.

Early in the morning and at the end of the day, McCleary's tall figure moved between the patients' beds, slow and serene as a ship, gently adjusting a pillow or the feeding tubes rigged above their beds. Suspended in a state between waking and dreaming, some men acknowledged the doctor, while others, cocooned in bandages, were unable to move or even speak. McCleary calmed them with a reassuring touch, first deciphering the man's expression or the attitude of his body to be certain this intimacy would be granted.

There was a strange precariousness associated with an expedition through the wards, and sometimes McCleary was aware that he was surrounded by men who were forbidden to touch their faces, as if halos of barbed wire circled their heads. On good days, there was a buoyant silence in the rooms that the doctor imagined as faith, a silvery presence that indicated the tick of healing.

In reading Mondeville, he had noted the author's belief that the world was filled with powerful agents of transformation that could aid or harm healing. Even color had power. If a patient suffered from uncontrollable bleeding, Mondeville directed, 'We must keep away any red things, whether paintings, coverlets, or any similar things, because like is attracted to like.'

Although he didn't follow Mondeville's theory that red could draw blood from a body, McCleary did believe that like was attracted to like. He knew that his face, his voice, and his gestures gave hope, healed, were his virtues. His colors.

The patients worshipped McCleary, and this distanced him from the rest of the staff. The junior surgeons acknowledged that his dexterity was superior to their own, his hands steady enough to balance a seed on his thumbnail, draw the finest catgut or horsehair, inspect an injury with a precise and fairy-weight touch. It was said – half in jest – in the staff quarters that the doctor's fingers, shapely and thin skinned, lacked the coarse whorls and ridges that marked other men's hands.

103

Though he was regarded with reverence, McCleary was occasionally overwhelmed during surgery as he struggled to suture skin to skin. It was a delicate and elusive task, as if attempting to fuse two wet surfaces. Or mesh snowflakes. He operated to achieve the best hope of scars, since it became apparent that reconstructing some faces required numerous surgeries and would take years.

As much of the work was innovative, it was his duty to record surgical techniques and observations for the benefit of others. McCleary's case notes were faithful and precise, but these dry descriptions were no longer a point of pride, as he was uneasy documenting procedures that had no precedent, nothing to be measured against, and uncertain outcomes.

The subtle changes to the men's physiognomy as they healed were impossible to describe accurately, even to another doctor. McCleary tried to hold a visual memory – the color and texture of each individual's wounds – but the pace of surgery blurred one shattered face into another.

However, when a graft succeeded, flesh unmistakably flushed with new color. The faintest tint was significant. As wounds healed, they faded. Red to lesser red. The measurement of healing was infinitesimal, the point of a thorn.

Following the intensity of battle overseas, the wards were overwhelmed with newly arrived patients, and guarding a clipboard held at an aggressive angle, Matron selected those who required urgent treatment. Every doctor was summoned to surgery.

McCleary had immediately ordered noncritical patients relocated to anterooms, the billiard room, the library, and even the corridors when the wards had been filled.

He had assigned Artis night duty, and by torchlight the boy calmly directed the new patients to their cots. Afterward, he perched on a stool in the library until dawn, listening to the men's restless breathing, prepared to summon nurses from the distant infirmary with a handbell in case of emergency.

At daybreak, the patients opened their eyes and gazed in wonder at the primly painted clouds on the ceiling, tranquil blue and white. One man studied the false sky for hours, claiming he'd sighted the outline of a familiar continent. 'But I cannot remember which one,' he muttered continually, quizzing the nurses, anyone who stopped at his bedside.

When McCleary entered the library, he followed the upward direction of the patients' eyes. 'All hospitals should have glass roofs,' he declared to a startled orderly. 'The patients could watch the stars when they couldn't sleep.' *To be surrounded by such regular order was surely joy*, he thought.

McCleary was suddenly aware he was the center of attention as the conversation grew quiet, the younger doctors glancing at him over their clipboards, the nurses self-consciously smoothing their skirts as if they were being judged. As he proceeded through the wards on his rounds, he sensed the patients' attempts to pierce his slightest expression and gesture for signs of hope or a blessing.

McCleary felt huge, important, his vision and strength unassailable, divine, as if his shadow had freakishly expanded around him, a sign of his distinction from other men. This was a dangerous fissure.

Shaken, he left the ward.

This incident intensified McCleary's loneliness, so that he wished to share the burden of his isolation. Oblivious to the abruptness of his behavior, he buttonholed Dr Kazanjian, who had just arrived, in the corridor.

'Should the patients be allowed to see their faces? Do you think my decision to remove the mirrors is correct?' With full concentration, he watched Kazanjian's face for an answer. Before the other doctor could speak, he added, 'Or will the first look at their own faces be too shocking after months of waiting?'

'I'm not certain if the shock would ever be lessened, no matter when they receive a mirror.'

'Is it possible they imagine their faces are worse than their actual appearance?'

'But the patients can see each other. Each man believes he doesn't look as terrible as the others. You've heard them joke.'

'So they have the illusion of hope.'

'It is our only weapon. Hope and time.'

When McCleary was courted by despair, a passage from *The Divine Comedy* occasionally came to mind, unbidden. Dante had placed the blasphemers in the seventh circle of Hell, condemned to lie on their backs, faces fixed to Heaven as God's fire descended upon them, eternally unable to turn away.

The corridor seemed to have been wholly altered since McCleary had entered the operating theater. Impossible to calculate the time that had passed. Hours. Days. A lifetime.

As he strode by a room he heard a muffled noise and guessed that something had fallen or a dog might have been locked inside. The patients were always adopting stray animals as mascots. Patients at Nutley had hidden a small donkey on the grounds for weeks without the medical officers' knowledge.

Although he had no desire for conversation or an encounter, he automatically opened the door. The small room was unlit, but after a moment he recognized the crumpled gray shape on the floor as a nurse in uniform. He was about to turn away when he saw she held a towel to her face, and the violence of her muffled sobs shook her shoulders, pulled her uniform into creases. She was a newly arrived nurse.

Should he disturb her? Sometimes an offer of comfort was intrusive, too intimate. She lifted her head, revealing a dull, swollen face, and he was dimly aware that she was saying something.

'Doctor, I'm sorry. I didn't think anyone would find me here. I'll leave right away.' She rose unsteadily to her feet, and he stepped forward to help. Her hand was very cold.

'What has distressed you, ma'am?'

'Nothing. Nothing happened to me. But the soldier boys.' Her voice rose. 'They don't tease me like the other nurses. They know I'm not comfortable with them. It's my fault.'

'The work is difficult. Your skill will develop by and by.'

'Will it? I . . . I don't like to look at the patients. I can't help it. I'm not brave.'

She knew too much. She must leave. Not unkindly, McCleary told her they could discuss everything in the morning. 'Ask the matron to give you something to help you sleep.'

The young woman practically curtsied as she left the room.

Outside the quartermaster's office, two orderlies mocked Artis for not enlisting. 'Hey, lily,' they jeered. 'If you were in the city, women would hand you a white feather. That's what they give cowards not in uniform. My cousin lied about his age and fought at Ribecourt. He wasn't seventeen years old. How about it, old man?'

Artis prepared to retort when McCleary interrupted, angrily ordering him to get a bottle of collodion. Grateful for the rescue, Artis located the bottle, brought it to McCleary, and waited silently until the doctor looked up.

'Sir, I wish to work in a hospital. To be a doctor. I can read and write, sir.'

McCleary put down his pencil and studied the boy's anxious face. 'Come along.'

In his office, McCleary ran his hand over the worn spines of the books on the shelves until he found *Gray's Anatomy*. 'This was my book in medical school. All the muscles and bones are identified. Memorize them. It's also important to keep your eyes open. Observe. You can lend a hand in surgery. I'll speak to Matron. We'll see if she will give permission to let you follow on my rounds.'

Artis didn't dare look at the book in his hands but blinked his thanks.

After he had gone, McCleary realized the boy had been plotting for weeks to talk to him alone. He hadn't noticed.

Screened by trees, McCleary watched two patients peer over the railing of the ornamental bridge. At this hour, with the sun at their backs, they would see nothing but the murky shape of their heads, broken by the spikes of yellow pollen floating on the tense surface of the water.

What would Julian see reflected in clear water? The silhouette of his head and shoulders would be unchanged, but his face would appear to have been altered with the violence of a beheading.

McCleary found Julian in the kitchen garden, and they walked the perimeter of neatly furrowed earth, thick glass domes protecting the frail young lettuces, their transparent curved sides black speckled where rain had spattered dirt. He was calmed by the symmetry of the space, the brick walls softened by weather. 'Isn't it restful, the order of a garden?'

'A sanctuary. Green and brown.' Julian hesitated as he pushed aside a branch, bumped against the doctor's shoulder. 'Pardon me.'

Because of his bandaged eye, he sometimes misjudged distance, becoming slightly unbalanced. Once McCleary had watched Julian pick up a glass and had the impression that he regarded objects as unstable, treacherous. When he entered an unfamiliar room, Julian's steps were tentative, as if the condition of the floor might change. McCleary was older and could distinctly see the young man losing his physical carelessness. The war had muted him.

'I'm well on the mend. It's only my feet that betray me now.'

Perhaps it was fortunate that no visitors were allowed, and the wounded could direct the anger of their adjustment at their caretakers. He understood that Julian's family lived at a considerable distance, and he'd never mentioned a sweetheart. It was better not to ask for an answer from men who would rather forget.

'At least I still have a face to shave. Or a scrap

of face for the lather boy to shave,' Julian said abruptly. 'I managed to shave under the worst conditions in the trenches, using a bit of broken mirror. Or sometimes a puddle. It was the only clear surface for miles. I'd peer down at the reflection of my face, wouldn't even take the cigarette out of my mouth. I longed for a lake. Transparent. Undisturbed. Blue.'

McCleary waited, anticipating the timing and arc of a question. Julian wanted to know about the future. Sooner or later, some patients found a way to ask.

'Can you repair my face?'

He must give a fair answer. 'Your bones are good. Thank God. Everything depends on that foundation. As for now, I wish your bandage could be removed, but the skin is slow healing.'

'How slow?'

'Forty days for skin and bones to knit. But it's impossible to set a schedule, as each body obeys its own clock.'

'Fine. So my face will be restored?'

Julian's voice was pitched high with tension, and McCleary felt it transferred to him, a bitterness that expanded into a tightness in his chest. He spoke in a low, measured tone to put the other man at ease, but this emotional control was also to help himself. 'Healing is never straightforward.'

'Not like death.'

'That's so.' Without thinking, McCleary had spoken against his own counsel, which was always

111

to give hope. Most men didn't push for a very specific answer.

'It must be a relief to rest your eyes from surgery. To see the garden.'

McCleary was grateful Julian had shifted the conversation away from a painful subject, and with an effort, he relaxed his hands. Rooks called in the distance, and he noticed a viburnum tree, its scent reaching them before its heavy clusters of cream white florets were visible. As they returned to the house, Julian began to speak about his wartime experience as if he were alone, with a mix of apology and pride.

'I'll tell you what happened during my last battle. The fighting around a château had shelled it into a ruin. The furniture was tumbled out on the lawn, covered with white powder from pulverized masonry.'

McCleary listened without interrupting, understanding that this was a process as logical and necessary as surgery.

'One of the infantry discovered the cellar entrance, and we went down the steps, into the deepest rooms with walls and floors of packed dirt. We found racks of wine bottles, supplies, foodstuffs. We shone our torches into the next room, and the light bounced back, blinding us. We stopped, fearing an enemy trap, but everything was silent. We proceeded slowly and discovered it was a storage room, filled with mirrors and fine furniture from the château. A mortar hit above, and everything that had been brilliant went dark. I wondered if I had died.'

McCleary imagined the star of Julian's torch eradicating his reflection from the mirrors, then the light suddenly vanished, eclipsed by the greater explosion above.

McCleary frequently wished that each time his eye focused on a patient all the power of his knowledge would converge and healing would be quickened. Didn't lovers direct their emotion toward each other with their glances? Unveil themselves with their eyes?

When he was in his early thirties, McCleary had been deeply in love with a singer, a dazzling soprano. He had attended her performances at the Aeolian Hall and Salle Erard on Great Marlborough Street, but he preferred to witness her voice lessons.

His choice had amused her. 'Such devotion,' she had said, laughing. 'A lesson isn't a real performance. I need a costume, an audience, to create the role.'

He hadn't known how to answer her, although he sensed her approval.

In the rehearsal room, he had simply watched and listened as she stood across from her teacher, only a hand span separating their faces. The teacher, a strict and dignified older man, had touched the back of her head, then pressed his thumb by her ear, the suprameatal triangle. *Don't open your jaw so wide. Imagine your tongue is forward. Now, follow me.*

113

Then the teacher had directed her imagination inside her body to the shape formed by her tongue, her ribs, the tightness of her diaphragm. Her vibrating throat. His hands had swooped and fluttered. The singing lesson was intense and intimate. Their eyes had never released each other.

Her singing voice came from the resonance of her entire being, every muscle and bone. Her body became a bell of sound. McCleary had been astounded by the emotion that poured through her. Afterward, when he had held her face in his own hands, it seemed sacrilegious to kiss the lips that sang.

Half a lifetime later, McCleary acknowledged that singing lesson. 'First you must cultivate an awareness of your body,' he would tell his patients, his eyes never leaving their face. 'Imagine your body is like a lantern, then pull the light inside yourself. Examine yourself. Find the injured place. Even if painful.'

CHAPTER 8

Catherine turned her head and focused on the strange detail of a gold button on a sleeve, then it was replaced by colors, blue and silver in a jagged moiré pattern. She recognized the familiar wallpaper in the corridor and became conscious of her arm, awkwardly bent over the edge of a folding cot.

'Where is Charles?'

'She's awake,' a man's voice said. 'Call a nurse to take her upstairs. You know who she is?'

'Why am I here? Charles? Charles?' She called his name again and again, struggling to move the blanket off her shoulders.

A nurse crouched next to her cot. 'Let's not move too quickly, ma'am.'

'I will not move until the doctor arrives.'

The stout nurse avoided Catherine's glare. 'Very well,' she said sourly, and firmly tucked the blanket around her.

A few minutes later, McCleary anxiously hovered over her, and momentarily didn't recognize the woman of the house. Catherine. A mourning widow. Strain ebbed into his eyes. He

115

slipped his stethoscope into a pocket and helped her from the cot. 'The room next door is quiet. We can speak in there.'

'No. Tell me now.' Her words were ready, loud, accusing. 'Where is my husband?'

McCleary propelled her down the corridor, her arm trembling, her narrow skirt abbreviating her steps, into a side room. After he had closed the door behind them, the ordinariness of light through the windows restored his equilibrium. He gestured at a chair, indicating she should sit down.

Catherine remained standing, watching his face, her fingers nervously tracing a carved detail on the mantelpiece. 'I saw Charles outside, but he wouldn't come into the house. He wouldn't speak to me.'

'Please sit down, ma'am.' He waited until she had moved to the sofa to speak again. His voice shifted into a slower pattern, his unconscious technique for postponing a terrible announcement. 'I'm afraid you are mistaken.'

'You don't want me to see him.'

'The man you saw wasn't your husband. I'm truly sorry. Trust me.' McCleary felt defensive, his white jacket stiffening around him like armor.

Her wild stare burned over him. This man had taken Charles. 'You lie. Everyone has lied to me.'

'You must listen.'

His words were a weapon aimed at her.

'But no one saw Charles fall on the battlefield. There were no witnesses. Surely he was saved, hidden. I've had signs, many signs from him.' Her hands were curved, beseeching.

'You have imagined this. Only your mind has put him here. Your husband will never return,' he said gently, his expression final and infinitely regretful.

Her body responded as if his words had the force of a weight, doubling over on the sofa.

A string of fine hunting horses was housed in the estate's stables, but shortly before the war started a few had been replaced by Charles's motorcars. The able young motor servant, occasionally called the chauffeur, had driven the Lancaster touring motorcar and the Royal Daimler as proudly as if they were his own, and had threatened to dismantle and bury the Rolls-Royce Silver Ghost should the military attempt to requisition it.

Catherine locked the smaller valuables in her rooms and had an orderly bring the Wolseley motorcar out. She drove recklessly on the untarred country roads, raising dust, the motorcar's speed exaggerating the cold of the wind pressing against her leather goggles and the blanket over her lap.

The city had been curiously bled of color. In St James's Park, the familiar banks of scarlet geraniums had been replaced with rows of cabbages by order of the Office of Works. On the north side of Piccadilly, the fashionable walk during the season, the women wore mostly blue or black clothing. Men were in khaki uniforms or dressed in convalescent suits of dark wool, some with empty sleeves pinned to their jackets.

There was less traffic on the streets, as many wheeled vehicles – even omnibuses and taxicabs – had been commandeered for war. However, the air was thick with fumes, and when Catherine removed her hat, a fine black powder had stippled its decoration of green velvet leaves like sinister pollen.

She walked through the streets of the West End, surprised to find the grand residences were still fitted with window boxes, the pansies blooming under the severe precision of striped awnings, creating the effect that this frail gaiety needed protection.

On the corner, a newsboy loudly repeated the headline of the paper in his hand: *Battle Rages Across the Channel*. Column after column in the newspaper contained names of the dead and news of the war, an unrelieved grayness that affected the entire street. Pedestrians slowed their steps, eyes trapped by this barricade, the evidence of death. The tense black telephone wires strung on poles overhead vibrated ominously, as if also conveying evil news.

In the lobby of the Empress Club, a guest gripped Catherine's arm, whispering, 'One widow can sense another widow,' and urged Catherine to consult a spiritualist medium. 'She communicated with my husband. She described heaven to me.

Can you imagine the comfort I had?' The bereaved woman wept, unable to pronounce the medium's name, and shakily scrawled it on a visiting card. *Mrs Kennedy, Spiritualist Advisor.*

Catherine stepped up into an omnibus, bracing herself against the railing as the vehicle swerved like a ship, and a stout woman in a uniform swayed down the aisle. Catherine stared in disbelief at the conductor selling tickets. A woman.

The signs in the windows along Oxford Street promised palm reading, crystal gazing, tarot cards. Catherine left the omnibus to walk, and two women gestured the direction to Fleet Street. On Devereux Court, she found Mrs Kennedy's name on a small brass plaque by the door, pressed the bell, and entered. A door unlatched with a faint click upstairs.

'You must walk up,' called a woman's faint voice. 'Take your time, dearie.'

A door opened on the dim landing, loosening a trapezoid of light from a room with a worn carpet and chipped paint of no clear color on the walls. A diminutive figure glided forward and invited Catherine to enter. Her coat was lifted from her shoulders by a woman who introduced herself as Mrs Kennedy.

'I'm pleased you've come to visit, ma'am. I sense it is precisely the right time. Sit across from me at the table. Pay before we start.'

Catherine's fingers shook above the coins striking the bare table.

'Is this the first time you've contacted your loved one?'

'Yes.'

The woman's braid slipped from its coil as she grasped Catherine's hand.

When Catherine pulled away, Mrs Kennedy insisted the contact was necessary to perform her work with the spirits. 'Let us sit quietly together. Picture your loved one. You wish news of a soldier, yes? Yes?'

Catherine was unable to remember Charles. Suddenly she had an image of the bedroom, and his silhouette at the window.

Mrs Kennedy's eyes closed and her head fell back. Her breath deepened into a loud, regular rhythm. 'He has been trying to reach you.' Her lips moved silently, as if language were useless, then she stuttered, 'He s-s-says you won't listen.

'Shhh. Wait. Now I see him among treasures. Among fine things, many paintings. A handsome man.' The woman's voice softened, her head dropped to one side as she intently listened to the silence.

Catherine heard nothing, but watched Mrs Kennedy with horror, unable to look away, memorizing every detail of the woman's face. 'But where, where is he? Tell him he must show himself to me.'

'Ah. He is happy with the spirits. He says . . .'

'He isn't dead,' Catherine shouted, shoving the table forward. 'He's in the house. He's home. You

120

stupid woman.' She grabbed the woman's shoulders, pulling the flimsy scarf at her neck. The room tilted until Catherine steadied herself against the table. She yanked her coat off the chair.

The spiritualist's shouts followed her down the staircase. 'He's lost to you. Do you hear me? Lost.'

Catherine heard only the pounding of her feet on the stairs.

That evening, a woman Catherine had met in the tearoom at the Empress Club invited her to a party at the Cavendish Hotel on Jermyn Street.

In the noisy, crowded hotel suite, Catherine was oblivious to everyone but the soldiers in uniform, wearing the familiar-colored jackets that belted and buttoned their bodies into identical silhouettes. For an instant, a fair-haired lieutenant standing with his back to her appeared to be Charles, then he shook his head, disagreeing with someone, and with that small gesture he was betrayed as a stranger.

Catherine turned away from the soldiers to study the women, tenderly identifying several of them as widows. Her sisters in mourning. Did they also feel hollow? Sleepwalking, numb, fixed to an empty core? Had grief changed the sense of their weight upon the earth? That's why it was important to keep moving. To feel alive.

She passed through the throng as if floating, invisible; no one jostled her. A line of spiky white orchids in vases marked the center of a long bare table, and she idly broke off a flower and tucked it into the chignon at the nape of her neck. A man handed her a glass of vodka. 'Try this. It's new. Been imported from abroad,' he said. The stuff was tasteless. She quickly finished it and asked for a second drink. Catherine was slightly dizzy, and the patch of a headache pressured her scalp. She didn't wish to eat, dance, talk. Nothing interested her.

A very drunk young man in khaki loudly demanded more champagne. Mrs Lewis, the hotel's proprietress, shouted that someone had already been sent downstairs to fetch the bottles. Mrs Lewis was gradually depleting the private cellars in the Cavendish with the full knowledge of the hotel's management. They didn't object, figuring the wine collectors would never survive the war and return to their prized vintages. It was anticipated that a direct bomb hit on the hotel would destroy the wine cellar regardless.

The fresh bottles of champagne arrived, were uncorked and triumphantly passed around. Quantities were spilled. Mrs Lewis called for quiet, and everyone solemnly repeated a toast to the unwitting donor of the champagne, Lord So-and-So. To his health. To his return, God willing. To the Tommies in the trenches. To the king.

As the revelers drank, a disheveled young man in white tie grabbed Catherine's hand and pulled her up the stairs, laughing drunkenly in protest, followed by the boisterous party. The door slammed open onto the rooftop, suddenly revealing a dark landscape of spires and chimneys. At their feet, weak lines of light squeezed around the edges of the oiled tarp spread over the skylight.

'Look! Look!'

A huge oblong shape hovered above the violet horizon, only faintly visible until struck by the needle-fine white lines of the searchlights. The zeppelin escaped the lights and flew closer, a silent monolith, an eye poised over the black map of the city.

Catherine watched the zeppelin's hypnotic, slow-floating progress. She felt herself soar into empty space, moving higher than the zeppelin, and with great clarity, she observed in the distance a shining channel of water, calm as a painted line. Beyond it was another landscape patterned with the bald scars of violence. The battlefield. Escape was futile.

Enraged, she pulled a mirror from her handbag and stumbled across the roof, waving it wildly at the sky, a flash in her hand.

'See me!' she screamed. 'Here! Here!'

A man angrily knocked the mirror from her hand. '*Are you crazy?*'

The crowd of partygoers watching Catherine laughed. What did it matter? Every evening held an incident of extreme behavior, soon forgotten. They defiantly jeered the approaching zeppelin, '*Live now, for tomorrow we die.*'

★   ★   ★

Catherine leaned back against the seat of the motorcar, gripping the steering wheel with one hand as she drove. Arched branches plunged together overhead, a blur of moving leaves, as if the world had reversed and a flowing green stream covered her.

An excited orderly watched as Catherine stopped the motorcar near the stable. The cavalry was here! he shouted. A unit had taken all the horses, unannounced. There was no point asking why the man hadn't tried to hide the best hunters from them. The animals had been shipped to the front, where they would pick their way around gaping craters and tracks left by machines of war.

On the steps of the house, Catherine spun around and flung her keys onto the darkness of the great lawn. What did it matter? The doors were always open, and there were never trespassers, only strangers.

Catherine barely acknowledged McCleary as they passed each other in the corridor. His tired face showed only a flicker of surprise, and this angered her, as if her grief didn't deserve more than a mild reaction. She hadn't forgiven the words he'd spoken. That Charles was dead. That she had never seen him. Her determination to prove him wrong was carried like hard coins in her pocket.

The other doctors and nurses were watching her. Now she understood the significance of their conversations, certain looks they'd exchanged.

She suspected that they had hidden Charles, swaddled his body in bandages, tempered his mind, and even if he lay in the next room, he would be unrecognizable.

When she was very young, Catherine had witnessed the effacing of her mother's sight, darkening slowly as a fog of tarnish on silver. Her mother described the narrowing world to Catherine, how bodies appeared to be rough silhouettes, heads were featureless, and hands blurred into irregular shapes.

'But how do you recognize me?' Catherine had tearfully demanded.

'I know your voice. Don't be sad,' her mother had answered. 'I'm comforted that you remain the same age for me. I will always visualize you as a child.' Then she had turned away from her small daughter without a loving gesture.

Catherine convinced herself that because her tears were silent and invisible, her mother was unable to see her distress. *But my voice, shouldn't she have recognized the sadness in my voice?*

So the moment had passed, and Catherine ran to the next room into sunlight, a luminous barrier visible only to her.

CHAPTER 9

An orderly had quickly ushered an unfamiliar woman away from the patient's ward into an unused anteroom in the east wing, where she paced for more than an hour. Fine, pale brown dust from her boots marred the shining length of the linoleum floor.

McCleary finally arrived, still half focused on his last patient, and was startled when she briskly swept the hem of her long skirt aside and reached for his hand before he could introduce himself.

'I'm Mrs Coleman. Please call me Anna.'

Remembering his position, McCleary stood up straighter, an elegant gesture that added ceremony to his welcome. He described the hospital routine to her as they walked through the maze of corridors and galleries, their footsteps sharpened against the gray linoleum laid over the parquet floor. 'Supper is at five o'clock.' He hesitated, uncertain where an artist should rank in the hospital hierarchy. 'You may dine with the medical staff, if you like. The nurses prefer to take their meals together in their suite.'

'I would prefer to sit down with the medical staff.'

'Fine. It will be arranged. You'll also need a place to work. The gardener's cottage is fully occupied, but the brew house, dairy, or rooms in the southern lodge might suit your requirements. An orderly will show you around the grounds tomorrow.'

'And my subjects? The patients?'

'You'll meet them in due time. Their wards are on the ground floor. Dr Kazanjian has briefed you on the job requirements?'

'Not in great detail.'

'We plan to use your sketches and plaster models of the patients' heads and faces as documentation and aids for surgery. And as a prediction. It's my belief that an artist's imagination can anticipate the course of healing.'

'So I will sketch their future faces?'

His eyes held a sliver of admiration. 'Yes.'

'So we are collaborators.'

'Don't expect every surgeon here to agree or express their gratitude. Tell me, how was your journey?'

She described uniformed soldiers sleeping on the stone floor at the station. The crowds watching the men board the trains for the front had been somber, nearly silent.

'Times have changed. Not one year ago, bands played as the battalions marched off to war. There were huge, cheering crowds.' *Hopelessness has possessed us*, he thought.

'On one of the trains in the country, no one offered their seats to the weary soldiers. The poor boys stood the entire trip.'

He stopped in the middle of the corridor. 'Mrs Coleman, there is no need to share these sad anecdotes with anyone else in the hospital. Better keep your observations to yourself. The men here have made terrible sacrifices.'

'Shouldn't they know the truth?' Her mouth tightened.

'I make exceptions for the truth at this time.'

A battered copy of *Gray's Anatomy* was open on the desk between McCleary and Artis as they discussed the structure of the face. The boy's finger traced the line of the nose on an illustration in the anatomy book.

'Name the muscles.'

'*Procerus, nasalis, depressor septi.*'

'Good. What is unusual about the muscles in the lower face?'

'They are . . . looser than the muscles in the upper face.'

McCleary pointed to the corner of his own lips. 'What does this muscle, the *triangularis* do?'

'It moves the sides of the lips down.'

'What emotion does it indicate?'

'Something unpleasant.'

'Exactly. Distaste.'

At the end of the lesson, McCleary closed *Gray's Anatomy*. 'You've done very well. Any questions?'

'No, sir.'

'Not a single question? There's no shame in asking to have something explained again.'

Artis smiled earnestly. 'I wouldn't hesitate to ask you a question. You have my word.'

'A wish, then? What do you wish for?'

'When I'm a doctor I wish to repair the *zygomaticus major*.'

'Ah. The muscle of laughter and joy. The smile.' McCleary's own lips swelled with involuntary pleasure.

From the first day of Kazanjian's arrival, he and McCleary had established a companionable relationship, developing a shorthand of words and gestures. They habitually worked through a problem side by side, Kazanjian sketching on paper or any available flat surface as McCleary gently coaxed the patient through an examination. Once, they had improvised a jaw splint from a silver teaspoon and gutta-percha soaked in hot water.

Keeping muscle and skin in place during healing was a constant problem with face and head wounds, as without bony support, the tissue would shrink and contract. To treat an injury to the soft floor of a man's mouth, Kazanjian had inserted small balls of tin secured by wires. The gentle pressure of this unlikely but flexible prosthesis preserved the shape of the mouth. Later the tin balls were replaced with a vulcanite denture.

Kazanjian's most ingenious creation was a device that immobilized an injured man's head for several weeks, allowing fractured bones to fuse. He soldered together a lightweight wire device that fit over the patient's head, resting on his shoulders, imprisoning him like a bird in a cage. The man couldn't move, wasn't able to turn away, and only his eyes were free.

Pickerill and another staff member criticized Kazanjian for pursuing far-fetched ideas, but he mildly pointed out that the army had determined that men with one tooth on each jaw that occluded were not allowed to have dentures. 'Now that is truly far-fetched,' Kazanjian said drily. 'Although I have heard reports from across the channel of outlandish treatments devised by desperate surgeons.'

'Pont has fashioned a nose from what material?' McCleary was incredulous when Kazanjian described one of the foreign doctor's prosthetics.

'Pont packs molten gelatin, glycerine, kaolin, Vaseline, and water into a greased wooden mold, carved to resemble the man's missing nose. Or approximate his nose. After the mixture hardens, the gelatin nose is removed from the mold and attached to the face with mastic, ether, and dextrin.' Kazanjian tapped his own nose. 'Then it is painted with gumlac madder and yellow ochre dissolved in mineral essence. I've never seen one of these creations, but they say once colored, the artificial nose looks very much like skin.'

'And does the gelatin wear well?' Doubt clouded McCleary's voice.

Kazanjian shrugged. 'The gelatin is soft. It won't stand up to heat. The patient must recast and paint a new nose every day.'

'A prosthetic is a patient's last option. Although there is plenty of precedent.'

'I sincerely hope artificial devices won't always be necessary.'

'Anything to help a man live a normal life is a blessing,' McCleary observed optimistically. 'There was a famous gunner in the Swedish army who had his jaw and chin blown off in 1832. Verschuylen of Antwerp made a solid silver mask for the lower part of the gunner's face, set with gold teeth. Inside the chin there was a small cup and drain to collect saliva. Apparently the man's luxuriant mustache hid the silver half-mask so he could pass scrutiny.'

'Did your father leave for the war?' Julian asked Artis from his perch on the edge of the fountain.

'He's not in the war. He left us to travel, Mum said.' Artis frowned at the anatomy book in his hand as if another version of his story could be read there. He was rarely without this book – McCleary's gift – despite its weight.

'I'm sorry.'

The boy composed a nonchalant expression. 'I don't care what happened to him.' Unwilling to let the subject drop, he added, 'No, I don't care and I haven't thought about him once.'

'My father left me too,' Julian said quietly. 'His leg was infected. He decided to take the risk of an operation instead of allowing the leg to mend untreated.'

'What happened?'

'He died soon after the operation. I was about your age.'

'Oh.' Artis was momentarily bewildered. 'But you're free of worry about him. I worry about everyone. Will this make me a bad doctor?'

'Dr McCleary would probably tell you a doctor must work around his worry.'

The second week McCleary had set up operations at the estate, Catherine invited him to make a selection from the racks of wine bottles against the flint walls in the subcellar. He had picked up a dusty bottle and reverently slid the edge of his jacket over the label to clean it. Clos Vougeot, 1893. Another rack held hundred-year-old brandies and priceless bottles of green Chartreuse from 1869 and 1877. Surprised to find a favorite he'd enjoyed as a young man, he had chosen several bottles of Chambertin, 1878, and hid them in a supply closet under tightly rolled bandages.

Following an exhausting ten-hour day in surgery, McCleary greeted Kazanjian, shrugged off his jacket, and collapsed into a chair. The two men sat in companionable silence, soothed by the order of the Pink Drawing Room, dwarfed by the ceiling's cavernous depth, which the fire in the grate struggled to illuminate. The weather was unseasonably chill. McCleary leisurely uncorked the Chambertin and poured it into two glasses, his last task of the day.

'Good evening, sir.' Kazanjian settled more deeply into his chair.

'I have had my measure taken today.' McCleary was obviously frustrated. 'But I remind myself that in medieval times, surgeons and dentists were classified under the sign of Mars along with butchers, barbers, tinkers, castrators of animals, murderers, and hangmen.'

'How are we counted in such proud company?'

'Because we work with sharp instruments to wreak violence on the body.'

'Soldiers weren't included on this sinister list?'

'Curiously not. Although we share knives and bloodshed.'

'Reason to give a patient pause.'

In the irregular light from the fire, the wine in McCleary's glass appeared as thick and obstinate as blood. 'One could almost imagine this was an ordinary evening with friends, good drink, and a fire. Is that apple wood burning in the fireplace?'

'Ah, could be. The boy laid the fire. It's quiet tonight. At last.' Kazanjian yawned.

'The scent of burning apple wood takes me back to childhood. A room and a fireplace. The book I was holding. My mother calling for me.' Suddenly restless, McCleary stretched his long legs. 'And curiously, one whiff of linden tree blossom and

133

without effort, I'm in Heidelberg, sitting in class where surgery was taught. There were linden trees outside the window.' In truth, war had tainted this memory. The medical skills he'd acquired in Heidelberg now saved young men who might have been wounded by the sons of his former classmates. He was unable to demonize these classmates, was only faintly disturbed by his lack of remorse, like a letter left unfinished. But these days, even learning could be interpreted in unforeseen ways. A patient in a city hospital had been sent away for 'observation' merely for reading a renowned foreign philosopher, now branded as an enemy. Perhaps the time would come when his own bookcase of medical texts, also written in the language of the enemy, would be suspect.

McCleary cleared his head of this thought. 'All the same, I'm glad to have a sweet scent as a memory of that time, rather than formaldehyde or chloroform.'

Kazanjian toyed with his glass; the dark wine swirled and tilted. 'At the base hospital, the fragrance of the wild roses near a triage tent was so strong it was noticeable even inside. It was my belief that the scent eased the men's suffering. Foolish, I know, to look for grace.' His voice asked for reassurance from his colleague.

'Not at all. I take great comfort from my reading of Mondeville. He wrote, "If the human mind believes in the usefulness of a thing, which is in itself quite useless, it can happen that the thing

134

actually helps the body through the power of the imagination.'"

'Perhaps I drew more comfort from the fragrance than the patients did.' Kazanjian looked rueful.

'It has been my observation that the placebo and absolute faith in the doctor are strong medicine.' McCleary leaned forward confidingly. 'I have heard the dental surgeon Morestin was driven to the front in a Rolls-Royce and performed dental work on high-ranking military personnel in the backseat. Now, I'm certain the officers were convinced they had the best dentist in the world.'

Kazanjian laughed. 'Their mouths were rinsed with champagne.'

'Champagne or not, the setting of a Rolls-Royce must have had a positive effect.'

They drank in silence for a few minutes.

'Strangely, tonight I'm preoccupied with memory,' muttered McCleary. 'When I was a young man, the Seine overflowed and flooded the wine cellars of the restaurant I frequented. I helped evacuate Voisin's, carrying the vintage Bordeaux and Burgundies from their sawdust beds to safety. Even now, the smell of sawdust instantly provokes an uneasy feeling, and I remember the force of cold water against my legs in Voisin's murky cellar. After we'd moved the most valuable bottles, we shared a superb wine, the sommelier's gratitude for our work.'

McCleary pictured the ruby wine he had drunk

that night, and his astonishment that he would be allowed to sample such a vintage. 'The meals I enjoyed back then seem like a fable today. Rationing has robbed all the glory from menus. I remember a dish with woodcock and snipe, a specialty at Paillard's restaurant. Durand's had *soufflé Pôle Nord*. There was superb sturgeon at La Rue's. I was once served *gigot de sept heures* that truly earned its name. My fiancée and I frequently supped at the Café Anglais near the old Opera House. After a performance, the Russian grand dukes, the Prince of Wales, and the Jockey Club members gave dinners in the first-floor room with its marvelous curved windows.' He stared into his glass, lost in thought.

'As I approach the end of my life' – he brushed aside Kazanjian's murmur of protest – 'I wish for one last feast. Although the ether in the operating theater has probably ruined my olfactory sense.'

Left unsaid was his desire to share this last pleasure of the senses with a certain woman and unwind a conversation of forty years ago.

Remember me, but forget my fate. Rehearsing her role as Dido, Queen of Carthage, for an opera, McCleary's lover had turned to him, singing these words, her voice as brilliant as her smile. She sang the word *fate* again and again until the *t* was correctly enunciated, sharp as swords, precise as stitches.

He had known her body intimately, as if she were his to heal. But this conceit of ownership had been his undoing, as she escaped him with her music. He didn't protest at the time, allowed her to leave, believing it was more important to take his gifts of touch and eye to his work. To cure his patients. He had sacrificed one passion for the other.

But even after all this time, his memory of her was exact; he could evoke her presence, her disciplined posture, her distant expression as she sang, which he secretly compared to her face when they were intimate. Recently, he'd thought of her more frequently than he had in years. Why was he preoccupied with her now? Was she still alive?

Thin wood-and-metal scaffolding bristled over many beds in the wards, rigged with ropes, pulleys, and weights that immobilized the patients' broken limbs. At night, the red-shaded glass lamps on the bed tables emitted a thick dull light, a fog of dense color, obscuring all detail so the room appeared to be filled with ships berthed at an infernal wharf.

A trolley rammed the door, and the patients jerked in their beds, startled from sleep by the loud crash. At the far end of the ward, a patient threw his blankets aside and leaped to his feet.

'The enemy! The enemy!' he shrieked.

When the shouting reached McCleary as he prepped for surgery, he spun around and raced to the ward. From the door-way, it seemed the entire room was in motion: the black figure of a man jumped from bed to bed, pursued by two orderlies, the fearful patients twisting in their webs of scaffolding, trying to protect their faces. A lamp overturned on the floor, throwing its light into a corner of the room like a flare. Medicine bottles scattered and broke.

'Where is the lieutenant?' The crazed patient tore at the bandages over his face.

The orderlies hesitated, reluctant to tackle him because of his injuries. 'There is no lieutenant here, sir. Just come along quietly,' they begged.

McCleary shoved his way across the room. Loose bandages trailed around the patient's head, and a sinister jagged line at his neck bled from a recent operation. He knew the patient's stitches would be rent, the slow work of surgery and healing destroyed. Was the man drugged or sleep-walking, insensitive to pain?

The patient ducked past the orderlies, toppled over onto a man huddled in bed.

'Get off! Get him off!'

'We're under attack!' With unexpected energy, the patient heaved pillows at the pursuing order-lies, and feathers erupted in a dizzy pattern, stark white when they spun into the path of the lamplight.

The crazed patient shook the precarious scaffolding over another patient's bed, and the man screamed as his suspended arms, cast in plaster, were violently rocked back and forth.

'Kill the enemy!'

The scaffolding creaked and collapsed; feathers

flew around two patients and the orderlies as they wrestled the patient down. He banged his head on the floor, moaning and sobbing. No one could quiet him, since his mouth, or what was left of it, was a dark ragged hole. A nurse pushed the men aside and stuck a hypodermic in the patient's arm.

There was nothing for McCleary to do. He slowly made his way to the operating theater, and it was some time before he was calm enough to pull on rubber gloves. During surgery, the clumsy operating lights, ill-balanced on tripod legs, appeared to be an apparatus of war. The open, unseeing eyes of the patient on the table were unnervingly blue. The man's skin possessed a vulgar whiteness, a thick waxiness, like a plant grown with too little sunlight, and his injury, where it had been painted with iodine, was a gaudy, florid orangey scarlet.

McCleary spoke with Kazanjian as they washed up afterward. 'This is all a performance, isn't it? A rehearsal for a freakish play in a theater. An *opera buffa.*'

Kazanjian's blink indicated agreement.

'I know you well enough to ask if I'm rambling.' McCleary kept talking as if he didn't expect an answer. 'I repair men's faces, and it is only temporary. Time follows behind me, unraveling my work. Nothing remains.'

'As we all unravel. No one is spared.'

For the first time, McCleary was aware that his expression was raw and unguarded, exactly like the men in his care. 'I begin to understand the concept of hell. Or the hell I've created,' he muttered. 'It is endless change. Hope without end.'

Early in the war, bone grafts for the face were taken from the patient's own rib; later the tibia and the crest of the ilium became accepted sources. McCleary had irreverently called this procedure 'looking for lumber,' and Kazanjian objected, claiming that bones were holy, the body's hidden foundation. Sometimes during supper or a rest period, the two medical men enjoyed mock debates about the individual merits of bone and skin, favoring the armchairs near the fireplace as the most congenial setting.

'To bones, your master.' McCleary saluted Kazanjian.

'To skin, your muse.' Kazanjian returned his smile.

'Friend, I am still of the opinion that bones are dull, stubborn things.' McCleary's voice was as solemn as a headmaster's for effect. 'Mondeville claimed that bones held no mystery, since death exposed them wholly to view.'

'Skin is easily destroyed, leaves nothing behind. Like a footprint in sand. Less than sand,' Kazanjian said. 'Bones and teeth are permanent. Saints of the church are memorialized with such relics. Splinters of holy bone.'

McCleary weighed his words. 'But while we live,

skin is our entire being. Skin isn't a shell or peel. I am – we are – one surface. The Greeks knew this. In *Metamorphoses*, Apollo flayed the satyr Marsyas as punishment for losing a contest. Ovid described it wonderfully. *"De la vagina de la membresue." "Marsyas was drawn from the sheath of his limbs."'* His voice was strong and musical as he recited from memory, 'The unfortunate Marsyas cried, *"Quid me mihi detrahis?" "Why are you stripping me from myself?"'*

He brought himself back to Kazanjian. 'It is a marvel that of the five senses, only skin is never without awareness. You can lose vision, hearing, smell, taste, but touch is never muted. The sense of skin is unceasing.'

'Until death,' Kazanjian said softly.

'Until death.'

McCleary slept poorly, waking into a no-man's-land, an unidentifiable early hour, convinced the lowering pressure of the moon had pulled at him. Where had this come from? He traced it to his reading of Mondeville's surgical instruction before falling asleep. 'Never cut on a full moon, as its power negatively affects the body's healing.' He must mention this to Kazanjian and the other surgeons.

CHAPTER 10

At the western edge of the estate, a grotto had been built of grayish limestone tufa, spar, and crystals, its entrance situated to command a view of the largest lake. One hundred and eighty-two years later, Anna found the entrance collapsed, grown over with vines, green sinews that knit the rubble tight to earth.

If the grotto's structure proved to be sound, her studio could be set up inside. She requested assistance, and the next morning five orderlies resentfully listened to her instructions.

'This will be a studio, a place to work. I must have light in order to paint. You understand?' Her voice was too loud, and she had already forgotten the men's names. She remembered faces, bodies, gestures. Not words. None of them had a profile interesting enough to sketch.

'See about the light once we get inside the place, ma'am. Hard to tell what you'll find there. Dirt and animal bones, I'll wager.' The supervisor spat into the grass near his feet. After the fallen stones, weeds, and branches blocking the path and entrance had been cleared away,

Anna stooped after the men to enter the rough doorway.

Inside the grotto, the dim light from small apertures spilled weirdly over the walls, rough and deeply pocked with an unrecognizable material. Fascinated, Anna gingerly touched the surface and discovered that the walls were covered with shards of mirror and shells, their shapes so blackened and grayed with dirt they might have been fished from the earth rather than the sea. In the eighteenth century, the mistress of the house and her daughters had decorated the nymphaeum with thousands and thousands of shells in an ever-expanding pattern, a project that had consumed years of their lives and was their sole surviving accomplishment.

The mark of the hand, Anna said to herself.

Above her, a man's head was outlined against the sky as he peered down through a small jagged opening in the roof, the broken remains of a nineteenth-century skylight. He suddenly vanished, and she dodged the twigs, leaves, and dirt showering down as the orderlies began to brutally enlarge the opening, changing the proportion of light and dark in the interior.

Anna had once visited a cathedral that had deliberately been constructed with a tiny pinhole in its dome. As the sun rose, a thread of light from the pinhole elongated over the numerals set into the marble floor, hour by calculated hour, transforming the cathedral into a vast sundial.

Now, gazing up at the hole in the roof, she was reminded of the men stationary in the trenches; the only visible sign of time passing was the heavens wheeling over their heads.

Iron pipes extended under the length of the greenhouse, funneling steam from a furnace in a distant brick shed up through vents in the floor, a functioning system for more than seventy years. There was less green under the glass roof now, plants were neglected, heat was haphazardly delivered, and there was a shortage of garden tools. If fuel rationing became more serious, the greenhouse would be abandoned.

Outside the greenhouse, Catherine watched as a shiver spread along the lower branches of the medlar trees within, disturbing their knobby fruit, the folded order of their white-flecked leaves. Concerned an animal or a bird had become trapped inside the greenhouse, she quietly entered and closed the door.

A black shape, half seen, moved rapidly in the irregular space between the trees. Someone was in the greenhouse.

'You're trespassing.'

The trespasser solemnly pushed aside the thin branches of the trees, her face remaining concealed by a brimmed hat. She moved closer and lifted the finely crosshatched veil from her face, surrendering to Catherine's gaze. 'Good day. I'm Anna Coleman.'

'Catherine.' She noticed that Anna's wide face had the tenderly tinted skin typical of women with reddish hair, and the lines across her forehead and fleshy neck had darkened with sweat to an intimate pinkish mauve color.

'The patients must enjoy visiting the greenhouse.' Anna's smile was confident.

'No one is allowed here but the gardener.'

'I see.' After a pause, she said, 'Dr McCleary said you'd generously allowed your home to be used as a hospital.'

'My husband believed it was our duty. Are you a nurse?'

'No. An artist.'

'An artist? Whatever will you do here?'

'I'm at the service of the wounded.'

'We're all in service.' Catherine regretted that her voice betrayed her unhappiness to this woman. 'Others suffer more than I do. But an hour doesn't pass that I'm not reminded . . .' Her words trailed off.

Anna nodded. 'The war cannot be avoided. Even at a distance.'

Catherine flushed as Anna solemnly evaluated her face, and even the position and weight of her limbs. Her scrutiny made Catherine uneasy, certain she'd somehow revealed herself to Anna. 'Keep the door closed if you come to the greenhouse again,' she said abruptly. 'A change of temperature injures the plants.' Catherine pulled the thin doors together behind her less gently this time.

Anna remained in the greenhouse, leisurely examining a rosebush, its jagged leaves curved like the hollow of a spoon, stems forked with fine, sternly upright thorns. After studying an object, she could sketch it entirely from memory, fit together its dissimilar parts. One curve echoed another curve, one line another line.

Surrounded by disparate shades of green, leaves of viridian shading to a sulfurous yellow and silver, Anna stretched her arms over her head, sensing the humidity dissolving the boundary between her skin and the air. She slowly unbuttoned and removed her jacket and blouse, unlaced her chemise. She plunged her bare skin into the enveloping heat.

Outside, at a corner of the greenhouse where black metal bars met at an angle, Catherine silently watched her.

The next day, she discovered evidence of Anna's intrusion everywhere – stalks broken, leaves withered as if the woman's eyes had robbed them of their green, buds that had browned, never to open. Her sanctuary had been spoiled.

During their first busy weeks at the estate, Anna and Kazanjian saw each other infrequently. When they had met by happenstance, she discovered it was strange to see him in an elaborately gilded room after the temporary, windblown rawness of the base hospital.

They stole an hour together and whispered

alongside the clock in the third-floor corridor, guarded by a somber portrait of a gentleman in a lace collar. Kazanjian's warm hand, with its faint odor of carbolic, covered hers for a moment, and she returned his smile. She already wished for a less fragmentary conversation with him, missing the intimate connection they'd once shared. At the base hospital, they had found each other at odd hours, usually outside the tents before dawn, and this time had a sacred quality, their hushed sentences meshing as men suffered around them.

Despite his fatigue, Kazanjian radiated quiet satisfaction, as his innovative techniques had earned the respect of the medical staff. He also enjoyed the almost supernatural aura associated with combat, and orderlies traded wildly exaggerated stories about Kazanjian's heroism. Although she had worked alongside him, Anna Coleman did not figure in their narratives. A woman who had emptied bedpans, swept floors, disposed of soiled linens, held a dying man.

But Kazanjian had others to serve now, and he escorted Anna back to her quarters, ill at ease in the areas of the house unconnected with his work. The jumbled hospital furniture, the temporary partitions erected in room after room had so confused the character of the house that Anna didn't notice the absence of mirrors until he remarked on it.

'Why, that is peculiar,' she said, her mind racing back through the rooms, wondering how this had escaped her.

They bid each other an unexpectedly formal good day. A dozen steps later, he vanished into the ward. She immediately felt his absence.

Catherine unsmilingly advanced into the grotto; the thick insulation of the air around her was as close and intimate as a pulse. Plaster had a clean, delicate odor. The stone floor released a mineral scent, flat and cold. Oil paint and turpentine were heady as perfume. Underneath, an elusive, sweet, and rich note.

'It's melted beeswax.' Anna looked up from her easel, answering Catherine's unspoken query.

Catherine didn't ask another question, her attention fixed on the mysterious shapes draped with rough muslin, the chalks and half-opened paint jars, the jumbled brushes and tools, stained from use. Sharp. Dirty. This untidy display was tempered by the soft, irregular glow of light cast off the walls of shells, cleanly frozen into a silvery pink glimmer.

'This is such a peculiar place. Hidden like a cave.'

'Surprising what becomes useful during a war.'

Catherine was critical of Anna's untidy, loosely pinned-up hair, her hands and smock blurred with chalk and paint. Anna could have been one of the women serving tea to departing soldiers at Waterloo Station. Unfashionable, earnest women, former suffragettes. She addressed Anna as if she were a maid: 'This is your studio?'

'Yes. I will sketch the patients.'

'For what purpose?'

'To document their faces. I can record skin color more accurately than a photograph.'

Catherine reached for something across the table, and her sleeve sent pencils clattering to the floor. Startled, she stepped back at Anna's harsh swearing.

'The lead inside the pencil breaks if they're dropped. If you wish to help, there's a smock by the door. Put it on. Your clothing is too fine for this space.'

Catherine wavered. What did this woman expect from her? She refused the smock. Anna watched her, and the concentration of her gaze made Catherine feel obligated, as if the other woman had forced a coin into her hand. No, Anna was beholden to her.

'Start by sorting the clay tools. On the center table.'

The tools were unfamiliar, made for unknown purposes, and Catherine slowly organized them according to the shape of their sinister metal hooks. She put them into a metal container with a clang.

Anna looked up. 'Please work quietly.'

'It isn't necessary that I work here at all.'

'Even the queen rolls bandages.'

Catherine coolly wiped her hands on a cloth. *How dare she speak to me like this?* Without a word, she walked out of the studio with her anger, unable to rid herself of the idea that Anna had dismissed her.

Several days later, Kazanjian stood in Anna's studio, eyes narrowed behind his spectacles, which blindly reflected the skylight that he craned his head back to observe. Shells were scattered over the floor, fine sharp shards dry and curled as leaves, and there was a delicate crack as he stepped forward. 'For luck,' he said.

'A blessing.'

He toured the studio, soberly examining the revolving modeling stands, large flat basins for soaking paper, barrels for wet and dry clay, plaster, water, the easels tilting on the uneven floor. Tools were arranged on two long worktables. Coarse gray linen smocks and aprons hung on pegs near the door.

He peered over a worktable at the images displayed on a length of linen nailed to the wall:

> menu card from Paillard
> pressed rose and a ribbon
> engraving of an *écorché* figure
> copy of an engraving, allegorical figure of 'Touch,' by Floris, circa 1561
> poste carte of *A Lady with a Dog* by Agnolo Bronzino
> photograph of Bernini's sculpture of *Daphne and Apollo*
> sketch of figures on rooftop of Palazzo Palagonia

sketches of base hospital
several photographs

She wanted him to turn away from these personal images but also wanted him to admire her choices.

'Your inspirations?'

'Yes. Mementos. Bits and pieces. Notes toward works in progress. The collection always travels with me.'

'I hadn't realized how you must have felt constrained at the base hospital without these familiar things.'

'I made do.'

'Yes, one makes do. For a long time, I was unable to part with the jacket I'd worn the night I was forced to leave my family and flee. Even after I was a grown man and it no longer fit.'

He had been as forthcoming only once before, when speaking of his childhood during their long journey by train. He'd worked in a thread factory when he was young, standing at the machines for six to seven hours a day. A blizzard of fine fuzz from the spinning cotton had continuously blown around the room, lining his nose and ears. 'My work in the factory honed my dexterity,' he had told her without a hint of regret or pity. 'It made me nimble.'

Kazanjian noticed a thin piece of scrap metal bent into a ring hanging from a ribbon that he'd jokingly presented to her at the base hospital. Now

151

she deciphered the question in his eye and her face became hot.

'Every artist is a magpie.'

Kazanjian gently took Anna's hand so her fingers rested on his open palm.

'Work has shaped my hand. A thousand brushstrokes,' she said.

'Why not a thousand pleasures?' He smiled at her surprise.

Anna enjoyed this unaccustomed union with him, then suddenly understood he wanted something more from her, his affection returned, mirrored. She ruthlessly corrected herself, withdrew her hand, but instead of revealing hurt at her rejection, Kazanjian's face was unexpectedly compassionate. Seeing this, she floundered, as if in a depth of water that no longer supported her.

'I must return to my work,' she said finally, her voice strangely breathless. She moved away from him, but their intimacy remained, pronounced as a change in temperature or light.

A week later, Catherine entered the studio, and without a greeting or explanation, Anna handed her a smock of roughly woven linen. Catherine held it, hesitating, a crude garment unlike anything she'd ever worn, not made for her body, not discussed with a vendeuse or fit and measured by a kneeling seamstress with thimbles, pins, silk papers. The smock was the uniform of an acolyte or apprentice, a commoner.

152

Anna's half-scornful face acknowledged this – and pleasure at Catherine's discomfort – as she waited. They understood each other. Catherine had never hidden from her maid while she was being dressed, but she turned her back on Anna, refusing the other woman entire satisfaction, and slipped on the smock.

Gradually, the two women developed a routine. After Catherine buttoned the smock over her dress, she stepped around and Anna handed her a list of tasks. Catherine welcomed the other woman's abruptness, since this eliminated the need for conversation. Each task was a fine thing, a translucent peg, a nail against time until Charles would seek her out. He would come to her.

She surreptitiously watched Anna, fascinated by the reckless animation of her expressions. The woman tilted her head, grimaced, squinted, and sighed in judgment. Compressed lips, the tapping of her fingers or a pencil indicated calculation, or some flaw or failure in the creation on her easel.

Anna's movements were repeated as flickering patterns across the shells and slivers of mirror on the walls, which had the effect of making the room seem claustrophobic and mysterious. On certain days it was musty; the air held a dankness emanating from the adjoining chambers deep in the hill, never explored because of poor light and the thin sound of invisibly running water.

Catherine's days were now shaped by measurement and repetition. The degree of color dissolved in water. The pressure of a brush wiped through a rag. The point of a pencil. She cut and sized paper. Arranged chalks by color, progressively light to dark, and fit them into slots in a wooden box. Some distinctions between the colors were so fine that her fingers felt dumb, her touch suddenly as insensitive as her eyes. Everything she did felt raw, primitive.

Anna sketched bottles, a chipped cup, an apple, situating them on the table at different hours and angles to find the best light. After this series of still lifes was completed, she arranged a roll of gauze in front of a piece of draped white linen.

White on white was the most difficult thing to depict, she told Catherine. 'Once as an exercise I spent two weeks on a chalk drawing of an egg against a white background. That was patient work.'

The rhythm of work slowly diluted the women's initial antagonism. At first, when Anna requested assistance, Catherine always had a startled reaction, as if surprised by the intrusion of a voice, by Anna's presence.

Catherine and Anna tenderly lowered a sheet of Whatman paper into a basin, and the film of water on its surface caught the light, transforming it into a dazzling white rectangle, sharp as a sail. The paper swayed voluptuously in the water.

154

'What do you think about when you sketch at your easel?' Catherine asked.

'Nothing. Anything. Everything. I'm in the color. I don't know.' Cutting short her confidence, Anna gestured at the basin. 'The paper has soaked long enough. It will become too soft. Pick up the other end. Carefully.'

Water streamed off the thick paper carefully held horizontally between them.

Anna nodded at the paper. 'See the marks?'

Faint lines – a lighter opacity – were scored across the length of the paper.

'The lines were impressed by the wire tray that held the paper pulp as the sheet was formed. A watermark is in the corner.'

'Like a scar.'

'Exactly like a scar.'

They worked in silence, dense with purpose, soaking papers then laying them flat to dry on blotters.

Catherine hesitated over her next words. 'When will the men – the patients – come here for their portraits?'

'Dr McCleary decides when they're ready. I only wait.'

'Won't you be bored to study the same faces day after day?'

'Not at all. A face is infinitely interesting. More interesting than conversation. Some people who sit for me chatter the entire time. About the weather. About their health. Their children.'

'Perhaps they don't feel comfortable posing. You might discover something about them that they'd rather keep hidden.' Then Catherine chose to remind the other woman of her position. 'I am always mindful not to look directly at the servants. It makes them uneasy. It isn't respectful.'

Anna made a scornful sound. 'My hand moves; I draw exactly what I see. That's my only responsibility.'

'You make it sound easy. Won't it be difficult to draw a damaged face? How can you look at them?'

Anna shrugged. 'My portraits of the patients will never hang in an exhibition, that's certain. They'll be hidden in a medical-office cabinet. Like the men are hidden here. The doctors – or the military – have decided that the men without faces are worse than cripples. Not to be seen. Not to be mentioned. But if every mother in the country could see the sketches I'll do of the injured soldiers, the war would end in a day.'

The look they exchanged didn't hide their pain from each other.

Anna often turned to Catherine, vexed by her silences, her selfishness, certain of the portrait she'd created in her mind of this woman. She constantly made demands of Catherine, figuring this was her obligation as owner of the estate. But gradually, as if Catherine were an object Anna studied for hours – delicate, elusive as white on white – her image underwent a transformation.

She realized the younger woman sought work as an escape. Every hour and day altered Catherine's memories of her house and her husband.

While Anna's attention was bound by hand and eye to her work, Catherine retreated into the privacy of her secret waiting. She seldom spoke of her husband. She exposed as little of herself as possible, only the smoothest surface of her character, a false agreeableness that masked the black and red emotions that possessed her. Cold and hot.

Both women were veiled. Neither of them would have acknowledged their mutual collaboration, as if seasoning a dish that neither of them wished to taste.

A fierce droning startled Catherine from sleep into wan light. The noise seemed to expand the ceiling into heavy flatness, weighing it down toward her. Enemy aeroplanes had come. She must flee the blackness that would follow. The house couldn't protect her.

Certain she was watched, followed, she swiftly moved downstairs in the dark, her torch held like a weapon. Outside, her eyes swept the horizon, the night sky empty, lucid. She'd expected chaos, fleeing figures. Had no one heard the noise of aeroplanes? Was she alone?

She swore the droning started low in the distance and slowly spread across the sky. No flame guided its progress, no gunfire. Catherine quickly moved away from the house, certain it was the target, keeping the fence that bordered the estate at her right side. A motorcar directed its headlights along the length of the fence, recasting its iron posts into an endless line of spears.

She ran along the path by the lake. Nothing appeared familiar. Each time her torchlight struck an object, its surface was grotesquely enlarged, seemed to surge toward her. A block of wood was too brown and coarse; the flecks and discolorations on the stones seemed to have risen from deep within their interiors. Colossal shadows loomed beside the path as if poised to descend. Near the grotto, an ominous shape became bricks carelessly piled by workmen. A tilted, angular block was a barrow, a rough pyramid a pile of branches.

The entrance to the grotto was invisible; she felt it as a plume of chill, distempered air. Her foot found a stone step, then a second and third step. Startled, she slipped, and her arms flailed in emptiness until her hand found the wall and her breath calmed.

She cautiously stepped into the silent grotto, the faintest lace of light from the doorway weaving itself onto the floor behind her. The rough, half-seen shapes of tables, chairs, and vats appeared forsaken, as if salvaged from another purpose. The familiar odor of stone and clay, the honeyed smell of turpentine and wax, were pronounced, as if intensified by her limited vision. The thin light of her torch greedily sought the shells on the walls, their pattern of spirals writhing in tight, hypnotic motion.

She'd never explored the second chamber, and now sand scraped under her shoes, and the echo revealed the emptiness of the space as she entered. Her breath slowed, allowing her perception to flow out against the width of the unseen walls hollowed into the earth.

She sensed an unevenness above, something static, threatening. Her torchlight swung up and pulled dazzling white stalactites from the ceiling. Her throat was exposed to their points. *Like fixed bayonets*, she thought. The torch slipped from her fingers, and its crack against the floor brought blackness around her.

Catherine's heartbeat thrust down her arms as she crawled forward, her blind fingers groping stone and sand, searching for the torch. Her hands raked the ground in a wider arc, then grasped cold metal. She switched on the torch, sending light careening against a wall, fracturing into brilliant silver angles. Suddenly something moved. She started, and the shadow moved. A mirror. The wall was covered with broken mirror. She laughed softly.

A thread of air led to the dark shape of a closed door. Another sound. The murmur of moving water. There was a soft splash, and in that instant Catherine perceived herself as doubled, observed by another. Her eye fit itself to a crack in the door, her vision expanding into the next room, where a man crouched in a circular pool, his naked back to her. His cupped hands released water over his shoulders, attracting luminous light to his wetted skin, as if her vision had glazed his body.

She blinked.

His head instantly turned, and the space between them collapsed as she hurtled into a memory of him, for she had seen this man before. He had stood outside the house that night. She had believed he was Charles.

CHAPTER 11

Brownlow, Artis, and Hunt, the head orderly, slumped against the greenhouse wall, a motionless frieze, as if a spell had left them suspended there. Sunrise transformed the glass squares above their heads into a fiery curtain, and Brownlow stirred and steadied himself on Artis's narrow shoulder.

'Let me rest against you. That's better.' His voice was thick, groggy from the effects of ether and a lack of sleep. 'God, look at the sun. How long was the last patient anesthetized?'

Artis blinked nervously, strained by fatigue and the unexpected contact with Brownlow's hand. 'Many hours. I lost count.'

'Young master, you must pay closer attention if doctoring is your goal. Don't take anesthesia for granted.' With difficulty, Brownlow pushed himself away from the boy. 'Anesthesia was once forbidden, and the art of creating twilight sleep was lost. Even so, some wise medical men considered any incision vulgar that caused a patient pain. They were masters, artists of surgery. They performed operations in minutes. A craniotomy took half an hour. Thirty minutes to open up a man's head, by God. Not one of our surgeons has that ability.'

Hunt was at rest, his big head laid on his folded arms. Clearly longing for sleep, Artis hesitantly observed that Dr McCleary was a kind man.

'A surgeon's only kindness is to spare a man pain.' Animated by the growing light, Brownlow launched into railing language. 'Anyone can cut open a body. And sew it up. But put a mind to sleep and bring it back, that is the skill of Morpheus. Sometimes I can scarcely believe that I have this gift.'

Artis addressed Brownlow's back as he lit a cigarette with shaking hands. 'On Saint Mark's Eve, you can wait on the church porch and see the spirits walk in. Only they're not spirits of the dead. They're spirits of the living who will die the next year. That's what my father once said. Gospel truth.'

'A pitiful hope, not truth. If you see spirits, they're a hallucination. A vapor mistaken for an image. The only haunting is in our heads. Sleeping potions can summon angels or devils.'

'But where does the mind go to see such things?'

Brownlow clutched the boy's arm. 'Through the divine gate. I can open it.'

Artis squirmed to escape his grip. 'I saw you did that to someone,' he whispered.

A treacherous crack opened with his words.

'What are you talking about?' Hunt shook himself awake.

The intense red point of Brownlow's cigarette faded against the yellowing sky. 'Let me show you something, Artis. Come with me. Hunt can stay and sleep.'

Brownlow and Artis crossed the field, the mist rising in spiraling, wraithlike plumes, making a frail attempt to halt their passage. A dark and ominous silhouette waited in the distance, a group of figures engaged in some conflict. Closer, what had looked like spiked antlers atop a half-human shape was recognizable as a stag's body with a man's head and torso, surrounded by snarling dogs. The goddess who had worked this terrible enchantment, Diana, stood next to him. The statue's frozen violence was disconcerting in this pastoral setting.

Brownlow sprawled at the statue's base. 'Here. Sit by me.'

Artis reluctantly obeyed.

'You have an interest in spirits, so I will share this.' Brownlow produced a rubber device, like a mask, and a small vial from his jacket pocket. He uncorked the vial and released a few drops onto a piece of cotton wool.

Artis made a face at the odor. Brownlow inserted the cotton into the rubber mask and held it over the boy's nose. His body relaxed on the grass, his thin arms spread out as if he had wafted to earth from a great height.

Brownlow watched with satisfaction. Then he too inhaled ether, quickly becoming agitated.

With clumsy confidence, he clambered up the stag and straddled its back as Artis watched, grinning beatifically.

Brownlow lurched from his precarious seat on the stag, shouting, 'Hear this! Call down the gods. I can match their power.'

He triumphantly raised his arms, and the transparent vial in his hand caught the light. He swayed, lost his balance, the vial dropped and shattered against the stag. For an instant, the odor of ether hung carelessly in the air, a foreign scent in the field, before the air stole it away.

The first patient was ready to be discharged, but the medical staff couldn't agree on an official procedure.

McCleary gazed at the men standing around his desk and took a deep breath. 'Our patient can't simply walk out the door and go home. Masefield's family haven't seen him since he enlisted. The shock of his disfigured face would be too great for them. And for Masefield himself.'

Pickerill didn't conceal his impatience. 'We don't have the luxury of debate during this crisis. Once a man is discharged, our responsibility ends. If he requires additional care, he can be readmitted.'

The others were startled by the vehemence of McCleary's disagreement. 'The men must leave holding the same trust they had when they entered,' he declared.

Too nervous to sit still, Brownlow began to rifle

through the drawers of a metal cabinet. 'Trust? Masefield's family will look at his scrap of a face and never trust medicine, the military, the government, or God again. I swear.'

'We have rules,' Pickerill said.

Kazanjian spoke from the back. 'This conversation seems like a trial.'

'Gentlemen, I volunteer to deliver mercy,' said Brownlow. 'I will dose Masefield's family with morphine to ease the trauma of his homecoming. It would be the greatest kindness to numb them into a welcome for their soldier.'

The others were silent. It was pointless to answer Brownlow, as he rarely listened or responded to another opinion.

McCleary felt anger eroding his self-control. 'Oblivion isn't a solution.'

'There are some who manage oblivion on a daily basis.' Pickerill glanced sharply at Brownlow, but he was studying the frozen, bubble-strewn glass heart of a paperweight he'd found in the drawer.

It was finally agreed that McCleary would prepare Masefield and his parents before their reunion. 'It's your show from here, Doctor,' Pickerill said with unusual warmth.

Later, Kazanjian asked McCleary why he was so determined to help Masefield and assume an obligation that was certain to be uncomfortable.

'Because Masefield must be allowed to have some say about his treatment.'

Kazanjian tactfully didn't interrupt McCleary's thoughtful silence. After a moment, he began to speak.

'Years ago, I had a patient, a young man burned in an accident. Morphine didn't help his terrible pain. He complained constantly, and the nurses resented him. I resented him. I always reassured him that I knew how badly he was hurting, how he suffered. His morphine was increased. There was no remedy for his condition.'

McCleary's unfeeling fingers held a cigarette, while in the calm center of his mind he visualized his patient. 'Finally I sat next to the young man's bed. *How do you endure this pain?* I asked. I will always remember his words. *I don't know. I never knew I had this strength.* The young man's face had an expression of relief and astonishment.'

McCleary directed the broad gesture of his hand at a wide and invisible audience of his peers. 'Do you know, after our few brief words, he complained less. Did he suffer less? Had words healed him?' He saw that Kazanjian was also puzzled by this, and there was no answer. 'Is there something in my work I haven't quite grasped? Or known how to relinquish?'

'Poetry, my friend. We need the blank believing leap of poetry.'

Although it was late, McCleary's walk to his quarters revived him. In his room, he allowed Mondeville's *Chirurgie* to fall open at random and read a quotation from Constantinus Africanus:

166

'Imagination rules all the other virtues, and consequently it may help or hinder recovery from illness.' This lesson was wholly directed at him.

An orderly maneuvered his way across the crowded ward, pushing a heavily bandaged man in a wheelchair.

'Coming through. New arrival. Everybody gangway.'

McCleary stopped, keeping one hand deep in his pocket as if in protection. 'What's this?' He gestured at the small red scraps littered over the blanket on the patient's lap.

'I'm sure I don't know, sir.' The corpulent, sweating orderly shrugged, impatient to move on.

Puzzled, McCleary examined one of the bright scraps, then searched the patient's blanket, uncovering a wilted rose. He gently laid it across the injured man's lap.

'The crowd threw flowers at the train station. For us,' the patient croaked, his jaw weighted with a wire support, plaster, and thick gauze. His good eye blinked, and his head wobbled from emotion or strain from the bandage doubling the size of his skull.

'As you deserved to be honored. Good luck to you, sir.' McCleary quieted his need to hurry. He respectfully touched the man's shoulder, and studied him more closely, deciphering an expression of pride on his damaged face. The doctor was suddenly ashamed that more and more frequently, he identified the patients by their bandages and dressings, not by name. There were so many injured men in the wards.

There was an unexpected movement across the room, and McCleary watched Artis hurriedly maneuver around the beds.

'Something has happened.' The distraught boy thrust an envelope at him.

Before McCleary even opened the letter, he knew Artis had been called up. He had come of draft age. A boy for the jaws of war.

'I'm brave as any soldier,' Artis said, but his eyebrows lifted toward each other near the nose, forming an expression of fear and distress. His voice became a whisper. 'Sir, I wish to serve. But I'd rather die than be injured like the men here. It could happen to me.'

McCleary felt his own face tighten. 'It's every man's duty to help, but perhaps you can continue to work here. You have a little time before you must report for duty. Keep this to yourself, understand?'

A smile shaped the boy's face. A true smile, involving the *zygomaticus major*.

'Have you boiled up the instruments in the sterilizer yet? And see that the operating-theater mackintoshes have been scrubbed and carbolized. Be quick about it.'

'Sir.'

McCleary vigorously straightened the covers on a bed, transferring his anger into movement until it became as slight as a scratch, a pinprick, the bite of an insect. He'd sacrificed for his profession and for the war. Donated a generous portion of his salary to Queen Alexandra's Field Force Fund. Relinquished the certain peace of retirement. His life would end in this hospital in the service of others. This certainty released a ruthless streak in his character, and he calculated that Artis should be spared as an exchange. A fair trade. Someone to follow his teachings. The boy would make a fine surgeon.

At the arranged time, Masefield's mother and father arrived to take their wounded son home. They were quickly conducted through an empty corridor and into McCleary's office. The doctor dispensed with formalities, abandoned his desk to sit next to them.

Masefield's mother, a faded woman in an ill-fitting dress, dabbed at her eyes with a handkerchief.

'Your son has made remarkable progress,' McCleary said gently. 'I must tell you that his face is still healing.' He didn't explain that young Masefield's face was salvageable and fortunately still had expression.

The distraught couple stared at him. 'We didn't know how badly he was hurt. He never let on in his letters,' the woman said.

'We will continue to treat your son as time goes by. There is always' – the doctor stopped himself from saying *hope* – 'improvement.' He didn't trust himself to say more than this, as he had already made them apprehensive.

'We're just glad to have him back. So many men . . .' She pressed her handkerchief to her mouth, unable to continue. Her husband crushed his cap in his rough hands and nervously watched McCleary.

'Your son is a remarkable young man and he has been extraordinarily brave. Now, he is waiting for you. Follow me, please.'

McCleary led them through a long stretch of corridor, his steps slowed to the solemn measure of ceremony he had practiced as an acolyte, giving them time and silence to prepare for the reunion with their son. They entered the patients' ward and proceeded down the center aisle between the beds. The patients didn't flinch or turn away from the strangers, but watched them pass. All conversation stopped.

McCleary briefly glanced at the couple beside him as they glimpsed one ruined face after another. He saw the initial shock on their faces replaced by frozen determination. The father's posture stiffened and he looked straight ahead. His wife nodded to the patients as she passed, not from pity but with a mother's grave acceptance.

At the end of the ward, McCleary opened a door and stood aside. The couple preceded him into the room where their son struggled to keep his hands folded on the table and not hide himself. His face was twisted with an agony of apprehension, but his mother cried out with relief and hurried to embrace him. The father touched his son's shoulder. They had passed across the battlefield. Scorched earth.

McCleary quietly withdrew.

As if the news of Masefield's successful discharge had filled a cup, Hunt, the orderly, and two patients decided to slip away from the estate to celebrate.

'We could drink in the village.'

'Why not? Man's got a right.'

Enthusiastic as poachers, the men hiked to a secluded spot and helped one another clumsily climb the iron fence, the injured men careful to keep their raw faces level. The doctors had forbidden them to incline their heads at certain angles, as pressure could damage their healing injuries.

Hunt could rarely encounter an object without interfering with it, and his stick slashed at the tall grass beside the road. A density of yellow butterflies reformed on the horse dung behind him. 'I've heard the petrol tractors can drive thirty miles an hour over the battlefield.'

'When they can figure out which way is forward.'

'And if the land hasn't been shelled into craters.'

They passed a lopsided lych-gate before an ancient church. The yard alongside was resolutely uneven; its tangled waves of long dark grasses seemed to billow and swell around the worn gravestones.

The second stories of the half-timbered buildings in the village overhung the street, creating the impression that they were unstable, thickly stacked blocks that cut off most of the early-evening light below. The high street was scarcely wide enough for a vehicle, and the men from the estate fell into line, proceeding in single file as cautiously as hunters. Invisible hands twitched curtains aside, and unidentifiable faces, pale ovals hung in the black squares of the windows, surfaced and then withdrew into the deep pool of the interior. A dog's angry outburst sounded from a passageway.

A villager carrying a parcel labored up the slanting street toward them, his boots bold on the cobblestones. He halted in front of the strangers, looking past Hunt's defiant glare at the silent men, their faces jagged with lines and shapeless with bandages. The villager's expression stiffened into fear, he stumbled backward, turned, and his running footsteps were an echoing judgment.

'Bloody fool.'

The men from the estate stood spellbound, solid as the stones beneath their feet. Hunt began to whistle, tentatively at first, then increasingly loudly.

'Company, forward! Right foot, left foot!' The men marched to Hunt's loud commands, altering the scene by their passage, as if they were carriers of misfortune.

At the end of the street, a child thumped a ball on the ground as her mother watched. The woman's skirt swayed around her ankles as she twisted toward the approaching men, her mouth shaped into silent dismay. She pulled the crying child into the house.

'It's dark as the trenches here.'

'More light. More light,' they chanted.

A window slammed open, freeing a man's harsh voice. 'You're not welcome here. You're bad luck, all of you. Leave this place.' The window violently shut.

Every window swung closed, linked by sound all along the street.

Peter, the slightest man among them, was hoisted onto the other patient's shoulders, making a peculiar statue. Peter's head – blunt and misshapen – bobbed above them, the black opening that was his mouth twisting, spitting out a wild guttural sound, his chest moving like an instrument, a bellows. They were grimly pleased by his angry, strangled cries, repeated again and again.

Something struck the cobblestones near Hunt's feet. Astonished, no one moved. The short patient with a wild thatch of hair furiously shook his fist at the blank windows. Small objects – stones, an apple, a child's wooden block – fell around them. Something struck Peter's forehead, and blood wobbled down his face. With a roar, Hunt scooped up a fistful of rocks, hurled them through the dark at the windows. Glass shattered.

'It's our street. Our sky,' yelled the dark-haired patient. 'No one keeps us away.'

'Our legs are strong as any man's legs. Our arms strong as any arms. Hear?'

The quiet that followed was weighed and watchful, a force held by the unseen villagers, and the men fought it with slow, mournful whistling as they strode through the deserted streets, surveying the territory they'd conquered.

McCleary was unexpectedly called out of his office by the matron. He let his irritation slip away when he saw her worried expression. 'Two men and a woman have come from the village,' she said. 'They wish to meet with you.'

'Strange. Did they explain the reason for their visit?' She shook her head, and he instructed that they should wait in a small room off the Main Hall, which was impressively decorated with carved gilt paneling. He decided to remain in operating uniform, a ready-made excuse to extricate himself if the situation became unpleasant.

McCleary's cordial greeting did little to change the visitors' belligerent mood, alter the angry lines on their faces.

'It's not a pleasant matter we have to discuss,' the younger man said, and he drew a deep breath to continue. 'Your patients came into the village.'

'Yes. I understand some of the men had a walking expedition.'

'They broke my window,' the woman cried.

'I apologize. We will see that you're compensated –'

The younger man loudly interrupted McCleary. 'We don't want the patients in the village.'

'They mean no harm. The behavior of a few . . .'

The stout man, who had remained silent, stepped in front of the others. 'It's their looks.'

'The patients frighten the children,' the woman whispered.

'Keep your patients out of the village. Lock them up so they can't come walking around again.' The stout man folded his arms across his wide waistcoat.

'If a soldier – a veteran – had a broken arm or leg, would you treat him the same way? Forbid him your streets?' McCleary stared down the villagers as if they represented the world that would judge his patients. The wall of critical, fearful eyes in their future.

The younger man stared at the floor to hide his discomfort, infecting the others with his uneasiness.

'My two boys are soldiers.' The woman wrung her hands.

The visitors relented after a lengthy discussion, conceding that the patients could enter the village under certain conditions. First, half a mile outside the village, they must begin to whistle 'It's a Long Way to Tipperary,' which would enable parents to bring their children indoors. The patients were restricted to one area of the green, where several benches would be painted red and reserved exclusively for their use. This would eliminate any

175

unexpected encounters between the villagers and the unwelcome outsiders.

The villagers took their leave of McCleary, proud of the sacrifice they'd made for the war.

After this intrusion from the outside world, the medical staff gathered for a hastily convened meeting in the Blue Drawing Room. They reluctantly agreed that the most badly injured men would be issued masks to ease them back into society.

McCleary was pleased to have their support, having previously laid out this plan in confidence to Kazanjian. He explained that this undertaking would start with a mask for a single patient. But McCleary's anger simmered as Pickerill spun out the debate, forcing them to cater to his unrelenting skepticism.

'Why such caution?' asked Pickerill. 'Surely there's a better chance of success if masks are made for several men?'

'The first mask is only a test and it will be kept strictly secret between us. If the mask doesn't work, there's no need to alarm the patients. Hardly reassuring for them to know they might need to hide their faces.'

'Let sleeping dogs lie,' said the matron loudly, and crossed her arms over her chest in the back of the room. She had spoken.

'Amen,' echoed another voice.

McCleary assured Pickerill that all the patients would be reviewed and a suitable volunteer selected. A disfigured man who had no further surgical options and could be trusted to keep the mask project secret.

Time, it was only a matter of time until surgical techniques would be perfected. Every case carried in on a stretcher increased the surgeons' knowledge. The masks were only a stop-gap measure. So they told themselves.

Kazanjian quietly suggested that Mrs Coleman should fabricate the masks, as she was experienced with metalwork and paint. He would assist her with technical advice and casting.

'Excellent idea,' McCleary said. 'Tell Mrs Coleman that after the first patient is selected, we'll have his photograph sent to her.'

'Photograph?'

'Obviously, the patient's face will have been radically transformed by his injuries. Mrs Coleman will model the mask from the man's original face, as he appears in an old portrait. At the least, he should look passably like himself.'

Pickerill acquiesced on this point. 'I don't mind assigning a woman to the task. But will Mrs Coleman be able to stand such close contact with the patients' faces without becoming ill or reacting badly?' Pickerill had stated what they all thought: *A woman has less competence.*

Except Kazanjian. 'Her eye doesn't judge.' He confidently smoothed the fine leather book in his hands that had been overlooked on a shelf.

★   ★   ★

After the meeting had adjourned and their colleagues had taken leave, Kazanjian studied McCleary as he eased himself into one of the remaining wing chairs in the Blue Drawing Room. 'What's wrong?'

'I have been a practicing surgeon for more than forty years. I should be able to passably remake a face. But when the face is held together by wires, straps, and gauze, I cannot anticipate the arc of healing. I lack vision.'

'Predictions of healing are never exact.'

'Unpredictable as clouds.'

'Diagnosis is like a jigsaw puzzle. There is a moment of confusion when you cannot decipher the picture. Then one piece drops into place and instantly a recognizable image appears.'

'But some men will require dozens of operations on their face. Success will be measured in millimeters. It will take months, years.'

McCleary continued to unwind the arguments against himself, unable to stop. 'I tell myself it's too early for conclusions, but when a man must wear a mask to cover what I cannot correct, I have failed. A mask isn't a cure.'

Kazanjian gently reminded McCleary that the mask was only a temporary solution, an object of service. A prosthetic. A crutch. 'It's only an intermediate step to help the patients,' he said.

'Many of the patients will fall into despair because of their damaged faces. Understandably, since their lives have been irreversibly changed. It disturbs me that nerve-shattered soldiers are treated for mental breakdowns at Maghull. But not a word of counsel for our *mutilés*. All I can give my patients is the illusion of hope.'

'Look to your own guide. Didn't you once quote Mondeville to me: "The use of falsehood in place of truth is allowable and justified if it helps produce true knowledge."'

The neat sound of shears came through the open window, followed by the scent of cut grass. McCleary was relieved by this interruption, since he struggled to speak. 'I have no one else to confide in,' he said abruptly, startled by his own words.

'I am honored.' Kazanjian's spectacles flashed white, reflecting the afternoon light. 'And you are overly critical.'

McCleary was weightless with relief at Kazanjian's calm acceptance of his distress.

McCleary had written to Macready, the adjutant general, and Sir William Robertson at the War Office, requesting that Artis continue assisting at the hospital to fulfill his military obligation. Exemptions were not unheard of for men toiling in jobs crucial to the war effort. Shipbuilders and shale oil workers were still exempt from service, although it had been reported that factory workers who had formerly been excused had been called up, their places assigned to women. Those who refused to fight on principle became conchies, conscientious objectors, sentenced to labor, exile in camps, or sometimes noncombatant jobs at the front.

Another group, slightly less resented, were young men with family connections and money, granted desk jobs in lieu of combat. McCleary mourned the loss of many of his oldest friends who could have pulled strings for Artis. It was yet another wearisome proof of his own age and decline.

It was crucial not to react to the patient's appearance. To see without being seen. For caregivers, a neutral expression was as desirable as riches or sleep. Maintaining this was unexpectedly stressful, and everyone working in the hospital wards coped in his or her own way.

At eight thirty every morning, the nurses knelt and were led in a fifteen-minute prayer by the matron. The stern nurses never wept publicly. Both men and women drank and suffered nightmares. Others walked about with brittle high spirits as if nothing was wrong. These individuals were the most fragile.

Occasionally, the doctors, nurses, and the boldest orderlies sought oblivion immediately after leaving the operating theater, collapsing in chairs or stretching out on the floor, too exhausted to find beds. Brownlow was once discovered asleep under a fruit tree in the orchard, the stains on his hospital garb nearly obliterated by a blizzard of fallen petals.

For McCleary, days became indistinguishable from nights as the silver disk of the light in the operating theater served as his sun and harsh moon. After surgery one night, he left the room's merciless illumination, forgetting to remove his operating clothes, his fingers numb, useless, as if they had been peeled away from his control in a dream.

Groggily, he made his way down the corridor. The scene depicted on the wallpaper – a hand-printed Chinese garden by Zuber – was eerily intensified by the new electric bulbs, and his vision filled with this restful landscape, the artist's perfect dream of green, a color that provided a reliable antidote to the effects of surgery.

A nurse in a white uniform and starched cap hurried past him carrying a basin of bloody water, and the juxtaposition of red with the green wall-paper was fantastic. His eyes closed tight against it, but he was unable to rid himself of this image.

A few patients had disobeyed McCleary's directive and secretly sought their reflections. They were unable to hide their distress from him, and there was nothing he could do but offer them gentle counsel, reassure them that the shocking image of their face was grotesquely distorted. For these poor men, knowledge was a poisoned apple.

Unconsciously, McCleary also began to seek out reflective surfaces. An inch of golden liquid in a wineglass. The curved face of his pocket watch. A lead glass decanter on a shelf. Near the stables, he noticed a reflective skin of water over paving stones. At the bottom of the cistern, there was a darker transparency, the water blurred by a fine fringe of moss. In winter there would be the presence of ice, soothing gray, a surface too smooth for the searching hook of his eye.

He daydreamed about the most perfect surface. A cut and polished diamond. Hammered gold. The back of an Amati violin, varnished by the hands of a master.

McCleary decided skin was the most perfect surface. Minutely jeweled with hairs, pores, imperfections, laced with veins finer than a line made by a needle or knife blade, opaque and simultaneously transparent; its impermanence was intrinsic to its beauty.

He wished for a perfection of skin for his patients. He imagined squares of skin the size of rose petals that would miraculously float down over the faces of the wounded men and cover their wounds – thick, silent, and painless as a snowfall.

'An interesting question. The most perfect skin?' Anna's hand stopped above the paper, chalk poised at a slanted angle.

McCleary waited expectantly.

'A young maidservant painted by Sweerts. Her skin was translucent, yet the texture of the canvas was faintly visible. This paradox is miraculous.'

'Your description is lovely, but I'm a medical man. My immediate thought was that skin is an optical illusion. Blood in the superficial arteries is red, but a layer of yellow fat in the skin makes it appear blue.'

'Renoir relied on an optical illusion for flesh tones. He painted primarily with neutral grays, a bit of red, and the color around the body created the look of lifelike skin. Unfortunately, the patients' masks won't have that subtlety. They'll look like painted metal.'

'You won't repeat this to the men, of course.'

'It would serve no purpose.'

'Thank you. I've always held artists in high esteem. I once knew a woman, a singer, very well.' His thoughts left the room, Anna's waiting presence, as he was struck by a sliver of memory, a beloved woman's lips as she sang, the color of her eyes and her dress. McCleary blinked and she vanished. He continued speaking in an uncharacteristic rush, embarrassed by his craving for Anna's answer. 'I believe artists are more perceptive than other people. You know, there is a question that has long puzzled me. Could a man who is unable to smile or frown lose his emotions? Is a smile, a facial expression, necessary to experience, say, happiness?'

'I don't know. It would be tragic if it were true. On the other hand, it would be a blessing if your patients couldn't feel sorrow.'

'I don't mean that this would make any man a lesser person, of course.'

'But perhaps this is your way of comforting yourself.'

183

He could tell the smile she gave him was forced, not a true smile. He thanked her and left the studio in somber spirits. He walked around the lake, briefly surfacing from memory of Anna's conversation to admire the distorted reflection of the red bridge in the water. A leaf weightlessly hovered, then touched the water, breaking the line of the lake's liquid image. He recollected that the orb of the eye was unchanging, expressionless, set like a static pearl in skin that quivered, twitched, stretched, struggled to communicate emotion. Only muscles created the radiant quickness of expression.

He had once watched a turtle that had been washed up on land, the creature's calm eye unable to communicate its bewilderment at the sudden lack of moisture, the intense weight of the dry air.

CHAPTER 12

The voices that carried from outside faded and the unwieldy circle of the straw hat in Catherine's hand was forgotten as she stared at the man in the chair. He sat sideways, his fair hair transformed into a ragged halo by the light directed into the studio from overhead.

'I have what I need. I'm finished for now. Thank you.'

Released from his pose by Anna's words, he languidly stretched his arms then turned around, slightly constrained by the bandage obscuring half his face. He was the man Catherine had seen in the pool.

His resemblance to her husband surfaced, slightly distorted, like a familiar object behind flawed glass. A scar curved near his right eye, which was wavering, deep blue, and there was little distinction between the pupil and the surrounding iris, as if its intense color compensated for the impaired vision of his bandaged eye.

'Julian is the first patient to sit for his portrait.' Anna's face floated behind her easel.

Catherine stiffly pulled on a smock, rolled up

185

the sleeves, and plunged her arms into wet clay, barely able to register its deep odor of decay and earth as its warmth slipped over her bare skin. She knew Julian had been called to her just as a bullet, a deadly projectile, the heat of an explosion, had been called to her husband. Countless hands had worked to heal this man, soothe his skin, hold a glass to his lips, a needle to his arm; he had been passed over water and land to meet her. There were no coincidences during a war.

McCleary stooped under the door's low arch. In his severe white hospital uniform, he seemed to be out of place, an actor in costume as he solemnly held up a handsome wicker hamper from Harrods. 'Ladies and my lone gentleman, I have brought a feast.' The hamper had been donated by a patient whose family refused to acknowledge he was unable to eat solid food.

Delighted by the doctor's offering, Anna motioned Julian to bring chairs to the table.

McCleary smiled at Julian. 'Hard at work, I see?'

'You've caught me out.' Julian grinned, his hands made a sweeping gesture, but there was the slightest hesitation, as he no longer possessed the confident carelessness of the able-bodied.

'Careful. Your balance may be affected.' McCleary gently relieved him of the chair, although his own hands were still tender from surgery.

Julian irritably shrugged him off. 'Even if I fell flat on my face, I couldn't be further damaged.'

186

'A cruel judgment,' objected Anna.

'I'm a disabled man. I'm not sentimental about ruins.'

'Nevertheless, you're a fine model despite your modesty.' Anna hunted down clean paint jars to use as drinking glasses.

'Here I am, the apple of an artist's eye, but my likeness isn't fit to be seen by anyone but a surgeon.'

'Julian, the sketches of your face will help others. They are a reference, a guide for me,' McCleary said carefully.

'So I'm repaying the debt of my care?'

'No accounting could ever compensate for your injury.'

Unaccustomed to commonplace chores, Catherine awkwardly spread a clean canvas over a worktable, hoping no one noticed her shaking hands. Julian's straightforwardness was shocking. She had expected he would be more apologetic, withdrawn. As Catherine's mother's vision had dimmed, she continued to receive guests at home, presided over dinners, teas, her favorite game of epigrams, but she had isolated herself from her family when she became totally blind.

At the table, McCleary sat next to Julian, discreetly sliding dishes within his reach, compensating for his patient's uneven eyesight. This courtesy was unnecessary, but he was accustomed to giving aid even in a social setting.

The tin of foie gras was opened, and they savored

its spicy gaminess, complex and heavy after the hospital cook's bland offerings. The doctor knew someone, a hunter with a large park who was on the venison committee, and promised to inquire about a donation of wild game for the hospital kitchen.

Catherine had no appetite and remained silent during the meal, then finally found her voice. 'I've never seen a table like this.' She gestured at the rough plates, the single bent spoon, the flowers sprawled in a bucket, the pencils that had rolled against the opened tins of food. A palette knife had been used to slice the cheese and potted meat.

'Why, this can hardly be an exotic feast for you.'

'It's very bohemian. I've never sat down to a meal without a proper tablecloth,' Catherine said self-consciously. 'Only at a shooting party, but it was very formal. Everything – the blankets, china, and silver – was sent to the field in hampers.'

'We must cultivate your spontaneity,' Julian said, not unkindly.

'Once on a dare, our host at Hatfield House rode his horse into the dining room. We all held our breath, afraid to frighten the horse as he jumped over the table. The crystal rattled, but nothing was broken. I stood very close to the horse.'

She had sought Julian's attention, but realized her anecdote had made a poor impression. Embarrassed, she studied Julian's hand next to hers on the table, his fingernails, wristbone, a

188

blunt blue vein softly looped over his knuckles. She surreptitiously glanced at his face, strikingly divided in profile, as his right side appeared perfect, and the left side was white, gauze-covered, stiffly mute.

McCleary poured champagne into the paint jars.

'I have a tale of champagne,' Julian announced. Anecdotes from the front had not dulled for Anna and the doctor. Catherine was dismayed, preferring that Julian remain a cipher with a hidden face and history, so that his personal information wouldn't affect her imagination.

'Our battalion had been in no-man's-land, unrelieved for weeks. I hadn't changed my clothing in twenty days. Our section commander brought out a bottle of champagne. He'd saved it from his wedding, as he'd married just before coming over. I'll never forget the taste of that champagne, its effervescence after water that always tasted of petrol. I was drunk on a mouthful, quicker than morphine.'

Anna began to rearrange the flowers in the bucket, breaking the solemn mood. McCleary watched without comment, reminded of the nurses who were never still, constantly greedy for the sensation of usefulness, basking in the spotlight of attention they brought to each patient.

Julian tapped his glass with a spoon. 'Let us drink to risk.'

'To brave souls who risk repairing the world,' said McCleary. '*Vivem*. I shall live.'

189

'Better said, sir. *Vivem.*'

Catherine felt the warmth of Julian's arm radiating through his thin shirt next to her. Had he deliberately moved closer? Did he glance at her a moment longer than necessary?

'How does the time pass for you here?' It was the first time she had dared to address him.

Julian shifted his body into a diagonal and he looked directly at her. 'Since I was wounded, I do nothing but wait.'

She turned his words over as if they were a box she examined. So he was a prisoner too.

'Can you move this way?'

Julian sat under the skylight, his body concealed by a loose, ill-fitting hospital uniform.

Anna studied the whole, undamaged areas of his cheek, jaw, and neck offered to her blunt chalk. His bandage was ungainly, and she imagined that in the dark, private fastness beneath it, his face was fragmented, monstrous, his skin a bitter red.

'How long will I need to pose?'

'An unanswerable question. Cézanne needed five hundred sessions for a single portrait.'

'So I have my orders. May I speak while you work?'

'Certainly. But I may not always answer.'

Anna didn't mind occasional conversation; it provided relief from the concentration of work. She had found that the relationship with her subjects could be as intense as that between lovers, or even a doctor and patient. A portrait was a continuous intimate struggle between observation and secrecy, and there was no protection from the artist's gaze.

According to Kazanjian, the muscles of the face were intricate and tough as lace, so delicately melded with the undersurface of the skin that accurate dissection was nearly impossible. Remove the skin, and the underlying muscles were distorted. The face differed slightly from the rest of the body in this respect.

Hour after hour, as Anna's eye focused on the few square inches of Julian's face, she remembered this tense, ordered web under the skin. His bandage had lost its troubling significance, neutralized by familiarity, and she depicted it as a white, unfinished area. She imagined that the power of her observation would magically wear away his bandage until his bare skin was revealed, whole and healed.

She had learned to work quickly at the base hospital, blocking the heat, her anxiety, unconsciously absorbing the rhythm of the activity around her. Anna had carefully surrounded herself with familiar things, and blank white paper, coarse charcoal, the thick colors waiting on a palette, formed a barrier, secure as barbed wire against disturbing intrusions. But even in the studio, she was afraid that an odor, a noise, a certain slant of light, would bring back troubling memories.

During her voyage across the channel, the scent of turpentine in a station had instantly conjured up the memory of scrubbing a man's naked back and shoulders, gray with dirt, using a turpentine-soaked rag in the triage tent. Wounded soldiers were cleansed with harsh turpentine, since soap and water weren't strong enough. Or there was no soap.

Julian was jarred by the slightest noise, which Anna fairly tolerated as a condition of his experience. He broke his pose at the clatter of a pencil on the floor, an unexpected footstep, the clank of a distant engine. When this happened, the twitching of her pencil or chalk betrayed her impatience.

'Silence is my battle cure,' he explained. 'I was overwhelmed by noise at the front. Sometimes the guns roared like rolling drums, an orchestra. Brassy. Majestic. Sometimes a sharp staccato or hiss. Machine guns clacked. There were thousands and thousands of continuous echoes, from every gully, shell hole, ditch, hollow under a fallen tree. Only the flies were louder. The noise was so relentless that dreams couldn't be distinguished from waking life. And yet, every morning the birds sang. Nightingales.'

She let him talk, her smooth chalk lines tenderly following the outline of his head.

'It was so disorienting that everyone asked themselves the same question, *Where am I?*'

Anna murmured sympathetically, continuing to sketch.

He continued in a softer voice, 'I swear the experience sharpened my perceptions. I can identify the progress of your drawing even though I cannot see it. Short strokes for shading. A confident, drawn-out scrape is a longer line, the slope of a nose, the arc of a silhouette.'

The chalk's contact with the paper, a delicate *shush shush*, seeped into the shells on the walls. Anna completed two additional sketches and paused to tidy her hair, fingers dulled with chalk. Julian was already fatigued, his torso compressed, shoulders curved forward. She ended the session for the day.

Gradually, Julian was able to model unselfconsciously and tolerated lengthier poses without discomfort. He seldom betrayed any distress about his appearance, never looking at Anna's work, and it was understood that without visual proof he could continue under the illusion that his face was undamaged.

Anna rarely questioned Julian about his family or studies, and silence was held comfortably between them as she documented his face. During his breaks, Julian would wander over and inspect her supplies, and Anna would recite the labels of the pastel chalks, as he loved the poetry of the names: Aucuba Green, Burgundy, Burnt Rose, Murillo, Nankeen Yellow. He would smudge a chalk on his arm, fascinated by the contrast of color with his skin, still slightly tanned from the time lived outdoors.

One day Julian abruptly put color to his experiences.

'Everything on the battlefield was gray or brown, as if all the life had been bled from the landscape. Any bit of color was precious as a jewel.' Julian recalled the huge crimson cross on the hospital tent, the green stripe on the ship that had conveyed him across the channel, the sapphire of a stained glass window in a country church that remained miraculously intact as combat had flowed around it and the area was taken, lost, and retaken.

When Anna studied a sketch or was distracted, searching for a misplaced brush or pencil – her attention focused elsewhere – Julian belonged to Catherine. With brief and secret glances, she memorized the line of his head and neck, the patient set of his mouth, the slope of his cheek and uncovered single eyebrow. His resemblance to Charles was elusive, shifting with the angle of his face, the light, and Catherine's mood. Or was it a trick of memory? How long would the true image of a loved one persist?

Catherine swore that Julian constantly sought her face, was sensitive to every breath, and followed her by ear, since he was unable to move his head while posing. She dropped an earring, and he instantly looked in her direction. Another time, his cool hand had found her arm at the sudden drone of an aeroplane, understanding that the sound disturbed her.

★　　★　　★

In the Pink Drawing Room, Anna caught herself jealously watching Kazanjian as he spoke to Dr McCleary; the two men appeared almost spell-bound, so complete was their attention to each other. Kazanjian had never shown her such intensity. She didn't interrupt, but continued to stare at Kazanjian, and just as a pattern can be discerned in a fountain's spray of water, she recognized that he would be lost to her. Everything that rewarded Kazanjian – the hospital routine, the approval of his colleagues, the challenge and gratitude of his patients – excluded her.

Even if she were to become intimately involved with Kazanjian, secrets could not survive in this place ruled by men. There would be talk, and they would transfer their harshest judgment to her work. Kazanjian would be unable to defend her. Her concern didn't extend to her husband. She had nothing to fear from him.

She was certain she had decoded her relationship with Kazanjian, just as she knew the amount of white added to red paint that made pink, the degree of green that would surface in the otherwise dissolving power of black.

Anna belittled herself for seeking Kazanjian's approval and relying on him for comfort. She hardened her heart against him, against the certainty of his future betrayal. In wartime, everyone shaped his or her own exile.

Breaking the line of her attachment to Kazanjian

seemed to heighten Anna's iron power of observation, so everyone around her appeared transformed, their desires intelligible.

Anna, Catherine, and Julian sat beneath a chestnut tree, taking luncheon in the field near the studio. Catherine handed Julian a cup of water, and their fingers touched. Anna observed their familiarity, the closeness of their bodies. She saw the angle of Catherine's head as she listened to Julian, the length of time she held his gaze. Catherine laughed at one of Julian's remarks, which Anna thought had been meant for her alone. Each of these exchanges had weight, like the swing of a heavy gate, a dropping coin. Anna was coldly furious. Julian was her subject, bound by the lines Anna drew, her vision of him. To document was to possess. From that moment, she determined to watch them, her eye a chink, a keyhole in a door, an open window that they would pass unaware. A thousand snares would be set.

They returned to the studio, and Anna noticed the synchronizing of the couple's steps as they walked together. Later, standing by her easel, Anna observed that Catherine and Julian seldom spoke to each other. This held the power of evidence for those who could read it, like the white space in a work of art. Her instructor at the academy had claimed that white had a presence equal to black and ordered Anna to reexamine her drawings. She had been skeptical but found that the shapes had

196

mysteriously reversed and the white space became stronger than black.

One afternoon, Anna straightened up, stepped back from her easel, and released Julian from his pose.

He grinned and swung around on the narrow modeling stool. 'I'd broken my pose long ago. You didn't notice.' He stretched his arms over his head, a luxurious, fluid gesture, and caught Catherine staring at him. She quickly withdrew her eyes, her face suffused with burning color. A brush slipped from her fingers into a bowl, and the brilliant red paint saturating its bristles dissolved into the water, swift and curved as flame.

Anna had followed this from across the room. It was impossible to hide from another woman. The attempt at deceit was like a cracked glass, its sharp edge hidden inside.

She expected their desire would swell and fill the space around them like a living thing, a seaweed expanding in water. This pressure diluted her abilities, made her hand hesitate, interfered with the calculation of her eye, was evident in the faltering progress of Julian's portrait, labored and imperfect.

The couple's tense impatience to be alone together was thick and exclusionary. Anna had become an intruder, an obstacle, a rock, an unwelcome witness. An outsider in her own studio.

★　★　★

It had become Anna's routine to walk through the rose garden between the ornamental lawns and the Italian garden. The original outlines of the flowerbeds had been lost, but the roses continued blooming, wildly overgrown, scarcely affected by neglect.

She took scissors from her pocket and began to prune the thinnest stems of the roses, holding her skirt away from the thorny branches. The path of the sun was interrupted, and Anna squinted up at a silhouette standing with the light behind him, recognizable after a heartbeat as Kazanjian. Weeks had passed since they'd had an opportunity to exchange more than a quick greeting.

'You were watching me.'

'Only in admiration.'

She flushed. 'Please don't.' She tucked a wisp of hair under her straw hat.

'Beg pardon. I didn't mean to distress you.'

He insisted they seek the shade of trees, as the midday sun was much too hot for a lady. He slowed his steps to hers, but she hardly looked at him as they walked around the flower beds, her skirt rhythmically brushing against the roses, petals falling in a frenzy of motion as if obeying a different pull of gravity.

In the orchard, the trunks of the trees were blacker and their leaves a denser green veil than they had appeared from a distance. Over decades, the apple trees had eased into unpruned irregularity, along with the climbing roses trained over their lowest branches.

After studying the roses' bluish green leaves and hooked thorns, she identified them as Aimée Vibert, a highly fragrant Noisette. 'Now I understand the gardener's scheme. The blossoms drop from the fruit trees, succeeded by blooming roses. So the trees appear to flower twice.' She smiled with satisfaction at having deciphered the unknown gardener's strategy.

Kazanjian pinched off a rosebud and gallantly offered it to her.

'Don't pick the roses now. They'll never bloom.' Kazanjian's face colored, and she turned away, unwilling to witness his disappointment. The surest way to thwart desire was to anticipate it. 'I apologize. Your gesture was kindly meant.'

His hands were in his pockets, and he wouldn't meet her eyes.

She willed the conversation to a neutral topic. 'Last summer, roses grew over the skylight in my studio. I had them cut back.' Remembering the spiked branches laced together over the glass, she again felt the oppression of claustrophobia.

'Did they block the light?'

'The leaves were always moving in the wind. The shadows were distracting.'

'I'm not a poet or an artist, but I appreciate quiet observation.'

'Sometimes I believe my skills aren't equal to my task. I cannot use light-colored chalks, the flesh tones, to draw Julian's damaged skin. He requires a palette of impalpable colors. Harsh pinks, red. A crimson portrait.'

'I also have a particular challenge. To observe a patient without immediately calculating what clever device I could create for this man. As if I'm more important.' He shyly looked at Anna to see if she would dismiss him.

She was touched by his revealing self-criticism. She studied him, and it was as if another person had become uncoupled from Kazanjian's sturdy figure in a rumpled jacket, and Anna feared she was unable to reject him. She leaned over and swiftly cut a rose, its stem brilliant white where it was open to the air in her palm.

'You see, I haven't lost my habit of pruning. I cannot help myself.' Her smile was forced and apologetic.

They returned to the house with little conversation between them. Anna sensed that the side of Kazanjian's body next to her was a walking outline of pressure and purpose.

Held upside down, the bowl released its mass of damp clay onto a canvas-covered board. Catherine slapped and pressed the gray stuff into a ball, cut it on a taut wire, and slammed the two halves together, expressing air. The rhythmic smack and pound of the clay reverberated in the room, and she was gratified when Anna looked up, distracted by the noise.

Catherine worked the clay until her hands ached and her wedding ring was webbed with pale dirt, the diamonds dulled. She plunged her grimy hands into a basin and stared into the clay-clouded water, imagining Julian's face there, then blinked and suspended her dead husband's face over his. Her fingers emerged from the water burning with cold, transformed into scarlet flesh.

Anna's voice interrupted. 'Julian is finished for the day. Bring clean water so he can wash.'

Catherine refilled the basin from a pitcher and, balancing it against her waist, slowly walked over to him. They stood face-to-face, the basin between them, as he rinsed his hands, then his dripping fingers briefly cupped her face. Water streamed down her neck.

Startled, she moved, and the water spilled, wetting her skirt, forming a gray pool around their feet, as if they were isolated on a fragile island.

The couple were oblivious to Anna, their intimacy surrounding them like the aura of gold leaf isolating holy figures in a medieval painting, the metal thinner than paper, protecting them with a curious impenetrability.

Anna's glance caught Catherine in its angle, and she watched as the younger woman's lips rounded, filled with color, while her pupils expanded into a fathomless, endless circle that was simultaneously yielding and forbidden, the only black pigment on her body.

When I've finished with the war or it has finished

with me, this is what I will paint, Anna thought. *Desire on this woman's face.*

She gently lifted a corner of the paper on the easel, and a rainbow of powdered chalk became airborne, its separate colors blending into gray as it streamed to the floor.

Catherine left the studio carrying tools in wooden buckets to the lake. She lacked the skill to use them, could only clean them. She crouched in the rough grass, skirt tucked between her legs, peering at her reflection in the greenish lake. Her face was indistinct, an oval that broke into glassy streaks as the tools plunged into the water, their sharp points glinting over dark weeds.

Julian was hidden from her like Charles, and she was unable to imagine an injury on Julian's skin, to visualize the harm that had been done to him. To dwell on this was to court misfortune. But she was determined to correct the hand that fate had dealt Julian. He would look at her and forget his own face.

That evening, she looked around her bedroom as if she had returned as a stranger. The candle remained in its silver socket on the bedside table. No tread on the carpet. Draperies in benevolent folds. The doors, windows, and walls were still sharp and secure. But the mirror was a bright and painful smoothness that held her image, momentarily unrecognizable.

★　　★　　★

The summer light in the studio intensified each passing day, deepening the iridescent, honeyed pinks and corals of the shells on the walls into riper color as if they were fantastic fruit. In this place, Catherine felt surrounded by Julian's vivid living presence, the color of his skin identical to the shells. She imagined if a shell were plucked from the wall, it would be threaded with tiny veins, delicate as a rosebud, bleeding from the spot where it had been removed.

The studio was becoming more precious to Catherine than her house with its fine carving, gilding, paneling, inlaid wood, stone, unchanging view from the solidly framed windows.

She brought certain objects to the studio as offerings to Julian. A porcelain vase for wildflowers. A lacquered Chinese tray. A carriage clock. Spoons of silver wrapped in thick flannel. A tea service banded with gold.

'How foolish,' said Anna, holding one of the teacups to the light. 'Fine things don't belong here. Take them away.' Black charcoal from her fingers marred the cup.

Catherine set down a dish with such deliberate force it seemed her intention was to grind it into the table.

'But we have so little comfort here.' Julian balanced a cup in his hand. 'I believe the lady wants to spoil a soldier.' He smiled at Catherine. 'In the trenches, the most ordinary things were precious. A clean cup. Clean water.'

Anna reluctantly agreed the tea service could stay but said she wouldn't be responsible if anything was damaged. She returned to the easel, her anger unsettled, and as she drew Julian's image, the charcoal made a thin, irritated scratching. She furiously rubbed out details of the sketch again and again, until the paper tore.

A negative influence held her hand, paper, and palette. Catherine must have been directing ill wishes toward her, like the invisible pressure that surrounded a bomb as it fell. Anna's knowledge of pigments, the composition of clay, the secret formulas of starch paste and pulverized pumice for paper, the scumble of paint over glaze of Venetian turpentine, thick oil, and resin was no protection against this woman. Or Kazanjian.

To defend herself, Anna relentlessly observed Catherine's face, the line of her body, her *contrapposto*, acknowledging that men regarded her as beautiful. She didn't trouble to neutralize her gaze, a courtesy she always granted to those who sat for a portrait.

At first, Anna directed only silent gestures at Catherine. She dumped a bucket of clay on the table, indicating with a contemptuous look that Catherine should prepare it again. The clay contained too much air. Another day, pencils had been scattered over the worktable as Catherine's lesson for neglecting to sharpen them properly.

Anna accused her of soaking a ream of watercolor

paper for too long. Brushes were cleaned again and again until they passed Anna's inspection.

Catherine suffered this scrutiny and harsh treatment, unwilling to argue, fearing that Anna's observing, infallible eye would decipher her heart. *I won't be found out.* Catherine thinned her desire for Julian, made it fluid and subtle to escape notice. She must remain in the studio to be near him. She was the servant here.

One afternoon, Catherine was bewildered to find a thick crimson curtain, which had once served in one of the bedrooms, dividing the studio in half.

'Today you will organize the chalks.' Anna spoke from behind the curtain.

Sticks of chalk, broken nubs and crumbs of color, were strewn wildly over the table. Catherine stared blankly at the curtain, listening as Anna resumed her work. She rolled a chalk off the table, and it exploded into powder on the floor, a scarlet starburst at her feet.

Anna jerked the curtain aside, releasing dust that added its transparent weight to the air. 'You're careless as a child.' She glared at Catherine. 'Arrange the chalks from dark to light colors. Begin with black.'

Catherine angrily gathered the chalks, her fingers immediately darkened to the knuckles by Charcoal Black, Slate Black, Sooty Black, Schwarz, Cinereous, Niger, as if dipped into an inky pool covering the worktable. Each chalk scraped and released a tiny puff of smoke-colored powder as it was pushed into a slot, and the repeated, rasping tattoo was certain to break Anna's concentration, like a piece of gravel in a shoe.

Julian stopped at the door and stared wonderingly at the curtain hanging across the studio, a deep red slash. 'What's this? A backdrop for my portrait?'

'The curtain allows me to work in private.' Anna's stern voice pierced the room.

Catherine could have touched Julian as he passed, but his expression was resolute, like that of an actor who had already judged his own performance. Why didn't he look at her? Why didn't he demand the curtain be taken down?

Anna's disembodied face hovered alongside the curtain, and with a magician's confident gesture, she swept it the length of the room, isolating Catherine on the other side.

Kazanjian stood with Anna in the studio, having made a surprise visit. She had prepared for this contingency and waited in a knot of anxiety as he studied the drawings tacked on the wall. Would Kazanjian notice the photograph of her husband, a heavy, somber man in a white suit? Isolated from the rest of the drawings, she had intended it would draw his attention. It seemed correct, inevitable, a truthful unfolding, that he should be reminded she was a married woman. But next to it was a drawing she'd overlooked, a portrait of Kazanjian surreptitiously sketched as he leaned against a post at the base hospital. The two men's portraits held his gaze momentarily, and the slightest flicker of acknowledgment altered his face.

'My portrait is an excellent likeness. This is your husband?'

'Yes. Photographed in our garden.'

With a swift motion, he turned his head away from this evidence of her life and abruptly said, 'Sometimes I am too careful, too deliberate.'

'But it is a mark of your expertise. You have infinite patience.'

'No. I am at fault, allowing my head to overrule my heart.'

Anna let this pass. She rarely excused carelessness, yet she'd left the sketch of Kazanjian where he would see it by her husband's photograph. He would misunderstand its significance, assume her sentimental attachment to his portrait. She had been betrayed by her own hand. *It is useful to recognize this behavior*, she thought. *So it can be prevented.*

The curtain was a permeable barrier, and Anna began to suspect Catherine was sending a code to Julian from behind it. Every day there were messages in the pattern of Catherine's footsteps, the scratching of her broom as she cleaned. The creak of the door and the cold rattle of pencils in a container were signals devised by her hand. The suck of clay as it was stirred. A sponge wrung out in water.

Sometimes when the silence grew too lengthy, Anna would demand to know what task occupied Catherine.

'I'm cleaning the badger-hair brushes and setting them on the table. Then the paper will be unrolled and cut.'

Anger constricted Anna's throat and tongue into silence.

There was a crash behind the curtain. Julian flinched and shuddered, and his fearful eyes met Anna's. After a moment, her gentle gesture indicated he should resume his pose. The sanctuary of routine, of his limbs fixed in a pose, would heal him.

She continued sketching with difficulty, unable to concentrate. The reddish dust from the conté crayon thickened over the half-finished, poorly observed drawing.

Julian waited on the modeling platform as Anna organized her drawing tools on a cloth. The crimson curtain hung directly behind him, and because of an effect of the light or an optical trick, the intense color coarsened his skin, drained its delicate subtlety. Red drew all color into itself, just as pain commanded everything in a body.

In Bronzino's portrait of Lucrezia Panciatichi, the deep brilliance of her crimson dress disclosed the faint green tint of her painted skin. Observing this, Anna had calculated that Bronzino underpainted his canvas with a greenish base, perhaps viridian. Later, she'd observed men suffering from fever affected in the same way; their bodies appeared waxen, drained by a condition under their flesh. Perhaps color rose through skin, as bubbles rose to the surface of water.

'Please remove your clothing,' Anna said without looking at Julian.

He wordlessly shrugged off his blue jacket, his gestures automatic, as he was accustomed to undressing before others, then removed his necktie, laid it with his shirt over the chair. He slowly unbuttoned his trousers.

Naked, he pivoted on the platform. 'Is it my profile you want?' His voice mocking, unnaturally loud.

'Yes,' Anna answered. 'Yes.' She was strong, an anvil; her breath hammered, repeating a noise that she slowly realized was the pencil between her fingers tapping on the table. The movement of her hand became a shiver.

She drew with a whispery scratch, the charcoal diminishing into Julian's image. A softer sound of her fingers rubbing the black powder into paper.

On the other side of the curtain, Catherine envisioned Julian's shirt slipping from his shoulders, the brush of cloth against his skin, his nude body a pale curve, a bent arrow that hooked her. She would become molten, turn to honey, perfume, or water, and flow under the curtain to reach him. Transform herself into smoke, pass through and pierce his bandage to soothe him.

CHAPTER 13

Weather had faded the bridge's painted brightness, and the lake reduced the color of its wavering, angular reflection another degree to a faded, brownish rose. Traces of the bridge's original color, hidden in its carved details, were secret proof of its scarlet past.

Julian and Catherine leaned against the railing, watching the green water sluggishly moving its flecked veil of chrome yellow pollen. He checked the sky and suddenly took her arm.

'Let's leave.' He hurried her across, their footsteps hollow on the dry wood planks. 'A bare bridge over water is too exposed.'

His words flew against Catherine's ears, softly insistent, and she shook her head, not wishing to be distracted from the sensation of his hand on her arm.

When they stood on the bank, he released her. 'I fear aeroplanes, ever since I watched them fly over the trenches. They were unnatural as lightning. Black crosses against the clouds.'

'A black cross?' She shivered.

'I felt like Gulliver. Unable to lift my hand or look away.'

'I've seen a zeppelin. So enormous it didn't seem to move at all but just hovered in the sky.' She remembered the blunt gray shape, the miracle of its weightless elevation, her anger as it filled the space above her.

'We're too insignificant to matter.'

'That's not true. You only act as if nothing matters. Nothing bothers you in the studio. You stand so still. How can you bear to have Anna stare at you? She seems so critical.'

'Little suffering compared to . . .' His words trailed away. 'I have experience with drawing myself. Military officials once quaked at the pencil lines my hand made on their maps. I had some importance. They relied on my eyes and my judgment.'

She noticed he pushed up his sleeves, a sign that he was uneasy.

'But never mind. I have prepared a surprise for you. Please close your eyes,' Julian instructed.

She held his hand and walked blindly forward, sensing she was being led under trees, as the ground was knobbed with the hard coil of roots.

'Now you may sit down and open your eyes.'

Tiny circles of bright color starred the grass around their seated figures, and after a moment she recognized the ragged petals of red, violet, and white. Dianthus.

With a shy smile, he effortlessly plucked one of

these flowers from the grass. 'See? Nothing grows here. I created this for you.'

Now she understood that he had picked the flowers and placed each one on the hillside. A false garden. Catherine felt as if she wept, but her eyes were dry. 'How beautiful.'

'It is the first bouquet I have ever given a woman.'

She desired to enter him like an infection, a worm, a bullet nestled at the point of impact, find the hidden place where he was wounded, mend him, and never leave.

A faint muffled noise reached them, then a second and third rolling wave of sound repeated the rhythm.

She cried out, and he put his arm around her. 'It's a freak of the air. A bombardment. They're fighting across the channel.'

'Don't speak of the war,' she pleaded.

For an instant, he appeared cold, glacial, split by the white bandage, then his kiss had a strange foreign taste that filled her mouth.

After a time, she gently stopped him. 'Will you reveal yourself to me?'

'No.'

Julian didn't soothe her anger but stretched out full length on his back. 'This is the most vulnerable position. Unprotected. I never imagined it was a luxury.'

He continued speaking so softly that she leaned forward to catch his words. 'My face is imperfect, but otherwise I'm whole, like any other man. I survived battle with nothing but my own map of veins.'

Framed by his blank white bandage, his face was flushed and creased with worry. 'Let us make an agreement. I will do anything you ask. But you must never look at my face. Why? Because I cannot look at myself in the mirror. You cannot have more knowledge than I do.'

Catherine leaned over him, and the veins in her arm became crooked rivers given another purpose as his fingers traced their lines on her skin. Julian wouldn't let her touch his face but worshipped hers with his hands and eyes. She slid her hand inside his sleeve and held the fabric between two fingers to anchor herself. She knew every expression his half face could command, except one. The lost, unguarded expression of intimacy.

His gentle weight against her was surprisingly heavy, and they slept together on the hillside. She awoke holding him in her arms, a man able to reveal his defenselessness only while collapsed in dream. She didn't dare to move, to change her position.

'This is impossible,' she whispered.

'Impossible?' He stirred himself awake, his voice harsh with astonishment.

'How will we hide our joy from others?'

The next day Catherine returned alone to the same place near the bridge, compelled to re-create her encounter with Julian. She found herself thinking of Charles, who had loved these hills, and had walked, ridden, been taken by wagon and motorcar, over the landscape he possessed, which was wholly tended by other hands. He never picked Catherine a flower from his own garden but bought her jewels. She immediately felt ashamed, using her husband to judge another man.

She lay on the grass in order to see the landscape from Julian's viewpoint, imagining she'd slipped into his skin and they were joined eye to eye, skull to skull. This was closer than she permitted herself when they were together, as she treated Julian's frail, dangerous face with its aura of medicine as if it were ice she'd break herself against.

Three o'clock in the morning was the charmed hour when those who couldn't sleep gathered on the tiny stage of the terrace to smoke, stare at the still-colorless lawn, and speak softly in the company of others. Occasionally, the light of a suspended cigarette carved a face out of the darkness, notching a chin, nose, lips into place.

McCleary had joined this group, grateful that the dimness obliterated everyone's identity. The tender muscles *orbicularis oculi* around his eyes slackened, and the dry whisper of the burning cigarette in his fingers was the only connection to his awareness. The quiet weighed on him, eerie after the closeness of the operating theater, the intimacy of bodies, the intense heat of the lamps over his shoulders. Was it morning? Had he slept?

A pall of haze obscured the ragged violet clouds on the horizon, and he reflected that it could be smoke from guns across the channel, the chaff rising from battle. Was it drifting gunpowder that made his eyes water and burn?

Anna had told him that when Krakatoa erupted in 1883, plumes of ash and smoke had drifted 'round the globe, transforming the sky, and even the sunsets in the far northern countries had become scarlet. Several painters had recorded this phenomenon, and thousands of witnesses had believed it was a harbinger of the world's end.

'That's what we deserve to see,' McCleary had answered Anna. 'Every sunset should be a blood-colored reminder of war. Let the mighty generals gaze upon it until there is peace.'

His thoughts turned to Artis. Military officials had failed to respond to McCleary's letters. He had telephoned the War Office and been startled when a female voice brusquely answered. He was not surprised when the woman claimed there was no file on his request, no documentation of his letters. He had considered appearing before the War Office Board, imagining himself – a gray-haired man in surgeon's garb – standing before a table of hostile officers. He would beg them to excuse Artis from service, would volunteer for a transfer to a casualty clearing station at the front. A life for a life. But what was the life of one man? A blink.

A figure emerged from the shadow of a standing urn, and he recognized Catherine. She sat next to him on the bench.

'The weather is surprising for this late in the season,' she said, as if to ease their strained relationship.

'Yes.' He didn't care to talk and wished her away.

'I couldn't sleep.'

'No one can sleep.'

'Every night is the same.'

He searched for another cigarette. 'Brownlow could give you a bromide, something to help your nerves. Many nurses need a draft, even after working several days with little sleep.'

'The constant noise bothers me, but I can bear it. Someday my house will be quiet again. Although it will always be haunted by suffering.'

'Ah, I cannot let your remark pass, ma'am. You could dismantle the house with the most delicate instruments down to bricks and timber, but there's nothing to discover. You create your own ghosts.' McCleary spoke to benefit himself, and in the leisurely lilting light of sunrise, he saw Catherine's dismissive shrug. 'Imagine that we occupy your house as if it were a stage. The characters will make their bows and take their leave when the performance is over.'

'I will remember you. Or should I say that I won't forget?'

'Hopefully you will remember me with kind regard.' McCleary flexed his fingers to ease their stiffness, considering his next words. 'It's fanciful, but to distract myself occasionally, I visualize the ballroom filled with your guests.'

Catherine was silent for a moment, and he was certain an image of dancing figures spun in her memory.

'On the afternoon of the grand balls, the lamp boys would light the chandeliers, hundreds of candles. It took hours and hours. My husband was a superb dancer. We were so breathless after dancing.' She clasped her arms around her body. 'The tables were decorated with sugar flowers, and huge floral arrangements stood between the windows. Lilies. The fragrance was overwhelming.' Her attention moved back to him. 'Even today, I cannot bear the scent.'

Catherine and Julian never spent the night together but found sanctuary in the vast lawn and woods. She now routinely dressed in dark-colored clothing in order to be inconspicuous, to move unobserved. They frequently met at the tall hornbeam hedge, where she'd discovered a hidden bay cut into the living branches, irregular, green, and secret, just wide enough for two bodies side by side. They met in deep woods, where soft pine needles had made a springy, straw-colored cushion for them under trees.

At midday, they occasionally risked an encounter

218

in the yew walk, a shadowed tunnel of gnarled, rough-barked branches. Nothing grew underfoot, no sun lit their faces or reached their straining bodies, intertwined against a tree. Under cover of dusk, they enjoyed the strange spaciousness of a forgotten amphitheater carved into a hillside the previous century, its gentle slope overgrown with grasses and wildflowers.

It was in this place that she haltingly explained herself to Julian. 'You'll think I'm mad or selfish. I am constantly afraid, but I've never felt so alive. It's because of the war.' She had expected him to be angry or scornful, but there was recognition and sad acceptance in his expression.

During their early intimacies, Catherine had craved the tension created as she held back, watched herself, careful not to disturb Julian's bandages, hurt his delicate face, wound him with words or expression. This changed. As Anna proceeded with his portrait, Julian became less cautious and self-contained, as if Anna's eye had freed him, the last veil torn away, the brick wall of his face finally revealed.

Gradually, he taught Catherine that her body was strung with a network of nerves, denser in certain sensitive places under her skin where he slowly, remarkably discovered them.

It was Catherine's desire to have Julian witness her intimate face. She became lost in his embrace, assuming multiple guises – like a mythical creature

– experiencing pleasure in each one. She was transformed into a shower of coins, a reed, a thing of
hands and lips, appetites and movements that she
experienced but did not control. Catherine didn't
recognize herself.

Anna had been delayed on her way to the studio.
Julian waited quietly, wearing only a shirt as cover,
his other clothing arranged on another chair.
Catherine folded lengths of canvas at a table facing
the curtain hanging between them. She gradually
became aware that their breathing was synchronized and, drawn by this rhythm, slowly approached
the curtain, then stood so it touched the length of
her body. Her face nestled into its velvet folds overlaid with a smoky scent from the fireplace in the
room where it had originally hung. Minutes passed,
marked by the slight, sonorous movement of water
in another chamber.

Catherine heard Julian stand, then he moved
against the other side of the curtain. Tenderly, he
pushed the fabric against her face and down her
neck. She closed her eyes. His hands found her
shoulders, and she pressed her weight into him,
curving like a diver. He became more aggressive,
intimate, as if tracing the outline of a continent,
forming a map of her body.

The curtain cushioned her hand as she touched
the undamaged side of his face, his brow, the
pressured orb of the eye, his nose, the hard line
of teeth, the rounded rim of his perfect ear. His

features felt primitive as a mask through the soft fabric.

He stripped off his shirt, and she imagined the angled cord of muscle in his neck, his shoulders, the hollow under his arm, then her fingers completed these images. His ribs and hip bone were prominent, her thumb rounded over its shape and then her palm curved against another bluntness.

Anna entered the room with the stealth of a goddess, undetected until the wrathful stamp of her sandal, the spume of her whirling gown. She violently swept the curtain aside.

Catherine recoiled as if she'd been struck.

Anna's eyes enlarged, filled with Julian's face and body. 'I'll start a new portrait tomorrow. It's time to sketch your naked face.'

Artis ground charcoal in a mortar alongside Anna, shy when they were alone in the studio.

'What did you do before the house became a hospital, Artis?'

'I cleaned plate for the butler. Cut and aired the newspapers. In the afternoon, I lowered the blinds, prepared the candles, and lit the lamps. I walked from room to room. Then everyone left for war, even the house steward and the stable boys.'

She didn't ask if any of the men had returned. 'Will you be called up to join the service soon?'

He didn't answer.

'You're tall enough.'

221

'But I want to stay here and learn to be a doctor. Dr McCleary has lent me his books, and I'm memorizing the muscles of the face.'

'A doctor?' She kindly masked her skepticism, having been discouraged from pursuing her own work when she was young. 'Ask Dr McCleary if it isn't true that a surgeon must also have the soul of an artist. Don't smile.'

He considered this for a moment. 'I only ask the doctor serious questions.'

Anna had once passed an entire summer furiously cutting and arranging roses in a still life, trying to capture their elusive color on canvas and paper. The roses had defied her, seeming to change color every hour.

Years later Jules Gravereaux, the great rosarian of Roseraie de l'Hay, explained this phenomenon to her. The rose petal itself was actually white, veneered by a film of color on both sides. Within hours of the rose's blooming, sun and wind evaporated the color, made it transparent, so red petals became pink and paler petals faded to white. Yellow was the most fugitive color. 'It dies almost as you gaze upon it, madame,' he had said.

Years ago, when Anna had seen her newborn baby for the first time, she was awed by the fineness of his skin and fiercely memorized every inch of his tiny body. Gradually the color of his skin had faded, a change too delicate for her eye to register, as the fragile boy began the process of dying before he was three days old. The color of a lost child.

Capriciously shadowed by leaves, Anna balanced on an unsteady bench, pruning the roses that had advanced fearlessly over the pergola. Her secateurs steadily bit through wood and weak stalks, eliminating buds so the few remaining on the stems would flourish. The muted peal of a distant church bell overlaid her pleasure at the calm deliberateness of this activity.

Kazanjian monitored her, watching closely as if Anna would tumble from the bench or discard some precious thing about herself that he'd miss. Sensing his desire, she recast him as a dark shape at the edge of her eye.

The thin stems cut from the roses – green whips studded with thorns – fell around him, streaking across his spectacles. He began to gather the branches on the ground, wary of thorns despite his thick gloves. Without looking at her, he said, 'Anna, we work well together.'

'Work is our entire experience of each other.'

'Yes. I've seen firsthand how you comfort others. You were a comfort to me too.'

Anna knew he was thinking of his grief at the young soldier's death. 'Dr Kazanjian, I once thought pleasure revealed the truth of a body. Until the war. Now I know the wounded body is the most truthful.'

'You're very harsh. I had hoped for a tender answer.'

Hadn't she made it clear he shouldn't declare his heart? His disappointment gave her strange relief. Released by her secateurs, a shower of leaves blurred green between them.

'May I ask you a question?' His face tilted up to her. 'You don't need to answer me with words, but allow me to watch you. Please don't turn away.'

She had dreaded this inevitable confrontation and set herself against him.

'Anna.' He was stiff with tension and held the branches as if arming himself for her reply. His voice was hoarse, nervous. 'Anna, how do you regard me? Do you love me?'

Anna's expression softened as she looked down at him, and she instantly understood that he had read an answer in her eyes. He was an intruding, observing presence and had discovered her. Panicked, she shook her head *No, I don't love you.*

'That isn't what your face revealed. You aren't telling the truth.'

'Your observation is wrong. You deceive yourself.' Anna's words were arrows.

He dropped the branches in his hands, bowed his head, and walked away from the pergola.

It took all her strength to grip the secateurs, press the blades together, cut through a thick and unwilling branch and crush her regret for the hurt she had dealt him.

★   ★   ★

Anna could gauge certain properties by touch or sight: the temperature wax could be manipulated, when the ground on a paper was dry. By instinct, she knew the plastic strength of clay, the amount of water a brush would hold, the amount of mastic and dammer to dissolve in linseed oil to produce a varnish with a luminous quality. Paint possessed a strangely carnal essence, and she could blindly identify some colors by the weight of the tube in the palm of her hand. White paint felt solid, thick with zinc and lead titanium. Reds were medium weight, except for the deepest shades. Black paint contained airy substances: powdered charcoal, ash, soot, dust, burnt bone and horn. Naples Yellow was light, containing very little oil. Brown was recognizable by another kind of sensation, a sober dullness.

How would Kazanjian's body feel to her hand? Anna imagined the tenseness of his muscles, the heat and odor of his skin. To replace these troubling thoughts, she allowed a single color on the palette – Crimson Lake – to fill her mind as if it were projected on a blank wall, a camera obscura. Then she focused on Rose Madder, Blue Verditer. This state of nothingness she created calmed her.

She couldn't lie to Kazanjian. But she would lie to herself.

Flakes of gray clay scattered over the table as Anna thoughtfully scraped out a bowl. This was busy-work, a spell against decision and indecision. She had watched soldiers polish buttons and boots, mend clothing, and carefully fold blankets over their cots, the fullness of repetition calming their minds, keeping away grief, despair, a dreaded event.

The previous night, her dreams had been sorrowful. Julian's unbandaged face was presented to her, his skin torn like paper and discolored by bruises, dark as leaves. After she had awakened, she remained motionless in bed, allowing a sense of foreboding to expand until tears held the edge of her eyes. Her dream had been a rehearsal. Now in full light of day, Julian's true face would be revealed without his bandages. He would be stripped of the frail privacy he had guarded while remaining ignorant of his own appearance.

Julian's feet ground gritty powder on the floor, announcing his arrival. Catherine had been sent away on some pretext so he was alone with Anna in the studio.

'You're here early.' Anna concentrated on sticking a wetted tape to the drawing board, and her voice was stiff with effort to remain neutral.

'You seem to be having difficulty,' he observed.

'The tape is too damp.'

'Let me help you.'

He held one side, and she pressed the tape down, her hands hesitant and clumsy. Finished, she nodded her appreciation to him and steadied the drawing board on the easel, a habitual action that now felt as if she were setting up a target.

Julian stepped onto the modeling platform, his footsteps uncharacteristically loud. 'Once my bandage is removed, you'll see me differently.' His low voice carried the authority of his encounter with suffering.

Anna stopped her automatic response to comfort him, although certain that he was correct. How could it be otherwise?

Julian carefully began to unwind the bandage from his face as if in slow motion. The gauze was weightless as a veil, thin as a crosshatch of white pencil lines, and his skin was visibly pink through the last transparent layer. The gauze strip gently spiraled free from his face, draping itself over one shoulder. He stood without moving, his face completely exposed.

His good eye – the deep blue of flint – fiercely held her gaze, refusing to let his witness withdraw. The pitiless overhead light intensified the unevenness of his ruined skin. The left side of his face was misshapen, as if the flesh had been crudely torn off and violently flung back in place, unformed as raw clay. It had no symmetry. His face a plowed furrow. A trench of flesh. An angry map of red.

Anna had willed herself not to react, but her eyes involuntarily closed against him for an instant, the infinite sadness of his expression already spreading in her memory like a slow stain, a diffusing cloud.

Then she straightened her shoulders and studied

him without flinching. Their mutual anguish was present but invisible, as an X-ray of the body reveals the bones but not the tension of the muscles that hold them in place.

Her chalk hesitantly began to record his face, and soon the paper was filled with an angry hatch of lines.

CHAPTER 14

An orderly backed the four-seat Vauxhall from the stable, then yelled until another aide grudgingly slammed the heavy wooden doors closed. With immense dignity, McCleary and Kazanjian climbed into the motorcar.

It was dusk, and the lorries speeding in the opposite direction on the main road cast their lights – white spheres blurred into a moving garland – straight into the men's eyes. The battering rhythm of these lights, the constant nervous motion of the vehicle, dizzied McCleary.

When he opened his eyes again, Kazanjian had turned around in his seat, his face obscured by bulky goggles, and was shouting over the noise of the engine. He wanted McCleary to understand that the city had changed since his last visit. McCleary pantomimed *yes*, since the streams of dust from the road seemed to drag away his words.

True to Kazanjian's observation, the pedestrians were somber and monotonous, even the women wore drab-colored clothing. A fashionable matron carrying a hatbox, striped in vivid green and white, jarred the palette of the street. McCleary commented that the woman should be commended for her gaiety.

The Third General Hospital was hosting a conference on new developments in surgery, and McCleary and Kazanjian slowly made their way to the director's office, effusively greeting colleagues who had been out of contact since war had been declared.

Kazanjian delivered one of the first lectures on the program. 'This is a new apparatus,' he announced, holding up a curious device, springy with wires, that looked nothing like a medical instrument. 'Vulcanite, plasticine, black copper cement, and modeling compound can also be recommended for support.' The audience murmured appreciation for his attempt at humor, more acceptable because of his accent.

Kazanjian explained his novel method of intermaxillary wiring, then presented several prosthetic devices and their applications. 'The greatest difficulty is preserving the bones, skin, and muscles in proper contour while healing occurs, which must be done in stages. I have devised a temporary bandage using the head as support for wounds of the midface, craniofacial dislocation, or destruction of the jaws.'

Crinoline – the same fabric used for petticoats – was soaked in plaster and reinforced with glue. These strips were wound circularly around the patient's shaved head and under the chin. Next, smaller strips of linen with rows of hooks at their edges were glued to the bandage wrapping the patient's face. The hooks were threaded to one another with rubber bands or Angle's wire and snugged tight, forcing the wound together. Old cut-up rubber gloves were installed as a lining to ease discomfort where the fabric touched the skin. The crinoline bandage immobilized the patient's face and provided progressive pressure to help cicatrization of the tissues. It could also be easily removed for cleaning.

For another patient, Kazanjian had fashioned a 'face bow' using stiff wire suspended from the headband of an army helmet to secure a broken mandible, shattered molars, and a detached lip.

The problem was a familiar one, but few of the doctors had worked out a solution. Kazanjian's lecture was well received, and he fielded numerous questions, addressing issues concerning trismus and closed-bite splints. With considerable pride, McCleary watched Kazanjian's face relax as he unfolded his case. He realized they were the mavericks at this gathering.

Later, McCleary took his place at the lectern before his medical colleagues, opened a portfolio, and slipped out Anna's drawings of Julian's face. It was late and he was the last speaker, but as he held up one drawing after another, the nurses and doctors stiffened into attention. To those sitting at the back of the large paneled room, Julian's face

231

appeared to be an unrecognizable, abstract shape, reddish and pinkish.

'We operate, we wait. We operate again,' McCleary explained.

After a brief, respectful silence, someone asked at what point did Dr McCleary know that everything had been done for a patient? That treatment had ended?

McCleary nodded to acknowledge the question. 'I rely on the patient's decision. He will tell us when enough is enough.'

The next day, McCleary made excuses to Kazanjian and escaped for a solitary walk from Trafalgar Square down Whitehall, preparing for another business matter. His eye was continually drawn to the wounded soldiers, many of them encumbered by jackets awkwardly arranged over their slings or crutches; their irregular silhouettes and limping walk made them highly visible on the street.

The secretary of state for war and the Army Council were headquartered in the War Office building between Whitehall Place and Horse Guards Avenue. McCleary was discomfited to find himself in the role of pilgrim where the machinery of war originated. Even the surrounding rooftops bristled with wireless telegraph installations. At the striking of eleven o'clock, there was a clamor nearby as two mounted troops of Life Guards changed in front of a massive building with a clock tower.

So many uniformed men crowded around the doors to the War Office it appeared to be under siege. McCleary patiently waited in line and presented his letter of introduction to Lord Derby, the recruiting sergeant, but the guards refused him access. The doctor tolerated their curt dismissal with the reserved force of a person harboring a secret, as he had the wild thought of making the threat that weapons were concealed in his medical bag, creating a false crisis, and vaulting into Lord Derby's office to plead Artis's case.

McCleary was some distance away, on Old Queen Street, before he became conscious that his face was slack, the corners of his upper lip were drawn outward and drooped, displaying his sadness, a physical reminder of his failure to aid the boy.

That evening, McCleary invited Kazanjian to dine with him, and he directed the driver to Claridge's. Sole was ordered from the card, and the waiter elaborately finished it at a side table with grated cheese, oysters, and croûte soaked in bouillon. It was a leisurely dinner and Kazanjian relished the flowers, the frock-coated waiter's obsequious service, the keys glinting on the sommelier's chain like silver fish.

The wine calmed McCleary, and he noticed that the candlelight and the golden ceiling created a strange, almost holy luminosity in the dining room. The women in evening dress – dark-colored silks – were as exotic and disconcerting as nymphs

233

at a shrine. McCleary was accustomed to the unadorned wardrobe of the nurses.

Across from their table, a woman slowly rose from her chair, gently gathering her skirt at her hip, a jeweled bracelet visible as a dazzling line across her wrist. McCleary intercepted her glance at her dinner companion, and their intimacy struck him like the shock of vertigo. He quickly drained his wineglass, not daring to look at her again, and as he set down the glass, he noticed the irregular brown spots on his hand, the skin slack and slightly transparent. The evidence of age.

I will probably never enjoy dinner with a beautiful woman again, he thought, marveling at this finality. He waited for a pang of loss to confirm this.

They left Claridge's to enjoy cigars and port at his club, the Marlborough on Pall Mall, and McCleary was relieved to find the backgammon tables and the elderly staff unchanged. He insisted Kazanjian take the chair nearest the windows and enjoy the view of the city before the blackout.

'I don't know how I will manage to sleep without interruption,' McCleary joked. 'Perhaps there will be an air raid.'

Kazanjian reminded him they would be leaving the city well before dawn, so there was little point in worrying about sleep.

'We won't be leaving for the estate a minute too soon. I might forget there's a war on and linger here in blissful ignorance.'

'I will gladly inherit your operating equipment and the remnants of the wine cellar.'

'Fine. You can return without me. I will remain in this chair, enjoying a happy and ancient age, gradually forgetting everything I know about Thiersch grafts. Troubled no longer by broken bones and their solution. Or fevered patients.' McCleary sent a cloud of cigar smoke up to the coffered ceiling and ordered another round of port from the waiter. He explained the club's generous custom. 'They serve ten measures from a bottle of port and twenty from a bottle of whiskey.'

The strong drink buoyed whatever troubled Kazanjian to the surface. 'What do you believe creates the most powerful memory?'

'Helplessness. Distress. Fear. Whatever strong emotion is associated with an event. That's the evidence from our wounded soldiers.'

'I remember everything associated with a particular woman. I suffer from it.'

'A woman?' McCleary looked at Kazanjian in astonishment, and his mind raced through the lineup of nurses, one rosy face after another. 'Well. We certainly cannot select our memories. Or what to forget,' he murmured. 'There is no choice.'

That night in his hotel room, the knot of concern for Artis loosened, McCleary remembered the woman he had loved. Years ago, he had impatiently pushed through a crowd at the Royal Italian Opera to meet her. They were eager to be alone and quickly left the hall. She was radiant, flushed after

235

performing, and expected this was the evening when he would speak about their future together.

They lingered over supper for hours, and finally, the strawcolored wine still remaining in their glasses, the moment for him to propose marriage passed, floated away. This had not been his intention. A diamond ring from Garrard was hidden in his pocket.

They looked at each other, not speaking. Without haste, as if giving him more time, she carefully folded her napkin and placed it on the table. Her diamond earrings trembled violently against her neck.

She had married another man. McCleary had occasionally read her name in opera reviews in the newspapers, as she became associated with celebrated soprano roles.

Years passed, but he had continued a dialogue with his beloved in his mind. *I've changed for you.*

It had been calculated that the skin took over one month to heal. McCleary imagined this as a slow and tremendous process, just as carbon silently fused to create diamonds. Perhaps it took the heart longer to fuse into the transformation of love.

He had once believed they didn't marry because he feared disappointing her. Now he had identified a finer texture within their relationship. She sang to free herself from the body's possessiveness, transcending the grip of muscles, the twine of nerves, the passing of time.

He was fastened to the internal rapture of healing in the dark, elusive pump of the body, a mortal measure of time.

Artis followed the sweep of Julian's arm as it encompassed the field, exuberant sweetbriar where it sloped down to the dim, almost invisible thread of the river. They'd hiked beyond sight of the house to the very edge of the estate.

Julian began to unpack drawing supplies from his haversack. 'We start the lesson. The school of musketry provided my supplies for surveying. The paper was printed with ten vertical and four horizontal lines. All the pencils were HB lead. No one knew why.'

He thumbtacked a sheet of the graph paper to a thin board and handed it to Artis. 'This string, precisely fifteen inches long, is threaded through a hole in the board. Like so. Now, before you commence drawing, hold the cord up to your face and tie a knot. This measurement will always ensure the eye is the same distance from the paper.'

Artis squinted at the pencil in his outstretched hand.

'Hold the pencil up at arm's length against the horizon,' Julian instructed. 'It will give an approximate measure and proportion of the land. Begin by drawing the skyline and always work toward yourself.'

The boy scowled. Orders. 'Were you a scout?'

Julian shook his head. 'I mapped the territory for the fighting engineers in advance of the soldiers, horses, and tanks. I stood alone on a road with paper and pencil, and little did I realize this was my last innocent look at the landscape. I drew the features that had military value, the fences, hills, and woods. A stone wall, tree, or ruin could hide a sniper's nest. During the bombardment, everything I'd so carefully recorded was obliterated. My maps were nearly useless.'

Julian responded to the boy's stricken expression with a shrug. 'The first rule is to ignore all detail. Draw only the outline of the horizon and the hills.'

Artis didn't understand the absence of detail.

Julian told him to leave out everything but an outline. 'For example, here's my face.' He drew a circle, adding two dots for eyes, a curve for the nose, a straight line for the mouth. He held up his sketch. 'No details, but you can recognize my face. Is it a good likeness?'

Artis took the paper and confidently redrew Julian's mouth, curved into a smile.

'Just so. But you would have been a more accurate draftsman if you'd erased the left side of my face.'

Artis looked at him, amazed.

There had been little sleep for McCleary. All night, the house and the lawn had reverberated with shouting and the slamming of ambulance doors,

238

then this urgency was swept into the small confines of the operating theater.

He was relieved to escape the house without meeting a soul, as every encounter brought a demand or a question. His pursuing Furies. The bane of his work. He carried nothing, hadn't even allowed himself a clipboard or stethoscope, believing this would make the terrible news he was to deliver somehow magically less true. Or official.

Outside, the lawn constricted ominously around McCleary, the unkempt grass acquiring a complex spiked pattern where it gripped the trees, brick-work walls, the marble curve of the fountain. The wrought iron bench had made itself nearly invis-ible under a horse chestnut tree, and he pushed aside the overhanging ribbed leaves to sit down.

The worn, rounded weight of his pocket watch was a comfort, and the blaze of the engraving hidden inside the lid was as clear to him as if he'd opened it in sunlight: *To M from D. Our Opera.* His beloved had cupped the pocket watch in her white hands before she gave it to him, still warm from contact with her skin.

'Dr McCleary?'

McCleary opened his eyes to find Julian studying him with concern.

'Why, I believe I fell asleep.' He straightened his shoulders, mindful of his dignity.

Julian stooped to sit next to him, awkwardly shifting to balance the left side of his body. His bandaged side. To stop his impulse to assist his patient, McCleary brushed the browning branchlets fallen from the horse chestnut off his own trousers.

'As you are in the business of restoration . . .' Julian's hand stopped McCleary's protest. 'You will appreciate my analysis of the landscape. It is entirely artificial, constructed a century and a half ago. The hills were carved from earth. The streams and lakes were redirected, serpentized into curves to beguile the eye. You may wonder why.'

McCleary's expression was thoughtful.

'The landscape designer rejected symmetry. Because a straight line holds no mystery. There you have it, Doctor.' Julian grinned.

'Ah, but the body itself is symmetrical.'

'Some bodies.'

'Yes, some bodies. My work is to restore symmetry.'

'When you were a student, did you imagine that would be your pursuit?'

McCleary shook his head. 'It was so very long ago. I've lost the outline of that memory.'

'My memory of my face has changed.' Julian spoke softly. 'I'm blind to myself. Like a black surface. It makes no sense, but I look at other faces in hope they reflect mine. Give my image back to me.' Julian fidgeted with his necktie. 'The nurses try not to react when they look at me. But they aren't skilled liars.'

McCleary sensed that Julian hadn't finished his thought. *Let me be a man of listening.*

'My face is more terrible than my memory of war, since it's inescapable.' Julian's good eye shone with tears, like water over marble, and he turned stiffly toward the doctor. 'I can read your expression. There's something you don't wish to tell me.'

McCleary struggled with the growing tightness in his chest. It was a moment before he could speak, and he started with an explanation. 'It is the body's perfect scheme that muscles begin and end at the bone. But the face is different. Some facial muscles connect only with each other. If damaged, these muscles can't easily be reconnected. There is nothing to hold them.'

'Why this anatomy lesson?'

'Julian, I can do nothing more for your face. For now.'

An infinitesimal pause, like silence after a cautious footstep.

'So surgery is useless? The drawings are useless?'

McCleary heard himself explaining that Anna would start new drawings of Julian's face. They would be used to help make a temporary device. A covering for his face. A mask.

'A mask?'

'It will be very lightweight. The mask will be modeled from a photograph of your face.'

'My former face.'

The finality of his statement rushed toward

them, sudden and violent, like a hissing arrow, wounding them both.

McCleary had the image of Julian's scars turning a deeper red, the color rising like mercury in a thermometer until the *pars lacrimalis*, Horner's muscle, forced tears to the eye.

Julian's hands covered his face, as if this contact could mend him. 'I should have been blown to bits.'

'Surgery will improve. There will be new techniques, new treatments.' McCleary regretted the tone of authority in his voice. The doctor's privilege.

'Be silent, will you.'

Quiet settled over their unmoving figures.

A pulse beat in Julian's neck, swelling a thin, taut muscle, the angle of a reed. 'How will anyone dare . . .' He choked as the words caught in his throat. 'How will anyone dare to love me?'

Words of comfort were useless. McCleary's eyes contained all his power of empathy, but it wasn't enough. He vainly wished for something that could absorb Julian's pain. Believing his own knowledge was inadequate, he'd searched his collection of Plato's works and found mention of the *êpodê*, a charm for the most effective words and course of action. But what *êpodê*, what 'beautiful discourse' was possible between doctor and patient, an unequal relationship, a betrayal?

Julian abruptly stood up and strode in the

242

direction of the lake, the blue of his suit gradually losing its detail until he was just a moving shape.

Among the newly arrived patients, a corporal with a forehead injury railed against the enemy's destruction of an immense and renowned library in Belgium. Three hundred thousand books, one thousand incunabula, and eight hundred illuminated manuscripts securely packed in wooden crates as protection had been ignited. The country's written history was immolated in nine hours. Sparks and a cyclone of papers were blown from the blazing library, and as the corporal watched, a single glowing page swooped toward him, the letters brightening as the paper became heated, then mutely disintegrating into hot ash even as his eyes grasped the words.

The burden of the new patients, and the whispered rumors that the war was not going as expected, took its toll on the staff. Brownlow stubbornly ignored protocol, his black hair grew shaggy, too long over his collar, his boots were seldom polished. Taciturn and sarcastic, strangely steady when drunk, Brownlow reacted to the slightest criticism or question without argument, simply shook his head or stalked away, his actions weighted with compressed fury, the anger of a closed fist.

Once an orderly and a patient found Brownlow slumped blank faced against a wall, and fearing his reaction, the two men hesitated for a moment before hauling the anesthetist, dazed from ether or drink, to his feet. They received no thanks or even an acknowledgment from Brownlow as he staggered away.

The nurse was a white figure ahead of McCleary, her flapping skirt reshaped into angular folds as she ran. He hurried after her, automatically steadying his stethoscope inside his jacket.

'Who is it? Who is it?' he gasped, dry breath painful in his throat.

The nurse didn't answer or slow her steps.

Someone shouted from the trees ahead of them. Suddenly, the fine light of a torch aggressively zigzagged through the darkness, revealing the gray trunk of a tree but leaving its uppermost branches black so it appeared towering, grown to an unfathomable height.

His breath still labored and unstable, McCleary peered up at a man crouching on a branch of the tree. A patient. He swiftly calculated that should the man jump from this height, his body would fall on soft ground. With luck, only a leg or an arm would be broken.

An orderly grabbed the torch from the nurse's hands, and then light twitched over Julian's ragged figure as if reluctant to pull him from the uneven concealment of the foliage.

'Stand back. Leave me alone.'

McCleary's chest seemed to suffocate his racing heart. 'Julian, don't hurt yourself.'

'Hurt myself?' Julian's laugh was incredulous. Gripping a branch, he unsteadily pulled himself upright to lean against the tree.

Make my words a rod of support, McCleary prayed. *Let my speech be a ladder.* 'Don't move,' he pleaded.

Julian's wild face swayed above them as if at the window of a burning building. He clawed at his bandages, pulling them free, and a white strip of bandage twisted as it floated down, caught in the torchlight.

McCleary winced, knowing Julian would bleed. A nurse gripped his arm and screamed, 'For God's sake, do something.'

McCleary shook her off. He was chilled, felt distant from the situation. He experienced this state each time he confronted the few square inches of a man's torn face in the operating theater. The face itself was small as a bowl, but it contained the world.

'Julian, please stay where you are. I'm listening.'

'Listening won't fix me. Words won't fix me.'

The wind simultaneously lifted leaves and the nurses' capes, as if they were joined by an invisible line.

McCleary waited in absolute silence, eyes locked on Julian's unmoving figure. 'You must honor your pact with me. Your doctor,' he said gently. 'This isn't an order.' He couldn't hear Julian weep but saw his shoulders shaking.

Minutes passed. The nurses clutched each other;

tension made them like stone. They couldn't look away. Spellbound.

McCleary again found his voice. 'Julian, if you jump, you might not die. You will spend the rest of your life in a bed. Dependent on others for your care. Fed with a spoon.'

Julian seemed to become heavier, lurched forward, then half-climbed, half-slid down the tree, collapsing into McCleary's uplifted arms. The orderly dropped the torch, and both men instantly vanished into darkness.

McCleary barely noticed the lack of light; he was faint with relief, the security of Julian's thin, angular body under his outstretched arm. Healing was his touch on this man's shoulder. Skin to skin. 'We will not speak of this again,' he whispered to his patient.

Then the torch was found, and the others silently stood back as the two men staggered between them, Julian's shirt stained with red, bold as a heraldic crest on a warrior's shield.

CHAPTER 15

After Catherine was told Julian was to be fitted for a mask, she drove until she no longer recognized the landscape and stopped the motorcar. She walked steadily, her feet moved, but she was torn in pieces deep in the interior of her body. She was held upright by some miraculous pressure, the tension that keeps the edges of a broken surface aligned.

She stumbled against clods of grass and dirt, then fragments of branches and roots, jagged and peculiarly darkened, burned or wet. At the site where the bomb had hit, blackened earth sloped into a huge crater, a measure of unclean water at the bottom. Her future was reflected there.

Anna rested against the balustrade on the second floor, her face unfocused above a tight lace collar. She ignored the rapid footsteps in the room behind her. *Let them pass by*, she thought.

But the footsteps ended as fingers gripped Anna's shoulder.

'You must help Julian.' Catherine was breathless.

'But I am helping him. He is my subject.' Anna turned back to study the view.

'Make a better face for Julian. I will pay for it. You'll have everything you need.'

'Should I create a face of gold for him? Blue sapphires for his eyes?'

Catherine winced. 'No. I know his face. I know what he should look like. It's better if I—'

Anna interrupted. 'I've seen other women in your situation. You only know him as he is damaged. A nurse at the front married her patient, a blinded boy of twenty with no arms or legs. She was a spinster and sixty years old. He didn't object. Figured he was lucky.'

'Don't mock me.'

Anna said nothing. Light from the room suddenly cast its buoyant weight across them, signaling the presence of an intruding nurse. A thin stripe of shadow glided across Catherine's face and neck, straightforward as a line of paint.

'Please. Make him a mask of glass. Or no, make it soft and transparent. Celluloid? Julian must be able to smile.'

'Have you really studied him?' Anna stared at her. 'His mask will be modeled on his portrait taken before his injury. I suggest you avoid looking at it. Better to remain ignorant in pursuit of bliss.'

'You're spiteful. You're incapable.'

'You cannot be Julian's angel,' Anna hissed.

★   ★   ★

248

The metal hutting erected at the southeast edge of the grounds was already inadequate for the number of incoming patients. The nearby Congregational church converted its school and lecture hall into a thirty-four-bed hospital, and the Wesleyan church fit sixteen beds into its schoolrooms. Both facilities were administered by a female commandant, a doctor, and a lady superintendent.

The local children had organized an egg-gathering society and would knock shyly at the church door with their offerings in baskets, each egg carefully labeled in pencil on its dull white surface *For a Soldier.*

There was no telephone service between the estate and the two hospital annexes, so Artis and a few chosen orderlies were the go-betweens, their bicycles and wagons laden with medicines, mail, X-ray charts, telegrams, laundry, and on one occasion, gallons of cream.

Women filled in as acting postmasters, and twice a day made the rounds, their delivery carts stacked with parcels, cables, registered letters, telegrams. The postmasters were also in charge of exchanging foreign paper money for the newly arrived soldiers, and one woman took particular pleasure in rifling through an enormous sheaf of colored bills as if performing card tricks.

During an errand to the Wesleyan church, Artis had stowed his bicycle behind a shrub and peered through the grimy window in the abandoned aviary, where Brownlow was quartered. Later, the men in the wards raptly listened as he solemnly described what he'd seen in the room: perforated metal cups, possibly to fasten over the face; leather straps; glass drop bottles; India-rubber tubes; papers; and shapeless black clothing haphazardly strewn over the poor chairs and table.

Later, Brownlow relentlessly quizzed Artis as if he knew about the boy's transgression.

'Tell me what physical sign indicates proper oxygenation under anesthesia.'

'The color of fingernails and lips.'

'What is the third plane of anesthesia?'

'The pupil is dilated, eye is dry and quiet.'

'How can you aid an unconscious patient who has swallowed his tongue?'

'Pull his jaw forward to move the tongue away from the pharynx.'

Artis fidgeted under Brownlow's critical gaze, expecting a reprimand, but instead he received a grudging smile. 'Very well.'

Artis leaned forward to meet the next question.

'Do you have secrets, young man?'

Artis blushed, shook his head.

'I'll tell you my secret. When a patient emerges from my ether, he sees the world but doesn't recognize it. In that instant of confusion, a man reveals total innocence. It is the most private moment, and the patient has no idea he's being watched. But I'm watching.'

★　★　★

Catherine made herself small on the grass, pulling her jacket tighter, tucking her skirt around her legs so she would appear less visible from the sky. Her perception mysteriously shifted, and she saw herself as if from a distance, the oval straw hat, the pale triangle of her skirt.

Artis walked toward her from the direction of the house, swinging the thick envelope he carried with the rhythm of his spoken words, a purposeful and unrecognizable chanting, *Orbicularis oris, orbicularis oculi.*

'What brings you here?'

He stopped suddenly, surprised to see her. 'I'm delivering this to the studio. It's for Julian.' He stood above her, awkwardly twisting the string around the envelope.

'You shouldn't disturb Anna. She's working. I'll give Julian the package.'

Artis continued to toy with the envelope.

Catherine removed her hat and shifted her weight back onto her elbows. 'I heard the ambulances arrive late last night. So many of them. I lost count.'

'The new arrivals didn't get settled into the ward until after four o'clock in the morning. I helped Dr McCleary. I didn't sleep.'

'It's wonderful you're such a tremendous help to the doctor. Please, there's no need to stand.'

Embarrassed, he sat down, leaning protectively over his bent legs.

'Give me the envelope, Artis.'

The sound of the field – insects, grass, wind – suddenly swelled and buzzed around her, intense as color. Catherine extended her arm on the grass toward Artis till they were as close as lovers. She waited for him to decide, watching as a faint blush of pink conquered his fair cheeks and moved down his neck.

With an effort, Artis suddenly moved away from her and flung the envelope at her feet.

She should have scolded him for this impertinence, but because of her greed to examine the envelope, she merely told him to leave at once.

Catherine's eyes swept her room, observing the placement of objects, shadows, the way they had been altered. The pattern of vines and leaves on the bed curtains appeared too heavy for the worn linen. A footstool had been moved. Perfume in a crystal bottle appeared browner, thicker. A pillow was creased. Was the mirror dimmed, newly flecked with tarnish?

On the bureau, the portraits of Charles behind the squares and rectangles of framed glass were subtly changed. Perhaps the photographs of his face weren't permanent but had been transformed over time, so slowly she hadn't noticed. She peered at a photograph of Charles taken at Bassano's studio; its dark grain seemed to fade and waver, dissolve into dots fine as sand before her eyes. Something must be done to halt this loss.

Julian's name on the envelope was black and

official. She studied the characterless script, allowed herself a fractional hesitation, then carefully slit open the envelope, irreversible as a plunge from a great height. She removed a photograph, the paper strangely light in her palm, and stared at a young man in uniform. Julian, before battle had slipped a razor ribbon over his face. His perfect features and carefree smile numbed her vision the way sudden, intense light temporarily shocks the retina into white blindness.

Charles had posed for a similar portrait. She placed the men's photographs side by side and couldn't judge if Charles and Julian truly resembled each other. Her confused eye carried one feature to the other man's face. She was the go-between, mortar, a collaborator with the two men.

Catherine wrapped herself in Charles's camel hair jacket, summoning the intimate sensation of his body. But her senses wouldn't yield to her wish, and her skin had no memory of the pleasure her husband had once given her. Everything slid away from flesh.

But there was a painted metal object, an oval that mimicked a face. Julian's mask. A shallow hollow to pour herself into. Catherine had only to claim it. Her anger at Charles for abandoning her was compressed into a triangle, one point like a dart at her back. Her decision was made.

She quickly started a fire in the grate with torn strips of stationery and blotting paper. While the fire burned, she calmly cut open the silk lining inside the crown of a large, flat-brimmed felt hat. Without looking at Julian's image, she inserted his photograph into the lining. She placed the hat in a box and covered it with tissue. Then she pried the photographs of Charles from their frames and, one by one, released them into the grate. The flames contorted his face, licked the transparent chemicals on the photographs into gray before their edges curled black.

The fire flared up, the heat pressing against her exposed skin. The glass in the empty picture frames on the floor reflected the moving orange and red flames back at the fire.

This is the funeral ceremony for Charles, she thought. *His pyre. Farewell.*

She resealed the one remaining photograph of Charles inside the envelope addressed to Julian.

At midnight, she placed it in a satchel and left the house for the studio. With every step, the tightness around her heart increased, as if gripped by a coil of thin metal.

The studio appeared to have condensed around its furnishings, and the air was thick and close. She didn't dare use a torch, but left the door ajar, admitting faint moonlight. Her breath felt solid in the grip of her chest as she set the envelope containing Charles's photograph on Anna's worktable. What was the risk? Everyone who had known Charles – all the servants – had left, gone to war or work elsewhere. Artis was the sole witness who might see Julian's mask and recognize Charles's face. She would watch the boy as if he were suspected of a crime. He was a living, breathing threat.

Her hand struck a jar, its glass shattered on the floor, and the sound rattled deep inside the thousands of shells on the walls, seeking to split their thin curves.

Catherine found herself standing outside, shivering, unable to recognize the hour, since the sky was fixed in hazy darkness. This calm static was false, as she sensed aircraft, or perhaps a zeppelin, silently growing closer, the vibration of their engines would soon be audible, and then a bomb's slow honeyed descent in a straight line.

She became a running, featureless figure on the ground, a target, aware her life could suddenly end without a witness in a black explosion, a spray of earth pulverized over the open field. Her bones, poisonous white lines held at angles by the tension of muscles, waited for a weapon, injury, death, to free them from her body.

Catherine watched as Anna cut the string and unwrapped the envelope containing Charles's photograph. She propped the photograph on the easel and silently studied it.

A point of fear enlarged and circled Catherine's throat, dried her mouth, spiked her flesh like a collar. Surely the artist's eye would decipher the false photograph, beginning the spiral of discovery of Catherine's guilt. Minutes passed until she trusted her voice enough to speak. 'Can you read a premonition in Julian's face? What do you see?'

'He was once a handsome man. And knew he was handsome, I'd say. Here. Look.'

I shouldn't touch the photograph. Catherine reluctantly took the photograph and found it unchanged, a paper overlaid with the thin veil of an image. Charles's black-and-white face. She returned the photograph to Anna, and her hand seemed chilled from the contact.

Catherine asked if Julian's mask would appear identical to his photograph.

'Depends on the eye of the observer. I trust Julian will resemble his photograph. But the mask is only my impression of him.'

'Impression? But you're making the mask from his portrait.'

'You're too simple.'

'What do you mean?'

Anna squeezed a brush into a rag, leaving a thick V-shaped paint stain on the cloth. 'A portrait is impressionistic as a landscape glimpsed from a train. It's impossible to capture anyone's true likeness. Perhaps I'm the only one who will believe Julian's mask resembles his photograph.'

'You speak nonsense.'

Anna calmly reached for a pencil. 'You can say whatever you like. Julian will live behind my mask.' The conversation was finished.

★　　★　　★

Anna announced that Julian's photograph had been delivered to the studio, but he took his usual place on the modeling platform without asking to see it. He wouldn't look back, dismissed the photograph as a memento of his former life. Anna's drawings were a point of pain he only indirectly acknowledged. 'Time enough to see my portrait when Anna has finished. My gift to the artist is patience. Now, explain the process of the mask to me.'

'I will model your face in clay as closely identical to your photograph as my skill allows,' Anna said. 'The clay face will be used to cast your mask in silver and copper. The metal mask won't be heavy, but so thin your skin will warm it.'

'A metal mask,' Julian repeated. He picked up a pencil, studied it intently, and carefully set it down as if this act took all his power. 'How can you pretend as if it's nothing to make a false face?'

Anna granted him the dignity of looking away.

From the moment Catherine handed Charles's photograph back to Anna, she willed herself not to think of him. This would break the connection between them. She would become unstained, traceless, perfectly transparent, and her guilt wouldn't be seen or sensed.

Catherine was unable to sleep. She arrived at the studio before dawn and pulled her finger through the webs strung by spiders across the door, an impermanent silver barrier. She never looked directly at Charles's photograph but was constantly aware of it, an icon, a malign presence, its surface flickering as she moved around the room, ready to trap her guilty image like a mirror.

The studio had become combustible, alive as a bomb, and she worked as if possessed, scorched if she rested or slowed. Only motion brought relief. Catherine felt she would splinter and was astonished that Anna could bear the constant pressure. Words were forced from her lips. 'How can you keep working? Looking at Julian's face, at all their faces?'

Anna didn't soothe Catherine. 'I muster the same courage as the doctors.'

Her words struck like a slap, and Catherine resolved to be Anna's equal. After the photograph had served its purpose and the mask was finished, she could easily steal it back.

To guard herself from the photograph, Catherine strengthened the line around her memory of Charles, refused to even dream about him. Until Julian would carry her husband's face, she imagined him as a blank too. But she tracked him relentlessly, traced the familiar scent of his body surrounding him plain and bold as sunlight. She listened to his voice, to his every movement, so if he should see the photograph of Charles and recognize the imposture, she was defended against his reaction, an accusation of deceit. She was prepared to fly.

Julian could find her exactly as a finger held to a point on a map. Once when Anna had been distracted, his hand on Catherine's neck was delicate, swift, and secret. Another time, their eyes met across the room and the clay in her hands suddenly grew supple and warm, as if it were Julian's flesh that she held.

Gradually, the photograph's presence seeped from the studio. She became startled by the slightest shadow or unexpected movement, the wheeling shape of a bird overhead, the sinister dryness of leaves moved by wind, a paper blown across the path.

But no obstacles deterred Catherine from shaping her gift to Julian, his safety. She considered that after the war ended, when everything in the world would change, a new identity was the best way to survive. Julian would wear a mask – Charles's face – and they would live together in twilight. She had saved him after the surgeons had failed, and he would never leave.

She'd done nothing terrible to accomplish this, merely exchanged one stone for another. The war was responsible for all destruction.

Catherine knew that if she waited, Julian would eventually appear on the terrace. The afternoon had passed, the lake flushing from silver to leaden gray without losing its eerie quality of falseness against the green field. Julian appeared to have been summoned from the air so suddenly did his familiar figure appear. He hesitantly sat down next to her.

'So I've found you,' she said, betraying her nervousness by an attempt at a joke.

Julian clasped her hands, and she welcomed the silence that surrounded them, since it smothered the memory of her deceit.

A nurse with a tray hurried along the open terrace doors behind them. The unfortunate woman stumbled, and audible above the sound of breaking glass was the sterile, high-pitched *click click click* of hypodermic needles striking the floor.

Julian's hands trembled, and he violently pitched forward on the bench, shuddering against her. Catherine felt fear run under his skin, and he stared, not recognizing her. Her hands became comfort, but her caresses were considered and distant.

She had made Julian an unwitting imposter, her changeling. Guilt was as internal as healing, building slowly as the freezing of water.

Because of the heat, the red curtain had been pulled to one side, and the studio again became a large open space. Catherine sifted dry plaster of paris through a mesh screen so slowly that her hand and arm ached, but despite her care, powder escaped and churned furiously in the air, whitening her hair and clothing, forming a frail snowfall on the floor. She sensed that Julian was looking at her, and for the first time, guiltily refused to respond.

'Catherine?' Anna called. 'This is the second time I asked you to refill the jar.'

'Yes. I'll take care of it.'

Anna's voice was unusually sharp. Was she suspicious? The lines on Anna's drawing seemed to deepen, writhe into a wild tangle, transforming Julian's face into an angry crimson scribble. Then everything in the studio began to demand Catherine's response: the blackness of charcoal, the redness of the curtain, the solid, unblinking white of paper. The powder dusted around the room seemed to have driven away the air, her breath. She pressed her fingers against her throat.

She feared the pencils would balance themselves on point, would scrawl the truth – *Catherine is a thief. She has stolen Julian's face.*

It rained steadily, creating grayed, indistinct shapes of the house and outlying buildings, the fountains, the statues of lead and carved Portland stone, proving how instantly the familiar was transformed.

Catherine left her windows open, eliminating the barrier to noise so she would have warning when discovery of the false photograph rippled across the surface of the lawn and spiked upward, toppling stones and brick walls. She would witness this from her window as measured footsteps ascended the stairs to her room. Soldiers would come for her. Or Julian, betrayed.

Tiny square paper packets lay in rows on a studio worktable, appearing so fragile that Catherine wonderingly asked if they were empty. In lieu of a spoken answer, Anna slowly broke the seal on a packet and tilted it to reveal the bright precious metal inside. The stuff trembled, registering the force of Anna's heartbeat in her hand. 'Gold leaf,' she whispered.

Half a dozen packets were carefully opened and set on the table, their golden contents floating like flames above the drab wooden surface.

Artis walked into the studio, and his confidence vanished at Anna's scowling expression.

'Both of you, stay where you are,' Anna hissed. 'Even a breath of air will disturb the gold leaf. It's fine as powder.'

Artis obeyed, remaining immobilized near the door.

Catherine was trapped. *Would the boy recognize Charles's photograph on the table? Would she draw his attention if she tried to conceal it?*

Artis glanced lazily around the room, then focused on the worktable where Charles's photograph was angled against a canister. His eyes narrowed in puzzlement or calculation.

Did he see Charles? In an agony of impatience Catherine stood still, waiting as Anna painstakingly refolded the packets of gold.

262

With a dry rustle, a paper capriciously slipped free from the easel, stirring the air, scattering and tearing the feather-light patches of gold.

Anna swore, Artis jumped forward to help, and in the otherworldly speed of a dream, Catherine unobtrusively placed Charles's photograph face-down on the table. The ragged bits of gold leaf were slowly gathered, wafted onto papers, a maddeningly slow task, since the fragile material fluttered up with each clumsy movement of their hands.

While they were occupied, Julian had entered and quietly removed his shirt behind the red curtain.

'You should have seen what happened, sir. Gold was everywhere. It blew around like magic dust.' Artis's excitement was always saved to share with the men.

At Anna's direction, Julian swung his legs up and stretched out full length on the table, allowing Artis to slide a block under his neck to keep his head level. 'This seems very formal,' Julian solemnly observed.

'For God's sake, let him be comfortable.' Catherine gently lifted Julian's head and padded the block with muslin, then draped a soft cloth over his lower body. When Anna and Artis were busy in the cupboard, Catherine boldly caressed Julian's naked neck and shoulder as he lay unmoving. Only his eye registered her touch.

Anna returned and methodically placed supplies

on the table. 'Casting your face will be a simple process. Not painful, but you may be slightly uncomfortable.' She noticed the white smudges Catherine's dusty fingers had left on Julian's skin but said nothing, as if an object in a still life had shifted.

Anna gently picked up a packet. 'Watch.' She held it to her lips, and with a puff of her breath, gold flakes flew, spangling Julian's bare shoulders and chest, like glinting confetti.

'Are you mad?' cried Catherine.

Anna shrugged. 'I don't need your assistance. You may go.'

Julian shifted imperceptibly to watch Catherine pass, as if following the movement of sunlight. Dismay creased his face, lines radiated across his forehead, bold as arrows.

'You must release the muscles of your face so I can remove your bandages,' Anna instructed. She deftly stripped off the gauze and handed the loose wrappings to Artis. 'Now, sir. I will make you handsome as you were. Relax.'

She dipped a fine brush in oil and painted Julian's eyebrows, lashes, lips, the curve of his closed eye. Cotton wool padded out the depressions made by his wounds.

Artis gingerly unwrapped three packets of gold leaf and put them within Anna's reach. She smiled at his exaggerated pantomime of caution.

'What will you do with the gold?' he asked.

'Gold leaf prevents the plaster from sticking to

Julian's skin and the cotton wool. Please don't move.' Her tweezers descended on a gold square, then suddenly stopped. 'There is too much light here. I can't see against the glare.'

Artis hunted for paper to rig across the skylight. Julian gently sighed.

'You may raise your arms if you're stiff.'

Julian stretched, releasing the tension in the room.

Artis maneuvered a thick paper over Anna's head to diffuse the light. They held their breath as her tweezers lifted an edge of a gold piece and floated it onto the cotton on Julian's cheek. It was delicate work, but finally gold leaf completely covered the cotton padding. His brows, lips, and lashes were also dusted with gold powder, which adhered to the oil.

'Finished.'

The effect was startling. Julian was a motionless, blind figure, his face partially gilded. It appeared that liquid gold had flowed into the depressions on his face and been frozen into place.

Anna leaned close, as Julian's hearing was affected by the protective padding in his ears. 'Keep your eyes closed,' she instructed. 'I will plug your nostrils with cotton wool. You'll breathe through a goose quill in your mouth. The plaster will be very cold until it hardens on your face. Everything will happen quickly.' She inserted the quill between his lips. 'Lift your hand to signal if you're distressed.' He made a guttural sound of acknowledgment.

Artis furiously stirred dry plaster in a rubber bowl as drops of potassium sulfate and water were gradually added until it thickened. Instantly, Anna scooped up a glob of plaster with a spatula and spread it smoothly across Julian's forehead. His hands clenched with the effort not to push her away as layer after layer of plaster obliterated his features, the erect quill marking his mouth.

'The plaster will become warmer and warmer as it hardens.'

Julian's chest heaved as he struggled to breathe, and Anna curved her hand over his shoulder. After a moment, his breath locked back into a measured pattern.

'It won't be much longer.' She spoke loudly so Julian could hear.

Artis reached under the cloth to briefly grasp Julian's hand.

Anna felt the plaster on his chin, gauging its hardness by touch and temperature. She gently hooked her fingers under one side of the thick plaster over Julian's face, and Artis copied her maneuver on the other side.

'Pull!'

The plaster mass was ripped from Julian's face. He sat bolt upright with an angry cry, his reddened skin streaked with plaster and fragments of gold, his arms shaking.

Anna calmly began to clean his face with a cloth.

'There. Every trace is gone now. Every trace. Nothing more to fear.' As she wrung the wet cloth into the bucket, the splash was echoed deep in the inner chamber, where the water in the basin flowed in complete darkness.

Catherine had waited until the studio was unoccupied to enter. She found what she sought on a worktable, a white roughly surfaced oval, cool and heavy to the touch. She turned the object over, hands trembling, and inside it was hollow, with Julian's face cast in reverse like carved hieroglyphics. Her finger traced the starfish of lines etched from the edge of his eye, the marks of suffering at his mouth, the deep triangle of his nose.

Holding the cast as reverently as a bowl, she lowered her face into it, her breath stirring the brilliant metallic flakes flecking its interior. She closed her eyes, imagining that this plaster mold – Julian's face – was a door she entered, surrounded by gold confetti that would mark her skin as it had marked his.

A sandstone bridge, squat and thick, spanned a stream that led into the smallest of the lakes, and Julian sprawled asleep on the grassy banks, a pose of complete abandon, one arm bent, shielding half of his face.

Without haste or caution, Catherine studied Julian as if he posed for her pleasure. She had no

267

sense of trespassing, since Anna and the doctors had long since stripped away his privacy. The thin bandages were a sterile white contrast against Julian's face, heightening the color of his skin, so he appeared to bloom with a feverish ripeness.

Julian woke and sleepily gazed up at her, his good eye faultless blue. He took her hand and turned it over as if it were a rare shell he'd discovered. Catherine closed her eyes. His touch became more intricate, his fingers wove and slipped knots, enmeshing her.

She had successfully hidden the truth of the photograph from him, neat as the fold in a paper. But now guilt became a vibration that rattled her breath, dissolved her eyes into water, hardened her hand into a false caress.

Suddenly he angrily pushed her away. 'Don't touch me that way.'

'What have I done?'

'You touched me with pity, like a nurse.'

Catherine was angry to be corrected and pulled away from him. 'You're imagining things,' she said coldly.

CHAPTER 16

C onscious of his rising panic, McCleary hurried through the medical-supply room and second- and third-floor corridors, turning away questions from a pair of concerned nurses and an orderly. On the board in his office he found the afternoon schedule, and his finger jerked down the listings until he found a familiar name.

McCleary opened the door to the Blue Drawing Room, startling Kazanjian as he sketched. A pencil rolled off the table, and the quick motion of Kazanjian's hand catching it in midair blurred between the reflections of the chairs on the polished floor.

'Excellent test. My reflexes are still in working order.'

'I'm no longer so certain of my skill,' said McCleary.

Kazanjian tactfully wondered how this was possible.

His kindly concern intensified McCleary's despair, and before it could overwhelm him, he vaguely mentioned difficulty with the matron. Just as Kazanjian was poised to ask another question, he declared, 'My emotions have betrayed me. I have begun to pity the patients. It is deadly for a doctor.' He waited, wrung by vulnerability, for the other man's response.

'You are too harsh.'

'No. Too honest. I wanted to – assumed that I would – retire from medicine confident of my abilities as a doctor. But I haven't been granted this conceit.'

'Every day in this place is a trial. Every hour.' Kazanjian observed him more closely. 'Ah. Something has happened.'

'Julian attempted to hurt himself. I'm to blame.'

'Just see that Julian is more carefully monitored.'

McCleary leaned against the table as if to flatten his feeling of sorrow. 'But that's not the worst of it. What's most distressing is that I sympathize with Julian's decision.'

'It is possible that a patient will slip away. Fixing a man's nose doesn't fix his mind. But there's no cure. Don't make it your portion.'

I'm losing control, McCleary thought. A warm color, a crimson wetness, lined his eyelids. He was well aware that Kazanjian wouldn't be deceived by the neutral expression he struggled to maintain on his own face. Gradually, a soothing silence shimmered between them. 'It's very late.'

'Good night, my friend.'

At brilliant dawn, McCleary walked aimlessly through damp grass, the cuffs of his trousers

270

soaked, his jacket no protection against the chill or the eyes of the matron, who watched him from a distance with secret concern.

He found himself staring at the statue of Diana and Actaeon, the statue's imperfections – grainy stone, pocked and rough as pebble – clearly visible in this light. *Why have I wandered here to stare at the ruined heads of a statue? All I see are faces.* At night, his dreams had become crowded with faces, their eyes angry and demanding, more disturbing than his actual patients.

Perhaps he needed rest. To spend a day in a museum studying precious fragments. Or Greek vases, their streamlined figures frozen in motion. Faces without eyes to return his gaze.

McCleary returned to his quarters and slowly readied for bed. The sunlight flattened the shadows of the iron bedstead into spiked black angles on the wall and whitened the bed-clothes. He could count every stitch on the counterpane, as if he were looking into a mirror that reflected the room more sharply than he could see.

The sense of comfort created by Kazanjian had vanished, his words morphed into a meaningless humming, a vibration lodged in the spiral of McCleary's ear, the cochlea, a spiral vestibule lined with a pulp of nerves.

A phrase of music brought relief, a *lieder* that his beloved had sung. '*Ich bin der Welt abhanden gekommen*,' 'I Have Lost Track of the World.' Gustav Mahler. Hearing this lieder for the first

271

time, he had been certain she sang exclusively for him, the words a reference to their intimacy. Her voice carried her emotion. There were no accurate words for love, just as there was no accurate description of suffering.

He closed his eyes. Minutes or perhaps hours passed until his consciousness dissolved into sleep. Had he been gifted with a more visual imagination, he could have pictured it rising over him like mist. Or a halo.

Catherine silently walked into McCleary's office. 'I did knock,' she said apologetically.

Flustered, McCleary asked if she was looking for something and picked up a stethoscope as if preparing for a patient, hoping this would send her away. He installed his hand in his pocket and waited.

'I don't like to see my house rearranged, but I am curious.' Her nervous gaze moved around the room, rapid as a blink. 'The light here is the same, although all the furnishings have vanished. But no matter.' She handed him a small envelope. 'I'm here on an errand. Artis is the only remaining soul who knew my husband, Charles, and I'd like to do something in his memory. I will pay extra wages every week so Artis may assist you with the patients.'

'Very kind of you, ma'am.' There was no point in mentioning that the boy might be drafted and deny him the extra wages.

'It's better that Artis works in the house, not in the studio. Sometimes he disturbs Anna. Young men can be so careless.'

'Artis is hardly careless.'

Catherine's nose wrinkled, her upper eyelid lifted, signaling her disapproval of his comment, and McCleary quickly offered to guide her through the offices.

He ushered her into the pantry, which had been converted into a diagnostics room. 'Let me explain what you see,' he said, proudly indicating a bulky piece of equipment and a padded table. 'The men lie down here, and the roentgen machine registers the image of their body, simply as a camera.'

On the corkboard, tacked-up black-and-white sheets of film hung stiffly, as if frozen.

'May I look?'

Without waiting for his answer, she held one of the translucent films to the light, and the curve of a skull blazed before her eyes, sharp and brilliant as the moon, the interior clotted with gray matter. She gasped. 'It's a head, isn't it? Is he dead?'

'No. He was photographed by the roentgen machine. We can see directly inside the living body without opening it.'

'It's strangely beautiful. The brain is a fog surrounded by bone.' She stared at him over the film in her hand. 'What I see is a true image?'

'You see the temporal nature of identity. The nose, lips, eyes – all flesh vanishes. Only bones remain.' McCleary was reminded of Kazanjian's claim that bones were the body's superior material. *Bones, our master.* His finger indicated a small, irregular shape suspended in the skull. 'Here, shrapnel. Cause of injury. The dark line is a fracture.'

What else could this machine reveal? The flush of the emotions on the brain? Her secret desire for Julian, her lies, her wish that Artis would leave the estate? Could it expose her deceitful red heart woven with veins, hidden in the chamber of the body, no longer the most private of spaces? The film slid from her fingers to the table.

'I wish I'd never seen this. The bone under the skin.'

He understood her stricken look. 'It is shocking. As if green were stripped from the grass. When I saw an image made by the roentgen for the first time, I realized what I knew about the body was incorrect in an instant.'

'Nothing is the same these days. I value different things. All my dresses and jewels have been put away.' Her voice faltered. 'But I have purpose, like everyone here. Not like before.'

Did she expect his blessing?

Catherine wanted to tell McCleary that what she had believed was permanent was an error of perception. *You know this; you recognize it too.*

His expression softened as if he were reacting to her unspoken thoughts. 'I'm an old man, and change is all I have to anticipate.'

'But you'll see the war end. It won't be long. Every week the newspapers say we're closer to breaking through the enemy lines.'

He was touched, not offended, by her dismissal of his frailty, and invited her to share the salvation he had discovered. 'Ovid claimed nothing perishes on this earth. Everything is renewed in a changed form and continues. I believe this.'

'But you're a doctor. You expect change.'

'Doctors are trained to witness life gradually diminish and to do what we can to halt the process.' His words were grave, but something in their intonation had the lilt and cadence of a question that seemed to require a reassuring answer.

'I don't wish to be forward, but you should allow someone to comfort you.'

They looked at each other for a moment, then Catherine abruptly wished him good day.

After she had left, McCleary regarded her with the tenderness he refused himself. A woman marked by suffering. Under other circumstances, he would have pitied or discouraged her intimate involvement with Julian, but now his objections seemed of little consequence. Silently, he directed her to pick up happiness like loose stones on a path or seek the quiet of a cloud, a tree, a bird, reflected in all their temporary perfection in water.

McCleary escorted Anna through the ward, and the patients whispered or signaled greetings as she was an easily recognizable figure in her smock of rough gray linen. He quieted the room, asking them to welcome Mrs Coleman, who had been assigned to sketch several patients for the purpose of advancing medical knowledge.

He had hardly finished his introduction before patients began quarreling loudly about who would be Mrs Coleman's model. The depth of their boredom was sobering.

Anna's first subject was a strapping man with the thick shoulders of an athlete, his jaw hooked by wires to a vulcanite cast suspended from a leather band around his head. More delicate silver wire was threaded through his nostrils, the ends secured with lead shot to keep his nasal passages open. When a nurse checked his bandages, the angry crimson of one injury was briefly visible on his cheek, and his fine body tensed in silent pain.

The men who were able to walk gathered to watch Anna sketch, and even the harried nurses and V.A.D. women slowed their steps as they passed the little gathering. Gradually, bolder individuals peered directly over the artist's shoulder and began to narrate a comical step-by-step account of the portrait as she worked.

Anna pleaded for silence. 'Please, move back a little. Let the model have some air.'

'But he'll suffer from so much attention, ma'am. His head will swell, even more than it already has.'

'We're only concerned for his health.'

The strapping man made a loud grunt, which

his fellow patients translated as his claim to be Anna's favorite model.

'I have no favorites.' She smiled.

'What, no wrapped gifts for us at Christmas?'

'Your one arm is gimpy and you've got no teeth to open a package, old man,' retorted another patient.

Their banter provoked ready laughter, as insulting jokes and merciless name-calling were familiar exchanges in the wards. Wit was the patients' suit of armor, and it was their conceit that these cruelties never drew blood. The able-bodied were excluded from participating, and the shocked, inexperienced young nurses would invariably and unsuccessfully attempt to make the men apologize to one another.

Several days later, during a modeling session, a patient begged Anna to finish her work as quickly as possible.

'Why, what bothers you?' She respectfully folded her hands in her lap. 'Are you uncomfortable with the pose?'

'I don't know.' The man was clearly unhappy. 'Before I went to war, the officers photographed me for the first time. They kept the photograph. Now you draw my face. I was a verger in Christchurch. No one ever took any account of my looks.' Then he dropped his head and whispered, 'Except for my best girl.'

Anna touched his hand. 'When the doctors have finished all your operations, I promise to do a portrait you can take home. It will be our secret.' Her promise was against McCleary's policy, as all finished drawings were to be secured in a portfolio and never shown to the models.

She spent days in the ward and became accustomed to their faces, obscured by a variety of splints, bandages, and specially made devices to secure their skull bones in place. Yet Anna never lost the impression that each man, bearing with a dramatically different injury, represented a particular fault or flaw, like Hogarth's engraving of lunatics at Bethlem Hospital, and only the ceaseless scratch of her chalk kept such chaotic madness at bay.

Once the portraits on paper were completed, McCleary's project was continued in the studio. The faces of a dozen patients and separate details of their injuries – a chin, a nose and upper lip, an ear with a bit of jaw, an eye isolated in a jagged scrap of cheek – were roughly cast in plaster. The masks hung on the wall like macabre trophies. Or death masks, their lopsided features fixed into a distorted expression, as if they'd witnessed an unspeakable horror.

While waiting for his face to be cast, a patient hesitatingly told McCleary that the display of plaster heads was disturbing.

'I would be interested to know why they upset you, after all you've seen,' McCleary said.

The middle-aged man, clearly ill at ease complaining to a doctor, quietly explained that these specimens looked worse than the real faces. McCleary instantly understood that the stark white plaster lacked the forgiveness of skin.

'It's a boneyard of hope,' mumbled another patient, standing unnoticed in the back of the studio.

Kazanjian surveyed the wall of plaster faces, muttered, 'The gorgon. Medusa's lair,' and fell silent, lost in contemplation.

Anna was overly sensitive when questioned or criticized in her studio, but she let his comment pass. Since their estrangement, Kazanjian had been unfailingly courteous, surprising, since she'd expected him to react with anger or cold distance after she'd refused him. After the bricks she'd raised against him. Occasionally, she had even wished to spend time with him, and this thought was instantly colored by resentment that his claim on her had somehow been reestablished.

She suspected that his patience was stubborn and infinite, although the working of his mind wasn't easily deciphered. He was a foreigner.

Weeks ago, Kazanjian and McCleary had treated a severely injured man whose nose had been obliterated by shrapnel. As if bodiless, reduced to the smallest point of his eye's focus, McCleary had considered the site of the future skin graft from every angle, hovering and twisting over the cavity in the man's face, anticipating the delicate pull of the sutures his hand would weave, the skin's resilience, the progress of healing after the passing of days and weeks.

One surgical option was a rhinoplasty devised by Dieffenbach: a patient's upraised arm was positioned alongside his head and secured with leather straps and plaster. A long, narrow strip of skin was cut from the underside of the arm, stretched over to the nasal area of the patient's face, and the end was sutured down. This skin 'bridge' – and the patient's arm – remained in place for weeks, until the graft took. McCleary hesitated, knowing that patients dreaded this protracted treatment.

Consulting Mondeville for guidance, McCleary had found a single sentence: 'Anyone who believes that the same thing can be suited to everyone is a great fool, since medicine is practiced not on mankind in general, but on every individual in particular.'

He had examined the patient a second time and decided to rebuild the man's nose with a tubed-pedicle graft, adapted from a technique pioneered centuries ago in India. Kazanjian then prepared a series of drawings that detailed each consecutive stage of surgery.

During the operation, a narrow flap of skin was cut from the patient's forehead, and one end was secured into a tube and allowed to heal. After fourteen days, the distal end of the skin 'tube' was moved down, positioned over the man's missing nose, and sewn with silkworm gut to his upper lip and cheeks. Until this fresh graft was established, the proximal flap remained connected to his forehead, allowing blood to circulate in the tube. To prevent the new nose from contracting, it was lined with a Thiersch graft.

The patient had borne the pain without complaint, although the scar tissue on his forehead where skin had been removed to create the nose was a crimson, pulsing swath. If the new nose graft failed to establish itself on the man's face, a Dieffenbach rhinoplasty would be attempted, again with no guarantee of success. There were no other options.

The fashioning of a facial feature was a process, and several more operations, some spaced a year apart, would be necessary until the grafted nose was properly reshaped, the bridge of the nose structured with a homograft of cartilage, and the patient was able to breathe without difficulty. New eyebrows would be created by transplanting grafts of hairy scalp taken from behind each ear. Delicate massage, gentle heat, and needling would aid recovery.

Enough time had passed since the graft that it could now be evaluated. McCleary looked down at the patient and fearlessly met his eyes. The man's worried expression – the corrugator muscle on his forehead – relaxed. The expectation of the silent observers surrounding the patient on the examining table was almost a physical pressure against McCleary. He glimpsed

Artis peering over a doctor's shoulder, fraught with concern, and gave him the slightest of smiles.

McCleary carefully, haltingly peeled away the bandages, alert for the slightest foul smell, which would betray the presence of necrosis. The last fine crosshatch of gauze was lifted free, revealing a very crude nose with the deeply pink, slightly swollen gleam of healthy skin, and simultaneously there was a murmur of relief from the onlookers.

'You can't see yourself just yet, sir, but take my word for it. Your operation has been a total success.'

Because of his wounds, the patient could not speak, but relief was inscribed on his body, and gratitude communicated by his hands, palms open, a gesture of blessing.

Suddenly, McCleary sensed ripples of joy, wave after wave of emotion, spreading throughout the ward, as actors in moving pictures silently reacted to something that happened in their mysterious black-and-white realm, invisible to the flesh-and-blood audience.

McCleary was quietly pleased when a senior medical officer at a city hospital requested drawings and models of the surgical techniques that had been developed under his tutelage at the estate. He understood that this was a tribute to his patients, enshrining the mortifications they had suffered in surgery's great history.

McCleary had no illusions about the long-term significance of his own contributions to surgery, predicting they were as evanescent as the body. Time passed over the face, wearing it like water over a pebble or shell. Everything could be worn away, damaged. Everything was temporary. He'd witnessed the beautiful and temporary fragility of the body, knew the angle at which a bone would break and the strength of the skin, a barrier frail as paper. For Kazanjian, time passed in a different manner, calculated according to a subtle marker, the slow, unseen knitting of bones. Hidden knowledge.

In the future, surgeons would be gifted with almost holy powers, their vision and the skill of their hands expanded with powerful devices, able to mend faces with fantastic methods and materials. Skin would be cultivated as easily as moss, away from the site of the body, or grafted from one face to another as simply as a swatch of silk. The very color and texture of the skin itself would be altered. Bones and teeth would be built up like coral in the wet lagoon of the mouth. Infection would be conquered, veins and nerves repaired with stitches finer than a scratch, the minute mechanics of a smile or even a dimple easily restored.

Medicine was a strangely personal yet anonymous practice. Although every surgical procedure had a precedent, very few individual surgeons received any recognition or credit. McCleary had first been aware of this as a medical student when he had been shown a rare and valuable book, published by Ackerknecht, that contained examples of every known suture up to the eighteenth century. Each suture had been carefully executed in thread on a thin piece of leather mounted on a page, but the originators of the techniques were not identified. A number of sutures were familiar and still employed in surgery, but others were impossible to understand, their purpose lost, a baffling arrangement of snug threads indecipherable as a foreign script.

The sutures were the result of hundreds of hours of painstaking observation and trial, their creators as anonymous as the craftsmen who had toiled in the great cathedrals.

McCleary had carefully organized his schedule, cleared half a day and an evening in the middle of the week, and marked his calendar with a red 0. No name, no details. He took the train alone to the city for the appointment, which he kept private.

Four hours later, seated in a red banquette against a velvet-upholstered wall at the St James, McCleary exchanged pleasantries with Mr Geddes, the distinguished director of national service and an associate of his godson. Over a lengthy dinner, they explored the possibility of mutual acquaintances and compared news from the front.

Finally, McCleary nervously laid out his argument for Artis's exemption from military service.

It was difficult to find caretakers for face-injured patients, as few medics or nurses could stomach the work. This young man had already proven himself capable of serving patients who had little reason to hope and were cut off from the outside world. McCleary was surprised by the tremor in his voice.

'It won't wash.' Geddes slowly set down his fork. 'Orderlies, assistants, junior trainees, nurses – they're all expendable. Every warm body is urgently needed for battle.'

'Could the young man be assigned to another hospital, perhaps a clerical job?'

'Policy now is to rehabilitate even soldiers with nervous disorders and send them back to battle. The most recalcitrant cases are treated with electrical shocks. Let me tell you, the soldiers soon choose returning to the front rather than continuing medical treatment.'

McCleary's dignity, his distance from this man, evaporated, and he suddenly clutched Geddes' hand on the table. 'I beseech you. The boy is like a son to me.'

Geddes pulled away and leaned back against the seat, a man long accustomed to making refusals.

McCleary stared at him stonily for several seconds, believing this was the face of the man who commanded Artis to his death. Then, with a false display of confidence, he motioned the waiter for the bill.

★　　★　　★

McCleary's fingers and eyes were unwilling to relinquish the cramped strain imposed by work, even though he had left the operating theater long ago. He hadn't faltered in surgery, his hands skilled and purposeful as a weaver's, each stitch made with needles and clamps was a line of bright blood, secure as yarn. Now he enjoyed neither relief nor happiness from the success of his labors but visualized an unending succession of wounded men, stiff and remote as warriors depicted on a tapestry.

With an effort he straightened up, summoning a stiffness to his neck, and to divert himself he gazed at the plump folds of the linen towels on the sideboard. Outside, the fissured clouds appeared weightier than the tall windows that framed them, and for a moment the faint odor of ether, the deep viridian gloom of the wallpaper vanished, and he floated into the billowing, violet-tinged sunset.

Kazanjian called McCleary from the next room to join him, and they maneuvered single file through the roughly plastered corridor that had once been used exclusively by servants. McCleary was in a mood to believe the corridor's construction was a personal affront, as he painfully struck his foot on the uneven floorboards and stooped under the low ceilings.

In the dining room, McCleary settled into a chair at the table, resigned to a lackluster dinner. 'Let us not mention great subjects tonight. I've no stomach for it.'

Kazanjian glanced at him as if figuring the degree of his tolerance. 'You'll have no stomach for tonight's dinner if the cook and the hobgoblins of rationing have their way.'

'Thank God tea hasn't been stripped from the menu,' McCleary grumbled.

'Tea could be next on the rationing list. They've added more restrictions in the city. Meat allowed only twice a week at restaurants. Brandy available by prescription. No rice thrown at weddings. Feeding pigeons punished by a fine.'

'I happen to agree with the pigeon feeding. The birds try the patience of any gourmet. At least our patients are exempt from rationing. An egg a day and all the cream they can drink.'

'They're better fed than the staff. Not that they'd ever dream of complaining.' Kazanjian lifted the lid from the casserole on the table, releasing steam and a slightly savory aroma, then ladled soup into their bowls.

'Good wine would improve this considerably.' McCleary stopped his halfhearted attempt to eat. 'In the interest of piquing our appetites, I will re-create a menu from memory, a significant meal enjoyed at the Ritz years ago. Now then. There was caviar to start. Then *boudin grillé. Ailerons de voilaille à la tzar.* No. Cancel that. I ordered a cut from a Pontoise calf, raised exclusively on milk and egg yolk. I remember the meat was white as linen. Perdreaux truffles darkened the sauce.'

They speculated on the selection of wines that

had accompanied this feast, and the names rolled off their tongues: Corton, 1878; Romanée, 1887. Kazanjian suggested two possible champagnes: Moët Brut, 1884, and Grande Fine Champagne des Tuileries. The dignified sommelier, who dressed in a gray frock coat by day and a smoking jacket in the evening, was always ready with Dr McCleary's favored vintages, even if a year passed between dinners.

Their spoons clicked companionably in their empty bowls. 'An end to our feast of words,' observed Kazanjian.

'Words and memory must serve, as the finest restaurants abroad have been shuttered. An entire generation of chefs fallen in battle. I heard from a colleague at Neuve Chapelle that the Maison Dorée closed and the staff relocated to a restaurant on the Île de Jarre near the dueling grounds.' McCleary smiled ruefully. 'I never would have imagined I'd be nostalgic for *duel à volonté*. Another lost art.'

McCleary searched the wards for Artis, eager to reassure him that inquiries had been made about avoiding conscription. There was no need to reveal his lack of success, and his determination to keep the boy at the estate overrode his qualms about this half truth.

Days had passed without the opportunity to catch Artis alone, as McCleary had constantly been interrupted by the staff and called away by emergencies. Time was running out. McCleary snipped this last thought as cleanly as a suture.

Remembering that Artis made a practice of cadging extra portions from the cooks, McCleary entered the kitchen. The huge room was warmer than the rest of the house, as the enormous stove was always kept stoked. The heat was relaxing, and he gazed around at the commonplace domestic things, spoons, sieves, and bowls, which seemed somehow peculiar, brought in from another life. Only a few doors and the length of a corridor away, medical instruments rattled and the anesthesia pumps hissed in the operating room.

He passed under a *batterie* of pots suspended from the ceiling, enjoying their rounded gleaming weight, a bough of copper instruments. An ancient pump curved over two deep stone sinks, and the silent, decades-long drip of water had left a line in the granite, just as knives had gradually sloped the wooden chopping block. The full stillness of the room was suddenly broken when the cook began to argue with the quartermaster in the back pantry.

Outside, McCleary shared a cigarette with Brownlow, noticing that the man's hands shook and he was wreathed with the odor of ether, familiar as grass. He asked for news of Artis.

'He's doing poorly,' answered Brownlow. 'Poorly or inspired as any other virgin soldier called to combat.'

'I've requested the authorities allow him to serve here in the hospital. They haven't responded.'

'He could plead insanity.'

'Like the rest of us.'

'He could work at Maghull hospital. At least the patients wouldn't shock him, since they're only crazy.'

'I imagine it would take a great deal to shock Artis at this point.' McCleary calculated for a moment. 'Brownlow, I ask you for one favor. Keep Artis out of the war. I cannot bear another sacrifice.'

Brownlow looked over his shoulder, checking the house, and his fogged attention cleared. 'God forbid he should be sent to the bloody trenches.'

'I've tapped all my military contacts. No one has offered assistance. I'm afraid they will do nothing.' McCleary knew that Brownlow was a hoarder of secrets, a mover of goods, possibly dabbled in black marketeering. He had always turned a blind eye to this, and now the prospect of becoming intimately involved with Brownlow made him uneasy. There was no alternative.

'How can it be done?'

'I leave the matter in your hands. The boy must be safe and never leave this place. It must seem as if Artis has had an accident. I think we understand each other?'

'Agreed.' Brownlow's mirthless smile wasn't directed at McCleary but at some hidden event in the future.

'I wish you well. I wish us all well.'

On the long route to his quarters, McCleary

chose to sublimate his lingering concern about Artis. There was only Brownlow to depend on.

Telegraph poles had recently been reinstalled across the fields, and the wire swags suspended between them linked the estate with clearing stations, train depots, the battlefield. Perhaps the force of the news racing along the thin wires kept the telegraph poles upright.

Startled by a faint noise, he stopped near a pole and put his ear against it. Did he actually hear something? A humming, a vibration? Did the wires sing?

He frowned, shook his head to cancel this sensation, but it was present, continuous as a fever, spread over the surface of his skin, sinking into his bones, evident in the weightless, elusive, shifting shape of his breath.

CHAPTER 17

Catherine's fear of discovery expanded, had no boundaries, the infinity of an unfocused photograph. She ate very little, food had no relation to hunger, clothing felt rough against her skin. 'I'm a sleepwalker who fears the evening,' she told Julian when he expressed concern, and allowed him to comfort her without further explanation.

From the isolation of her deceit, Catherine sought out McCleary, who appeared frailer, and extended him small courtesies, leaving boxes of candles, bottles of wine, a fruitwood humidor custom made for her husband on his desk. The activity of packing these gifts soothed her.

One evening, she found McCleary alone in the staff mess room.

'You must be relieved when it's quiet.'

Startled, McCleary looked up from his tea. 'God, yes. Excuse my language. I've seen too much today.' The mechanics of courtesy were beyond his strength. 'Another round of the wards before I sleep. Tonight I'm just as happy Matron put the lamps low. Makes my work easier.'

'Easier? Why?'

'I clasp the men's hands, make contact so they know I'm present. The darkness covers my face.' His voice thinned. 'Sometimes when I'm fatigued, I swear they can read my emotions, quick as a flash.'

Catherine asked if the patients could also sense his feelings with his touch.

'When I examine a patient, I give myself over to him. An act of witness.' McCleary strayed from her question, and his words seemed lifted from another dialogue. 'When I ask about their spirits, they claim everything is fine, but I see that they lie. A man can smile, and yet his eyes could remain sorrowful. Strangely, I've found that the upper face is subtler, more truthful than the mouth.'

It was out of character for McCleary to discuss such things with a woman. A civilian. He found it curious that he modified the severity of the topic to make it comforting for her. Or perhaps for himself. He scanned Catherine's face.

She made no answer but gazed out the window, where the summer light still preserved its intensity.

'You're a doctor, but nothing you've said is a comfort to me.'

'You are correct. I am truly unable to comfort anyone. I've lost the skill of lying. In fact, I am even unable to save Artis, although I have tried.'

'He will go to war?'

'Only a matter of time.' McCleary noticed the woman's cheeks swelled, an involuntary reaction indicating relief.

Through the window, he watched Catherine leave the house, and as her figure lost its detail with distance, he had the impression she expected someone to overtake her. She was afraid. Was it the sky she feared or strangers? Hands reaching for a gun or brick? Men. Enemies. Invaders.

Casualties arrived at the estate in ever-increasing numbers, the damaged proof of a recent major military drive. Night after night, rectangles of light from the windows lay across the lawn near the main doors, an illuminated carpet marred by the passing of men and their shadows, hurrying to the burdened motorcars, ambulances, and lorries.

Every corner of the house reverberated with activity, even the abandoned west wing, where lanterns could be seen moving past the thick, uneven fifteenth-century windows, as new territories were claimed for patients.

The old brew house and the head gardener's cottage were commandeered, and beds maneuvered into awkward angles in the cramped rooms. Dangling above them, fragile and untouchable, were bunches of herbs the gardener had secured with string and suspended from the rafters to dry.

Julian's few possessions – his pocketknife, surveying tools, sketch pad, compass, a pocket book by Wells on India paper – were hastily packed by a harassed, red-faced orderly, who announced Julian was moving upstairs. He thrust the untidy bundle into Julian's arms. Good day to you.

A place had been found for Julian in servants' quarters at the top of the house, a small unswept room with an aged calendar on one wall, empty trunks, and blurred squares on the floorboards where unidentifiable furniture had been removed.

McCleary had discreetly asked the quartermaster to relocate Julian, explaining that he was among the able bodied and there was a shortage of beds. Unmentioned was the darker possibility that should Julian's mental health deteriorate, it would be a terrible example for the other patients. Better that he was sequestered.

Catherine woke into a gray dawn, immobilized, muscles stiff as if submerged, unable to swim or save herself. Directly overhead, level as paper on a table or ice on a lake, the mirrors covered the floor of the attic, their surfaces glittering with malevolent purpose. The specter of waiting had returned.

It was impossible for Catherine to re-enter the studio. Days went by in isolation except for the occasional perfunctory conversation with a nurse or an orderly. One afternoon a nurse told Catherine in passing that visiting officials were interviewing several patients, perhaps something to do with their pensions. Catherine assumed Julian was in this group. In truth, she was reluctant to see him.

A valuable Chinese screen had been retrieved from one of the storage areas and was unfolded as a fresh object for Catherine to study in her rooms.

The glassy lacquer was bituminous black, and the decorative ponds and pagodas so abundantly gilded that Catherine's misshapen reflection glided across the three joined panels, a reassurance she was still present, could cast a shadow.

Emboldened, she sought company and spent hours in the Tapestry corridor rolling bandages with a jittery V.A.D. girl who spoke endlessly about her desire for a new hat and her craving for sugar since the stuff was rationed. Catherine had never been soothed by women's company, so her reaction to the girl's chatter surprised her.

Catherine walked a circular path around the studio, unable to enter, convinced it was the hour Artis would recognize the mask as Charles. Each branch that caught at her skirt and the stones that stopped her feet confirmed this, tried to keep her away from this confrontation. She stepped through the studio door as if the threshold would crack beneath her.

She set to work, staying in the shadows, hiding in the flourish of the broom, the motion of brush and rag. As Artis assisted Anna, Catherine directed the force of her concentration at him, to stiffen the boy's hands, his neck and shoulders, and strike opacity into his eyes, to distract him from turning his memory against her.

The negative mold of Julian's face had been painstakingly sculpted, corrected to resemble the photograph of Charles, and then cast in clay. Artis and Anna gently maneuvered the plaster mold of Julian's face, filled with liquid clay like a bowl, and wedged it upright between two blocks on the table. With a great show of decisiveness, Anna placed a canvas-covered board atop the plaster mold, rapidly inverted both pieces, and set them down. 'If the clay was too thick or too thin, or contained air, the cast will crack when it is removed from the mold.' She tinnily rapped the mold with a knife handle, loosening the firm clay inside.

'Now to unveil the face I have created.'

With both hands, Anna delicately shook the mold to release the clay from its adhesive suck, and the face slowly, heavily slid free.

Catherine stifled a cry.

Formed of damp gray earth, Charles's face appeared to miraculously emerge from the surface of the table, the right eye closed as if he were sleeping. Where the injured area of Julian's face had been protected with cotton padding, the clay was blank and irregularly textured, as if wallpaper had been ripped from its surface.

'May I see?' Artis spoke from the far end of the table.

'Step right up.'

Catherine waited, lips tightening into a line, the tension spreading, stiffening her face and hands until she begged Artis to speak. 'What do you see?'

Ignoring both women, Artis coolly studied the clay face, a fragile object that could be damaged

297

with the gentlest pressure of a finger. His hand hovered over the thing, as if preparing to violate it. 'The mask isn't right.'

'What's wrong?' Catherine's frightened voice broke into the room.

Artis was clearly puzzled. 'I didn't think Julian would look like this.'

'I imagine each of us has our own vision of Julian's real face,' Anna said.

But Artis wasn't satisfied and wheeled around to stare at Catherine, a question in his eye. She couldn't answer, made herself a stone. He shrugged.

Catherine looked from Artis to Anna in shocked disbelief, both of them deceived by the face in front of them. Charles was safe. She had passed.

The aura of danger surrounding the mask lifted away, clean as an erasure. The mask became a shallow oval, an object of service like a metal spoon that lifted food to the lips. A utensil for the face.

Catherine suddenly wanted to laugh aloud through this moment, disrupt their seriousness, their solemn evaluations. She found herself giddily inviting them to dinner in the State Room; she would open the oldest wines in the cellar, make them each gifts of particularly precious silver objects from the house.

All to celebrate an imposture.

★　　★　　★

Each of Charles's jackets had required twelve separate fittings by his tailor at Poole's, the linen lining measured, basted over padding, and steamed to mold his body into an approximation of the ideal masculine physique.

Catherine unpacked Charles's Inverness cape from the wardrobe and pressed her face into the folded fabric at the back of the neck, anticipating traces of Eau Impériale, the cologne he had always worn. Wool. Nothing but the smell of wool. Her fingers rubbed over the stitching on the collar as if it held a hidden code.

She carried Charles's clothing in a valise to Julian's new quarters and stood in the doorway, surprised by the lack of light and the sparse furnishings. Not even a lock on the door, although servants had recently occupied the room. She draped several jackets over the lone wooden chair until it nearly tipped over. A tall hat from Truefitt balanced on the bedpost. Walking sticks, worn needlepoint slippers, and a pair of boots were arranged in a row under the small high window. Even if Julian suspected they were her husband's clothes, he would never pose the question to her and would wear them to please her. A man could shift clothing with greater ease than a woman.

When Catherine had finished, she proudly surveyed the display of her generosity, the jackets on hangers strung along the mantel, neat as wings, still bearing faint creases from another man's body.

★　　★　　★

Anna resented the space Kazanjian commanded and his lack of consideration, as a collection of his materials – colorless liquids, beakers and vessels like fragile toys – had been installed in her studio. She categorized these objects as offerings, lures he placed to entice her. A man's baubles. In response, she moved her own supplies and worked from the opposite end of the table. This also served to eliminate her pleasure in watching him at work, for his hands were dexterous and graceful.

For his part, Kazanjian observed her maneuvers, said nothing, was noticeably formal and self-conscious in her presence. Yet, anticipating her needs, he would stealthily slide a pencil, brush, or modeling tool forward on the table so she could find it at her fingertips. The first time this happened, Anna experienced an instant of not knowing what to do with her hands, and their eyes met, hers clouded with confusion.

The clay model of Julian's face had been cast again in plaster and coated with yellowish paraffin in preparation for its final electroplating. The layer of wax had thickened the sharp edges of the plaster face, smoothed it into a dull, honeyed surface, eerily similar to flesh.

A fine camel's hair brush trembled slightly in Anna's hand as she dusted Julian's plaster face with plumbago powder. Released from her brush, the weightless particles of powder soared into the air around her, transformed into wavering insta-bility, as seaweed moves in water. The powder floated down, settling over her hands and arms like dark, fantastic lichen.

She stood back to study the mask, its nose, cheekbones, and chin gleaming with bronze powder so it appeared solid, more permanent than the plaster it disguised.

Grudgingly, Artis stepped aside as two orderlies shoved an unwieldy metal box and a battery into place on a bench, then connected it to a generator. The men roughly indicated that his observation wasn't welcome, so he drifted over to Anna and Kazanjian.

'Will you cast the mask in silver today?'

Occupied at the cluttered worktable, they nodded briefly. As Artis showed signs of waiting for a more detailed answer, Kazanjian announced that the plaster model of Julian's face would be immersed in the lead-lined crucible.

'Crucible?' Artis carefully printed the word in a tiny notebook.

'The alchemists made the sign of the cross over their vats, thus its name. Watch you don't touch it. The liquid inside is sulfuric acid.'

Kazanjian dramatically pulled on thick padded gloves, so it seemed a giant's hands had been transplanted onto his wrists. Despite the cumbersome gloves, he expertly lowered the plaster face, suspended on wires, into the acid bath and secured it on a cathode hook. He made an elaborate ritual of this casting process, which Anna suspected was intended to impress her.

Artis cautiously moved closer as Kazanjian called the boy's attention to a pair of shimmering gold-red metal squares submerged near the plaster face in the crucible.

'The two copperplates are wired to the anode. The single liquid battery generates an electric current which deposits copper on the mask. Each metal has an allegiancy.'

Anna imposed her knowledge over Kazanjian's explanation. 'The wax will melt out, and Julian's mask will be cast in copper. It will be one thirty-second of an inch thick. Thin as an eggshell. The final layer of silver will add an almost weightless luster to the mask.'

Days later, Kazanjian dissolved pure grain silver first in nitric acid and then in distilled water, two parts to twenty-eight parts. When cyanide was added to the Florentine flask of silver acid, it magic-ally, silently boiled, becoming opaque. The copper-plated mask was resubmerged in this liquid.

McCleary had been invited to observe the last step of the casting process, and the doctor slouched on a stool, his feet secure in its rungs. He noticed the tension between Anna and Kazanjian and that she addressed him abruptly.

Kazanjian snagged the mask in the crucible on a hook and lifted the dripping face free as if salvaging the victim of a beheading. The mask was deposited on a slab of soapstone, acid puddling along its edges, a hard object, its shine obliterating all identifying features.

'The object has a strange beauty,' Anna said quietly.

McCleary found himself fidgeting to break the silence and was relieved when Kazanjian inspected the thing, as if his own curiosity had been put into effect by the other man. 'Looks like it's fashioned from silver bone. Seems close to your interest in structure, Dr Kazanjian.' His arms tightened across his chest, and the muscles around his eyes subtly betrayed his concern. 'How will Julian keep the mask on?'

'I've calculated it is light enough that a pair of spectacles will hold it against his face. Or it can be secured with a thin ribbon tied around his head.'

Anna peered closely at the silver mask, her face visible through the eyehole. 'Why, under a hat, the mask will hardly be noticeable.'

'The man who wears it will notice.'

She swiftly stood up to defend their work. 'Nevertheless, Dr McCleary, it is the best that can be done.'

'Of course. I didn't mean to suggest otherwise.' McCleary was accustomed to the temporary binding of cloth and bandages, and this bloodless, seamless, impenetrable mask didn't fit his definition of *heal* or *cure*.

Craving solitude, McCleary made excuses and slipped away, although he didn't escape Kazanjian's worried eye.

★   ★   ★

303

Before Julian's mask was cast, Anna had imagined that it would fit against his face as closely as a liquid egg was contained by its shell. The outer painted surface of the mask would be smooth as oil. Or painted porcelain, its delicate detail uncannily fine, lifelike.

Julian would speak, say her name, the mask would magically become soft as tears on his face. The same salt warmth, the same familiarity. No. The mask would shield Julian's bones, cover his muscles, keep its stiff, unmoving falseness. Only an enchantment could restore the movement of his face.

As a young woman, Anna had studied in Rome, her footsteps echoing through the galleries, the stone floors cold even on a July afternoon. In one museum, she had circled a statue of Apollo and Daphne for a considerable time.

The marble figure of Apollo reached out to seize Daphne, but she arched away from him, her bent fingers sprouting into twigs, hair thickening into leaves, and skin hardening into bark. By her transformation into a tree, Daphne escaped Apollo's pursuit, his attempted rape. Anna had marveled at the sculptor's skill. What audacity, to capture a fluid act of metamorphosis in unyielding stone, to depict Daphne at the instant her soft flesh roughened into bark. As she was and as she would be.

Anna needed several sittings to find the exact color of Julian's skin. To create flesh tone – white red brown yellow – she calculated and combined them in her mind. The physical quality of paint, the sheen of its oil and varnish, mimicked the natural luster of skin.

Anna painted squares of silver metal with a range of colors and held each one to Julian's cheek until there was a match. A number was written on the back of this square, the key to the proportion of its colors.

Anna had been fascinated when Kazanjian explained that gold could not be fused with gold. But gold melted with a trace amount of silver, zinc, or copper alloys increased its hardness and durability, its ability to bridge the bones of the jaw, circle a finger as a ring.

The gold filling in a tooth or an eye made of glass would not be rejected by the body. Tinfoil could hold injured skin in place while it healed. Bones could be transplanted and fuse to one another. She missed Kazanjian's curious knowledge. His unconventional expertise. Her sadness turned to anger, and it was in this mood that she criticized Catherine to Julian.

'She's a selfish woman. Spoiled by money. It's a wonder Catherine can pick up a spoon for herself. Even the clay on her hands is an imposition.'

Julian's face was directed up at the skylight. 'I can't judge Catherine,' he said simply. 'I'm lucky to be alive. Luck has made me less critical.'

Julian seemed so young. Anna lifted the paintbrush from his mask to listen.

'I've done so little during my life. At university, it was considered a great adventure to sleep outdoors or to set out cross-country with only a compass. Once I walked alone to Myddleton Lodge to see the maze planted in the shape of a cross. I didn't speak to another soul for two days. I was so daring.' He smiled ruefully. 'And now I don't feel safe in a field. Or anywhere else.'

His blue eye fiercely demanded her attention. 'I have no mirror. I don't ask what I look like. The doctors see their own handiwork, not a face. But you study me every day. What do you see?'

Her fingers stiffened, the brush became a useless stick of wood in her hand. 'I don't know what your life will be like. Isn't that your actual question?'

'I'm grateful you've never reassured me everything will be fine.'

'When I draw or paint, each movement of my hand is a wish for your recovery.' She was filled with sadness, as lantern light is contained and released by its glass.

The silence in the room was jagged; it pushed against the walls, escaped outside, where birdsong defeated it.

Catherine returned to the studio, certain it would be empty, unguarded, and found the worktables had been transformed in her absence, grimed with charcoal, chalk, and plaster dust. She couldn't bear to touch anything, remembering once gathering flowers as a child and her fingers becoming blackened with coal dust from the distant silver factories that had settled over the fields.

Catherine circled the room, careful nothing disturbed or jarred her, as if what she contained would spill if she moved too quickly. Her head was level on her neck, her footsteps were confident. She would wait until everything was ready, the clay dry, paper smooth, landscape cooled by shadow, hands of the clock aligned. No haste. Not yet. The moment to act would arrive.

Charles's photograph was propped up on Anna's table, ringed by jars of paint. Catherine calmly laid it down, her hand knocked over a jar, and thick red paint slowly, inexorably spread over the photograph. She watched for a moment, then carefully wiped the paint off with a rag, smearing the emulsion on the photograph, erasing Charles's features so he was barely recognizable.

'It's done,' she said loudly.

There was no edge, no end to this swell of happiness. She glanced around the room, certain nothing could harm her. But then her eye fell on Julian's half-painted mask, a curved shape with a black eye socket that drove its hollow into her chest, torqued all sensation around it.

CHAPTER 18

A mahogany sideboard in the breakfast room had remained strangely overlooked, stranded while efficient metal cabinets and tables had been installed around it. McCleary treasured this magnificent piece of furniture as if it were his own property.

He moved aside the containers cluttering the sideboard and delicately rolled back toweling to reveal its surface, inlaid with a scene of the nymph Syrinx as she was being transformed into a reed, escaping Pan's amorous attentions. Her tormented figure was pieced together from pale pear and satinwood, *Chloroxylon swietenia*, surrounded by a garland of holly wood, stained brilliant green with oxide of copper. The fine detail of the inlay had been created by an intricate technique of burning with hot sand. Polished, the wood reflected light like a golden bowl; scraped with a knife, it released an aromatic scent.

Over a period of months, McCleary had carefully examined the sideboard and speculated that it might have been made by Seddon or Adam. His sensitive fingers touched its surface, marveling at the absolute smoothness, the perfection of its joining, without unevenness or cracks. For a moment, the odor of disinfectant vanished, the rattle of the orderlies' carts in the corridor was silenced, as he studied the image, secret and guarded as the private act of moths at a candle, fish caught in light passing through water.

At a slight sound behind him, he dropped the toweling on the sideboard as the distraught matron burst into the room.

'Come quickly,' she shrieked. 'Oh God, she's hurt.'

McCleary called for Brownlow, and they raced upstairs followed by the plump matron, red faced from her efforts to keep up. The door to the room was ajar, and a young woman sat on the windowsill, moonlight striping one side of her body so she was gray and a deeper gray. When she turned, McCleary saw her arm was covered with black lines, and a deep stain spread on her skirt. She had cut herself again and again.

She'll have scars, thought McCleary, an odd consideration, but he'd suddenly remembered the young nurse's red hair and transparent skin. He gestured at Brownlow to stay back.

'Hello, Margaret. You must be unhappy about something.' McCleary's voice spread a tide of calm into the room as he slowly moved forward, almost seeming to float in his white uniform.

Margaret silently watched him until a board creaked under his foot, then a silver instrument flashed in her hand, and she held it against her wrist.

The men froze.

'Don't come closer. He's gone. I know it. He's gone.' Her voice was dull with resignation.

'Who is gone? Talk to me.'

'My fiancé.'

'Tell me what happened, Maggie.' McCleary extended his hands, palms out, demonstrating his vulnerability. He leaned slightly toward her, then took a step, lowering his hands so as not to alarm her with this intrusion.

'Give me the scalpel.' Brownlow's commanding voice broke in.

'No!' She quickly touched the scalpel to her arm, and a black line expanded with blood.

McCleary shoved over the washstand with a crash, creating a wedge of distraction so they could seize her bloody arms. Brownlow pinched her neck, her head wobbled, and she collapsed into his arms like a stupefied lover.

The injured nurse was sedated, bandaged, and put to bed. Afterward, McCleary motioned Matron from the room into the corridor for a whispered exchange.

'Tell me, do you have any idea what happened to this young woman?' he asked.

'Margaret visited her wounded fiancé in a city hospital. He had told Maggie that his wound was trifling, but she's a nurse. She examined him and found a green stain on the bandage around his ribs, smelled it, and knew he had gangrene. There was no hope for him. He would die. Maggie pretended everything was fine and kissed him farewell.' She struggled to keep her voice even. 'She returned here, and that's when she cut herself. Maggie said she wanted to die and join her fiancé. But she didn't want him to see her upset.' The matron struggled not to weep, and regained her customary sternness.

McCleary strode into his office, secured the door, and gazed wildly around the room, seeking sanctuary. The nurse had been willing to die for her lover. He mourned the dryness of his own life. No intimacy, no one touched him for pleasure. But his hands gave comfort from pain or death to those under his care.

There was an ancient tradition of *consolatio* advocated by Cicero, Seneca, Plutarch. Troubling passions and distress were remedied by reasoning, consolatory counsel, philosophical treatises.

His internal vision telescoped and he saw his own body stripped, the exposed nerves visible, a robe of pulsing threads. Like the wounded, he too had need of *consolationes*.

It was unusual to find Brownlow in the staff dining quarters, as he seldom socialized with his colleagues. Brownlow would grab a sandwich or a mug of soup from the cook's helper and eat alone on the terrace or outside the pantry, as if time away from monitoring the flutter of an unconscious

311

man's breath was frivolous. This afternoon, he sat down for luncheon with several bored orderlies and began to lecture them in an intense, hushed voice.

'One hundred years ago, Chauliac soaked sponges in lettuce juice as sleeping drafts for surgery. The juice of the morel and hemlock also caused insensibility. Tinctures of black henbane, *hyoscyamus*; ivy; and mandrake were known to witches. Soporific and anodyne.' His voice rose. 'And yet, some argued against pain relief for women during childbirth. It was the female's lot to suffer, they claimed. Queen Victoria consented to chloroform during delivery of Prince Leopold, and that settled the matter.'

Brownlow's audience grew restless, but they continued eating, as leftover food on a plate was a punishable offense.

'What genius to celebrate Morpheus. Now, I ask you, why?' he hissed, glaring at the group, not waiting for an answer. 'Because Morpheus doesn't recognize the conditions of happiness or sadness. Only sleep.' Exhausted by his rant, Brownlow fell back in his chair as the orderlies filed out.

A day later, Kazanjian found Brownlow and Artis slumped blank-faced against the wall in the ruined Chinese temple. Wads of cotton wool littered the weathered floor around them, and a bottle transparently gleamed where it had rolled, released by

Brownlow's open hand. A bitter odor invisibly thickened the air, and traces of small charred pellets remained on an iron plate over a small brazier.

'You little fool!' Furious, Kazanjian roughly shook Artis until his eyes opened and he stared groggily at the angry man standing over him. His dry mouth gaped.

'I saw things. White wanting to be a color,' the boy croaked.

The next morning in Kazanjian's office, red-eyed, stuttering with shame, the boy swore this would never happen again. Artis would keep his distance from Brownlow. He gave Kazanjian his word, and the doctor in turn promised to keep his adventure from Dr McCleary.

At an equal distance from the grass-choked amphitheater and a circle of viburnums, a pseudo-Gothic pavilion had been built in the eighteenth century according to the fancy of the estate's owner. The pavilion was one room of considerable size, and the enormous arched windows on all four sides made it strangely private, as anyone approaching was immediately visible. Decay had been a stealthy and steady visitor to the pavilion, cracking glass and stone, hiding the ornament that had tumbled from the edifice in the long grass.

'What was that?' Inside the pavilion, Brownlow, Hunt, and another orderly fell silent as they sat cross-legged on the blackened floor. A broken window admitted sounds from the field, and after a moment, their voices rose again, filling the glassed-in room.

'It's owed to us. To the men. It's the least that's owed by them that's in charge of this bloody war.' Hunt spat on the floor.

'I don't agree. It's not for us to decide Artis's fate.' The orderly leaned back, withdrawing from their circle.

'We act to protect the boy from future suffering,' Brownlow insisted angrily. 'It's our only choice.'

'I'll have no part of this business. The authorities will have your heads.'

'Who will do the deed?' Brownlow made a sarcastic invitation.

The light gathered itself and struck at an angle across the pavilion, bringing clarity to the rusted chandelier, its scrolling armature bent as if by harsh wind on a cliff. No one moved, and they avoided one another's eyes.

'Very well. Gentlemen, we will compete for the task. All is fair, as they say. I'll prepare the choices.'

Each man drew a broken straw from Brownlow's clenched fist. Then he opened his hand, displaying the remaining straw, the evidence that he had won. His face fleetingly revealed his dismay, then his expression was masked. 'Never fear. I will treat the boy gently. There can be no mistakes. God have mercy.'

★　　★　　★

314

McCleary had intended to fit the mask on Julian by himself and was dismayed to find Anna and Kazanjian already making preparations at a worktable.

Anna looked up briefly. 'Good. We can begin now that you're here.'

She tied an apron over her smock, and McCleary noticed she'd lost weight. Julian sat with his back to them on the modeling platform, removing the bandages from his face.

The mask lay facedown on a rough cloth, its curved silver interior exposed. The thing seemed so final, a fortress. Somehow, McCleary had never let himself visualize that the mask would cover Julian's entire face.

He peered closely at the mouthpiece, faultlessly joined; the cup and drain fit inside the chin area had the useful precision of a pocket watch. Something stopped him from touching the mask. Respect for Julian? Pity? A misguided sense of privacy? The wish that the mask would vanish?

'The eyelashes are the finest copper wire.' Anna took the mask and drew her fingernail along the soft lashes. 'The eyelid is much thinner than the band of a ring. That will make it easy to wear.' Her expression challenged any criticism.

Kazanjian had inlaid a glass eye into one socket of the mask, an opaque orb, neat and snug as a seedpod, crested with a permanent eyelid.

McCleary placed his hand next to the painted face on the table, skin to false skin. 'Not a brush-stroke visible.' Reluctantly, he lifted the edge of the mask, and his fingers trembled at its unexpected lightness. 'Admirable. The mask is lighter than a leaf. A fine piece of work,' he said, hoping he'd mustered passable enthusiasm.

'Thank you, Doctor.'

Anna awkwardly announced that the mask was ready. Did Julian wish to see it?

'Perhaps he'd like to be alone, Anna,' Kazanjian said quietly.

'No, I'm fine,' Julian said. 'But I don't wish to see the front of the mask. Why should I have a view no one else does of his own face?'

Julian's words were so soft that McCleary strained to listen, as if there were an echo. He recognized a distance between them – a group of healers, cogs in a great machine – and Julian, the isolated subject of their effort. He looked at Kazanjian, and the strain of anticipation and strange shame in his colleague's eyes mirrored his own.

Anna picked up the mask, cradling it as gently as McCleary touched his patients.

During their interaction, Kazanjian had remained in the background, but as Anna held the mask up at eye level, he put his hand on her arm. McCleary caught the raw glance Kazanjian directed at her and suddenly – with a shock of wonder – perceived that they had fallen in love.

Anna advanced over to Julian and with profound tenderness placed the mask – face side down – in his hands.

He held the painted object without looking at it, then angled away from them, claiming his privacy, and slipped the elastic strap over his head to secure it in place.

Anticipating this moment, McCleary had rehearsed words of encouragement, but he found himself unable to utter a sound, and even his breath was stifled as Julian turned around.

McCleary's gaze froze on the mask, a cold metal face with a slit for a mouth that seemed to leak its flesh-colored stiffness down into Julian's body. It was a closed thing, a prison. His failure. Julian would wear it like a shield on his face.

'Is it uncomfortable?'

'No more than a glove.' Julian's muffled voice sounded false, and it seemed uncanny projected from his immobile face. His head moved this way and that, as if seeking light.

McCleary tenderly examined Julian's face, noticing the clumsy distinction between the painted mask and the heightened fragility of his bare neck. He touched the line of the mask where it lay against Julian's cheek. No sharpness, no pressure. He felt a wetness on his fingertips and realized Julian's tears had leaked from under the mask.

Julian pressed his hands against his chest, as if to contain his heart. 'The mask is hard against my skin.'

McCleary said nothing, but – rapid and unbidden as a roiling cloud – pity swept over him.

His curly hair flattened by perspiration, Hunt pulled out a bottle of spirits he'd already sampled and passed it to the orderly gracelessly recumbent beside him on the straw-strewn stable floor. Brownlow watched them impassively, turning up his shirtsleeves, his only concession to the heat. Although it was past eight o'clock, the room was stifling with the lingering odor of manure and straw mingled with the newer scent of gasoline from the motorcars, the newest occupants of the stable.

Emboldened by liquor, Hunt loudly addressed Brownlow. 'You're very silent this evening. No secrets to share?'

'I can't stop my ears if a man has a loose tongue in his head.'

'Your vapors make everyone talk. You know everyone's business.' Hunt continued, gaining confidence. 'Someday you'll blackmail every one of us.'

'If only you were bloody interesting enough to blackmail, Hunt. Thus far, nothing in your life is worth tuppence.' Unperturbed, Brownlow stretched his long arms. 'I'd rather have a man bleat for his mother under anesthesia than weep in pain. It makes a better tale. More profitable.'

'I'm no bleater,' Hunt protested. 'Noise don't reveal a man's character anyhow.'

'Neither does a face,' added the orderly.

'No mirror could convince us of that, my friend. Survive enemy bullets and death for something far worse.' Brownlow's claim brought silence.

'You shouldn't say those things, sir.' Artis spoke up from the corner.

'Don't talk about what you don't know, young master. You'll do well to keep yourself respectful.'

The men's exchange carried an unspoken intent, and Artis half-sensed this undercurrent.

'The lad will know everything soon enough. He reports for duty tomorrow.'

'Heigh-ho, to the trenches we go.'

'Let's give him a proper send-off. Here's the bottle.'

Pressured by Brownlow to take a turn, Artis gulped from the bottle, quickly becoming a childish, giddy drunk.

'So where's our good doctor?' the orderly demanded. 'Strange that he's late.'

'I don't imagine this is an occasion he's antici-pated with pleasure.'

'Dr McCleary will be here?' Alarmed, Artis propped himself up on a bale of hay.

'He's supervising the consumption of drink.' Hunt giggled.

McCleary's tall figure interrupted dappled light from the dirt-speckled lanterns, and the men scrambled to their feet as if it were disrespectful not to stand in his presence.

Artis stumbled drunkenly over a bulky object

and aimed a wide kick at a sandbag on the floor. 'What's this?'

'There you go.' McCleary steadied the unbalanced boy, keeping one hand on his shoulder. 'Now then. I'd promised to help with your military obligations. I have made inquiries with several military officials. Nothing has come of it.'

Sobered, Artis heard this without flinching. 'Yes, sir. Doctor.'

'I can arrange for you to stay and help in the hospital. This will be your service to your country. What say you?'

Bewildered, Artis stared at McCleary and the men around him, then answered with a clear voice. 'I wish to stay. What must I do?'

'Trust me. Trust that I will help you, but it will be painful. Only briefly.' The doctor straightened his back, his tense shoulders betraying his nervousness.

The patchy light in one of the lanterns hesitated, and the orderly crouched to relight it.

'Drink this.' Brownlow put a cup to Artis's lips, and soon the sleepy-eyed boy sprawled on the sandbag, his fine hair an aureole against the rough fabric.

Brownlow and Hunt easily hoisted Artis to his feet, then gently bound him upright against a post with a thin rope, leaving his right arm free.

'What are you doing?' the boy groggily demanded, plucking at the rope.

McCleary observed these preparations without comment, his mouth fixed into a grim line.

Hunt heaved a sandbag atop a pile of hay bales. He flattened Artis's outstretched right hand against it and secured it in place with rope. Increasingly agitated, Brownlow kneeled, unpacked a syringe from a small kit, and solemnly prepared it, a silver line, its sharpness seeming out of place against the coarse straw.

'Keep him steady.'

Artis grimaced and tensed as Brownlow daubed his hand with a dark liquid and the syringe found its mark in his open palm.

Sweat ran down Brownlow's face. 'It's too dark. Gentlemen, your lanterns, please.'

The others hurriedly moved the lanterns closer to Artis, and the broad brushstroke of light eliminated the details of their faces, bleaching their figures, and even the bales of hay appeared to be transformed into a solid mass.

Hunt handed Brownlow something bundled in a cloth, and he carefully unwrapped a small object, a neat angle that fit into his hand. The lantern light striped the thick muzzle of a Browning pistol.

'Artis, keep your hand open. Understand?' Brownlow lifted the boy's chin and stared into his eyes. 'Courage.' He briefly turned to examine the pistol, took a few steps back, cocked it, and aimed at Artis. His arm wobbled, and he dropped the gun. 'My eyes.'

McCleary held out his hand to take the pistol himself.

Shamed, Brownlow ignored him and with the same intensity he commanded in surgery, squinted down the barrel at Artis and pulled the trigger. The force of the gunshot jerked his hand back as Artis shrieked.

CHAPTER 19

At four o'clock, the light through the open door of the studio was faintly bronzy green, a color it seemed the grass outside had relinquished.

Kazanjian slipped a gold pencil into his pocket and opened a sketchbook to a drawing of his hands holding his spectacles, which Anna had quickly executed during their train journey. She had claimed it was his most accurate likeness.

He smiled thoughtfully and studied Anna across the table.

'We have a history of objects between us.' His voice carried a sympathetic humor that masked the possessiveness in his statement.

'It strikes me that you're a man who finds objects useful.' Her eyes acknowledged their shared experience. Their intense conversations at the base hospital had lasted until the night moths and biting insects were irritatingly thick around the small lantern and their frantic shadows visible against the tent. Then Kazanjian would escort Anna to quarters carrying the lantern, which he referred to as a proper gentleman's accessory.

Their code. 'Your lantern always accompanied us.' At the memory, Anna's smile did not fade as quickly this time, and she bowed her head to hide her expression.

She was occupied with the task of making pastel crayons, preferring to fabricate them herself, as commercial pastels faded, their fugitive color derived from coal tar dyes. Her sketches of the injured men must be a permanent record, outlasting memory, flesh, and the enemy.

Gum arabic, strained oatmeal gruel, and cadmium red pigment had been ground together into a stiff mass until its texture and consistency were identical to those of pastry dough. Drops of honey were added to counteract brittleness, so the pastels would glide, not crumble on contact with paper. As Anna rolled bits of this brilliant mixture into small balls, her fingers and palms became reddened by the cadmium, appearing to have been rubbed raw by the contact. Under the influence of this violent color, she began to tell Kazanjian a story.

'Some time ago, an older woman commissioned a portrait of her six-year-old grandson from me. I had trouble sketching the boy's face; his expression was so unhappy. He was uncomfortable even when he wasn't posing. I observed him carefully, tried to puzzle him out. He haunted me.

'One afternoon, I put down my brush, went over to the boy, and carried him to the settee. He allowed me to remove his jacket and shirt. I found bruises on his back. He wouldn't speak about it. I let him sleep in the hammock under the trees for the entire afternoon.

'I implored my husband to do something to stop the child's ill treatment, but he dismissed me, suggested the boy had had an accident. Children are clumsy, he said. I can do nothing. I discovered the boy's family was prominent, and they had helped fund the hospital where my husband practiced.

'The next time the boy and his grandmother came to my studio, I took her outside and told her someone had deliberately hurt him.'

Anna looked directly at Kazanjian. 'The grand-mother said he'd never been like other children. She was actually scornful. She turned her back, and her hands shook so badly she couldn't open her parasol. The poor child ran after her down the walk. They never came back.

'Sometime later, the boy was admitted to the hospital with a fractured arm. But not a single bruise. My husband told me this just to confirm the correctness of his judgment.'

Kazanjian muttered an unintelligible oath.

'I told my husband never to speak about the boy again. I put his portrait away but couldn't forget the child. By the time we volunteered to work at the front, my fury at my husband was ice cold.'

She opened her hand to reveal crimson powder creased in her palm, neater than blood.

Kazanjian touched her arm, caressed Anna's

stained hand, her red palm, red wrist, revealing his knowledge of her, his hands equally skilled as her hands.

She couldn't see, couldn't calculate, responded without strategy, touching his face, wreathing his head with the odor of turpentine that clung to her skin.

He kneeled, resting his head against her skirt.

At that moment, they could have been hurtled to the ceiling of a grand palazzo, transformed into painted figures, a mythical god and goddess in the repose of love, the flourish of their silken drapery, their perfect flesh displayed against a brilliant cobalt sky.

'Forgive me,' Anna said, stepping away from him.

Catherine craved privacy, a bough, a protective arch over her head. The constant pressure of the injured men's vigilance, the veiled observations of their caretakers, the unceasing monitoring of recovery, had completely permeated the house. Julian's aloofness was a relief, and he held it so unconcernedly that he seemed to be merely passing through the hospital, with no need of aid. He had refused the luxury of Catherine's room and possessions, which intensified her determination to increase her power over him.

She quickly passed out of view from the windows and made her way to the lower orchard, partially enclosed by an ancient wall. Many decades ago, the peach trees had been wired flat against its orange brown bricks, tamed into horizontal lines, a decorative torture that removed the branches from the third dimension. At certain hours, sunlight revealed the neat wires that bound the living branches, the sudden winking glint of thin metal hammered over bark.

Charles's familiar silhouette appeared at the end of the path alongside the wall. He continued toward her, the trees irregularly altering his gray jacket with violet shadow. Frightened, she swore his image must be projected from her deepest memory, yet she couldn't control him, make him stop. He was a ghost.

At a sound – the *tap tap* of his walking stick – this day-light specter vanished, replaced by a man with a white-wrapped face who stood before her and with shy, self-conscious pride, boldly put his hand in the pocket of a fine jacket that once belonged to her husband.

Catherine embraced Julian with relief, not disappointment.

They walked together, Julian lifting branches away from the brittle circumference of her straw hat. The afternoon was unusually warm, the sun a pour of dull heat that cushioned her cheeks and throat, blotted moisture around her arms.

'Look. How perfect.' A branch and its thin leaves shook as he twisted a peach from its stem and slipped it into her pocket.

The fruit still held warmth from the sun, making

a comforting weight against her hip. They fell silent; he was preoccupied, gazing at the trees with a blunted air as she anxiously observed him. She had watched her mother's unseeing face in a similar way, alert for the slightest foil of expression, which created the same waiting helplessness she now felt with Julian. Only his words or touch could temper the mood between them.

He stopped and put his hands on her shoulders so they looked into each other's eyes. 'I must tell you. They put the mask over my face like settling a crown on my head. It was so cold it seemed to burn my skin.'

To ease his pain, Catherine took the sensation of the frigid metal into herself, like a fire eater, a sword swallower. Nothing could burn her. She pressed his hand against her breast, but even this contact didn't ease the tightness held in his body.

Catherine began to fear the distance the mask would take him from her. Their happiness would be destroyed before Julian could be transformed or healed. But the blind path was laid.

I'll make a boat for you, a raft, a vessel. To take you away,' crooned Brownlow, crouching at Artis's bedside. The boy was oblivious, still recovering from surgery, his gauze-bandaged arm swaddled in a thickness of folded towels. Brownlow's bullet had torn exactly through the center of his palm.

A nurse bustled around the bed, aggressively

snugging the blankets close to the boy, making it clear to Brownlow that she was in charge. Her scowling, ruddy face was a coarse contrast against her smooth white cap.

'The boy will recover from his accident. But he isn't fit for conversation. Don't be bothering him now.'

'Certainly, Nurse.'

Brownlow unsteadily moved back, colliding with Dr McCleary. In the hasty glance they exchanged, McCleary thought the other man's eyes passed scornful judgment on him. Or was it complicity? He was in a state to mistake any gesture for criticism.

Eclipsed by McCleary, the respectful nurse hovered unnoticed as the doctor's calm hand measured the drowsy boy's pulse. Artis's face was slightly pinched with pain, his features seemed closed in, simple as a cartoon, upper lip contorted, brow narrowed.

McCleary smoothed the boy's forehead where a blue vein twisted across his temple before losing itself under a spike of damp hair. Artis's lips were only faintly pink; healthy blood hadn't yet flushed the skin.

'Forgive me. Speak to me,' McCleary whispered, wishing to seize the boy's consciousness and drag him back into awareness.

Naming the body was a charm against the unexpected nature of a wound, and McCleary recited muscles of the hand from memory: *abductor digiti quinti, abductor pollicis longus, extensor carpi radialis brevis, extensor carpi ulnaris.*

Visualizing what was inaccessible, he descended into the boy's hand as smoothly as a glissando, the jagged ends of bone; lean, purposeful striations of muscle neatly secured with silkworm gut and horsehair. The beautiful compactness of the body's interior.

He sensed healing was progressing satisfactorily, although any injury or medical procedure carried risk, and even a scratch could develop into sepsis, shock, blood poisoning. Dakin's Solution was commonly used for infection, but it was an unreliable antiseptic. Just to be safe, he would order a nurse to apply oil of balsam, an aromatic and ancient remedy, to Artis's hand.

The details of the accidental shooting had been explained to another surgeon, and after examining the boy's wound, he confirmed McCleary's original diagnosis. But now McCleary realized he'd sought this second opinion to create distance and absolve himself from the shooting and its aftermath.

It was certain that Artis's dexterity was compromised, and that he would recover only partial use of his injured hand. Holding a spoon, a bayonet, or a scalpel would be difficult. The boy had been delivered from war, but his dream of becoming a surgeon was ruined. This would be explained when Artis was stronger. McCleary would make certain he would have no material needs in the future. His solicitor would draw up the necessary documents.

McCleary leaned closer to Artis, forcing himself to smile. 'I will tend you with care. I promise you, young man.'

Artis slipped into deeper sleep.

McCleary shook himself, remembering Artis was a patient among patients. Other sufferers needed his attention too. Suddenly, he was distracted by the unexpected scent of ether.

Unnoticed, Brownlow had quietly re-entered the room. 'You've lost your apprentice, Doctor,' Brownlow hissed. 'But I'm certain he'll be right as rain.' The pupils of Brownlow's eyes were unfocused pinpoints, constricting with his pitiless aggression.

McCleary didn't trust himself to answer.

'I don't imagine the lad will want your medical tutoring after you arranged his injury, however well-intentioned. But I could train him as an anesthetist. Perfect dexterity isn't absolutely necessary.' Brownlow licked his lips, his fingers twitching in the pocket of his jacket.

'A profession that doesn't require steady hands, as you constantly demonstrate.'

'I'm a slab of flint compared to you, Doctor. I don't weep and wallow over my patients.'

'Please lower your voice. Artis doesn't have the disposition to work as an anesthetist. And I don't have the disposition to stand by and watch.' McCleary angrily shifted his weight, and his foot struck something that rolled out from under the bed. An ether bottle. He understood Brownlow's intent.

Brownlow's words tumbled out. 'I meant no harm. The boy will only wake to suffer. I help him in my way.'

McCleary retrieved the bottle of ether, cold as ice.

'I deliver men into nothingness. But nothing comforts me,' babbled Brownlow, his face fused with anguish.

Brownlow's loneliness was beyond any solace McCleary could offer, and he waited until the man's words ebbed into silence. 'It is a mistake to believe we can have companions. We're alone with our work.'

Along the drive lined with shadows, an unfamiliar woman determinedly hurried toward the house, hampered by her skirt, which she repeatedly kicked with her canvas shoes. An orderly stalked close behind her, his feet silent on the grass.

Catherine was a spectator, watching the two figures appearing to be involved in a silent, unfamiliar game.

'Halt!'

The woman ignored the orderly's shout, and continued without breaking stride.

The man lunged, seized the woman's arm, sending her hat – a black feathered cartwheel – flying. With a soft cry, she jolted to the ground near her hat.

'Ma'am, you're not allowed at the hospital. No visitors.' The orderly helped the woman to her feet, her face dazed with disbelief and indignation.

'Here, what are you doing?' Catherine pulled at the orderly's arm until he released the woman, and she backed away, sobbing into her gloved hands. A bouquet lay crushed on the grass, intended as a gift for the visitor's sweetheart, son, or husband.

Catherine and the orderly stared at each other in mutual incomprehension. *How did this woman get past the gates?*

The woman evaded them and bolted up the steps into the house.

'Stop her!'

Inside, the female intruder careened down the corridor, her gaze striking the faces of each bystander in a search for her loved one.

'Richard! Richard!' the woman cried. 'Where are you?'

She was possessed by such fierce anguish that the bewildered nurses, doctors, and orderlies stood aside, none of them daring to interfere. The woman shoved a supply trolley out of the way, the tiny orchestra of its glass instruments nervously heralding its collision with the wall.

She plunged into a room, and the patients playing checkers at a table were startled by this gasping intruder, her dark hair unpinned, falling to her shoulders, dress stained green at the knee and hem where it had been crushed against grass.

A man in a black wire mask stood up. The woman's eye met his single eye, her mouth opened with astonishment as she saw an injured man up close for the first time, and her scream swept in the outside world, the pitiless, constant judgment all the mutilated would encounter away from the shelter of the hospital.

A young patient with a thickly bandaged head, his eyes slits across two red, swollen circles of skin, angrily tilted the table; the game pieces clattered to the floor, then spun into a silence that obliterated the bustle in the corridor. A crowd gathered around the woman, who had fainted in the doorway.

McCleary trudged purposefully behind Kazanjian, Hunt, and Brownlow along the narrow path, launching the long stalks of the butterfly bushes into trembling motion as he brushed against them, scattering their faded, grainlike, almost phosphorescent gray flowers. To the north, dryness seemed to radiate through the browning stalks of mown grass across the pasture, prickly stubble readied to catch the first frost.

McCleary dismissed the joking conversation that reached him over their shoulders as frivolous and unnecessary. Why couldn't they enjoy silence, the enormous space of quiet? He increasingly craved solitude. Ten strides later, he was glad of their loud company, as he was again possessed by a heaviness that weighed his legs, stooped his shoulders, dulled his voice and the sympathetic brilliance of his eye. This ill feeling had no internal source that a pathologist, an anatomist, or the uncanny, infallible vision of an X-ray could detect. In truth, the operating theater had become the only place he felt truly secure, where time could be accounted for as a heartbeat, tunneling its rhythm through a stethoscope. Bodies were a safe and familiar landscape, with their subterranean levels of muscle, veins like a river, bones located in flesh like stones unearthed in a field.

The heavy hamper he carried pressed into his palms through his thick deerskin gloves. Although he was always careful of his hands, this discomfort barely registered, as if he had become detached from the troubles of his body.

They reached their destination, an orangerie with panes missing from windows and roof, its metal structure thinned by rust. Inside, a craggy shape in the center was the tumbled remains of a fountain. Huge stone planters that once held tender tropical plants – India jasmine, Bourbon palms, citrons, rare vines from Sidon and Smyrna – had been rolled into corners. Weeds had flourished during the summer, now tangled, fading green spokes protruding from the stone floor. Characteristically ill-tempered, Brownlow stamped them flat.

The men simultaneously removed their jackets, a constricting reminder of service. McCleary dusted a bench with a crumpled newspaper, then cautiously sat down.

The Fortnum and Mason hampers had been a gift to a patient who had subsequently auctioned them in the billiard room to Brownlow, now swiftly unpacking tins of pickles, peas, preserved ham, cheeses, Charbonnel chocolates, a cake with candied fruit. He gloated over a small gleaming tin. 'Gentlemen and doctors, we are blessed. We have wild-game paté. Lift your forks.'

'I couldn't even scrawl an X for my name at this point.' McCleary stretched his cramped and aching hands. He thought to save a delicacy for Artis, perhaps a slice of cake, then guilt overlapped this generous thought.

'A glass of wine won't be too burdensome.' Brownlow dexterously uncorked a bottle and poured the wine into beakers, their chosen drinking vessels. 'A fine Margaux, courtesy of our lady hostess.'

'The fresh air has made you rave, Brownlow.' McCleary held out a beaker to be filled, trying to catch the man's eye and gauge his condition. Brownlow's moods had become more mercurial, and he habitually forgot, rather than forgave, those who frequently quarreled with him.

'Brigands with our spoils,' Kazanjian said solemnly.

Hunt giggled. 'Like *Treasure Island*.'

The men hailed the hampers' former owner and Fortnum's delivery team, two stout women in the store's signature green uniforms.

As the glass reached McCleary's lips, he

inhaled the faintest scent of iodine from his stained fingertips, the connection to work always present. The bitter odor was lost as he swallowed wine and was immediately engulfed by its richness, surprised that taste still had the power to command his senses. A memory crackled, an image of ivory light, silver candlesticks, the black shape of a ruffled skirt. He struggled to identify these fractured clues. A restaurant, a dinner with his beloved. What had she whispered to him? Or had she hummed a bar of music? Handel? 'Ombra mai fu'? Perhaps an orchestra had been playing.

Swept by a sense of loss, McCleary realized he was staring at Kazanjian, who had the good fortune to find love in this unlikely setting. He studied his friend for signs of transformation, radiance, the blessing of Cupid, but Kazanjian's stolid face gave nothing away. McCleary smiled, resolving to speak with him and share his pleasure. Or was it best to leave something so private unsaid? He found it difficult to conduct discussion on the intangible, preferring physical objects or a verifiable condition as subjects.

Brownlow and Kazanjian's conversation about two patients grew louder and impassioned, heated into an argument. Kazanjian briefly touched the other man's arm to make a point, and the anesthetist shook himself and drew away, unable to bear the contact.

'Even the masks made by Anna Coleman won't

337

give the patients a life. For all the good it does, they should wear flowerpots over their heads.' Brownlow's eyes appeared black, huge, unfocused, and his grin challenged anyone to contradict him. No one spoke up, knowing argument was useless, as Brownlow routinely ignored other opinions.

'He isn't wrong,' muttered Hunt.

'Thank you, sir.' Brownlow snapped a salute in his direction. 'I overheard two patients in the ward begging another to make a wish because it was his birthday. Guess what he wished for?' He continued without pause. 'The poor blinking sod wished that he would be struck blind, so he would never see anyone's reaction to his disfigured face. The other patients agreed. I thought to myself, Yes, blindness isn't so far-fetched for someone with a ravaged mug. Imagine the relief.'

Hunt whistled in astonishment at Brownlow's disrespect.

McCleary couldn't let this dismissal of his work stand unchallenged. 'There are many routes to a cure. The masks will activate the patients' own healing.'

'Problem with you, Dr McCleary, is that you're always so pious. Like a saint giving blessings to the patients.'

'You're drunk, Brownlow.'

'No, I'm a bloody visionary. Sober enough to know that in our secret hearts, we rejoice that our faces are whole. Our proud lips can kiss. Our eyes blink. We don't recognize the damaged men as equals. No, we see them as gargoyles, and this completes the injury the enemy started.'

Brownlow's words struck a chill in McCleary, which spread and numbed him. There was truth, like something unhealed, in his words. And shame too. He dully realized that the others were looking at him for a response.

McCleary found his voice. 'Yet even when a man's face is damaged beyond recognition, his true identity doesn't change. Even after death, something remains. Call it what you will, nothing on earth is excluded. Ovid knew this and described it wonderfully.' His fine voice became more resonant as he forgot his surroundings, and the lines floated clear in his memory:

'All things are always changing,
But nothing dies. The spirit comes and goes,
Is housed wherever it wills, shifts residence
From beasts to men, from men to beasts, but always
It keeps on living. As the pliant wax
Is stamped with new designs, and is no longer
What once it was, but changes form, and still
Is pliant wax, so do I teach that spirit
Is evermore the same, though passing always
To ever-changing bodies.'

The others were silent. By a trick of shadow, the narrow metal scaffolding on the roof of the greenhouse appeared to constrict, drawing

339

closer over their heads as if it were a descending net.

'I'm not buying it.' Brownlow clambered unsteadily onto a bench and stood to address them, intense as a preacher. 'The only place our spirits pass is inside our own brains. And then lights out. I see proof of this every day on the operating table.'

'Aye. Let him dry out,' said Hunt. 'He sees things half the time. Sleepy on his feet from fumes up his nose.'

Roaring, Brownlow leaped from the bench, swinging wildly at Hunt, and they fought across the rough floor, shouts echoing around them.

McCleary had no memory of how he came to pull Brownlow free and wipe the dark thread of blood running from his mouth, his gesture of comfort automatic. He held Brownlow's arm, and the panting man looked at him wonderingly.

McCleary remembered a night in Heidelberg when he'd slashed an opponent with a saber in a duel and, to his shame, had been unable to stanch the wound with a tourniquet from a torn shirt. Someone had helped him the same way that evening, had taken his arm and led him away, unaware that his own face had been cut. Had violence always been attached to his practice of healing?

McCleary felt the ticking pulse of the saber scar on his face and released Brownlow's arm with an abruptness that surprised both of them. 'That's enough.'

Brownlow turned away, his face sorrowfully composed for tears.

CHAPTER 20

The supper sent to Catherine's room was cold under its metal covers, the soup in a dented tureen, a greasy cutlet on a thick china dish from the hospital pantry. She stood over a small table to eat, a cloth protectively draped over her gown, but the spoon's scrape across the bowl, the coarse crumble of bread, the very act of eating, was repulsive. She had no need of food. Her fingers released the spoon, and it clattered on the plate.

A cloak around her shoulders, she hurriedly left the house, dressed to meet Julian. The long grass struck her skirt in rustling, regular waves as if she moved along the water's edge.

The pavilion's walls of stone and glass were indistinct, deepened to gray under an equally gray moon. One summer's eve a violinist had played fox-trots and tangos in this windowed room, which had been crowded with dancers. Women had drifted outside seeking a cooler atmosphere, and their pale silk gowns carried light diffused from the candles like pollen into the dark field, where servants waited with glasses of champagne, their silver trays blossoming with moving reflections.

Now the image of this scene seemed overly bright, fantastic, as if even her memory had been affected, muted by war.

A strange odor found her; she knew it had wafted across the channel. It was the odor of fear and mourning, a harbinger of battle that had followed the men to their sanctuary at the estate. This was certain as gravity, cold as Mercury, and with another turn of the tide, spin of a planet, the enemy's pointing finger on a map, grasses would suddenly flatten, revealing bare earth, leaving her unprotected and alone as the sky inflated, arched itself enormously overhead.

Inside the pavilion, her footsteps revealed the cold echo of an unoccupied space, and her awareness sharpened to fit the opening of the windows, a route of escape. Too fearful to pace, she steadied herself against a wall, fumbled with a candle, and its feeble flame revealed broken glass, a floor patterned with pebbles, and the wiry disorder of birds' nests in the eaves. The chill of the room enfolded her bare skin, a surface inviting inscription.

Julian would be here soon. In her mind, she had stripped his face of features as wind strips leaves from a tree. Darkness would cover what she didn't wish to see of him. On a battlefield, everything was aimed at one point. A target. Wasn't a lover's body a location to find in the dark?

A noise outside.

Fear snapped like a cloth in wind, twisting her attention around to a man emerging from the blackness behind the door. The illusion of his appearance was betrayed by wavering candlelight that caught the subtle reflection of his moist eye, revealing its live blue-and-white opacity in the mask that was Charles's face.

Her eyes stared cruelly, dangerous as a thrown weapon, a flaying knife. She couldn't look away from this man. Not Charles. Not Julian.

'So we begin.' His words were shapeless, rising and falling from behind the mask in a strange voice.

He moved close enough to touch her, but her head turned away; she couldn't look at him directly.

He ignored her rejection – or was unable to see clearly – and gently opened her hand, pressed a small shell into her palm, smooth and unmarked as a bird's egg, the line of its opening curved like two lips.

'This is for you, Catherine. Hold it with the slit upright. I will touch the shell as if it were your body. Watch, think of yourself.'

She looked up and for the instant of a glance, his mask revealed its stiffness, a primitive imitation of flesh, its surface textured with feathery brushstrokes, fine as a bird's plumage.

Their bodies touched, he cupped her hand, and his finger slowly circled the shell's narrow opening.

The rhythmic sound of his breath, a faint whoosh, was intensified by the mask, and it seemed he exhaled and inhaled through its entire surface, his flesh fused against it.

Catherine resisted, tried to step back, but he wouldn't release her; his finger stopped moving when she trembled. But there was nothing to fear, as his hand held only pleasure. He was unaware of her deceit, his unwitting imposture. She closed her eyes, to convince herself it was Charles who held her.

Julian watched her face, patiently waited, then began to retrace a circle on the shell, his breath quickening, loud and intimate.

She felt the shell's thin membrane absorbing warmth from her skin and willed herself to slip into it, to dissolve this suspense. The room, his presence, the tense angle of her body vanished, and she became heavier, then lighter at his command, a chain of sensations ending as she blindly pushed him away, gasping *Who are you?*

The candlelight intensified into a fiery streak that spread over the mask, glowing where her fingernails had scratched him in passion.

An orderly adjusted his spectacles and tossed an envelope addressed to Mrs Coleman onto her worktable.

'What's this?' Anna studied the envelope. An official communication was seldom welcome in wartime.

'Will you be reading it, Mrs Coleman? Should I wait for a reply?'

'Not now. No.' She instantly forgot the orderly and tidied the table, slowly covered a bowl of clay slip, cleaned her hands with a cloth, put the letter in her pocket, and left the studio.

She entered the infirmary, not realizing she had sought Kazanjian until she found him.

'A pleasure to see you, ma'am.' Kazanjian was formal and remote, as if to defend himself. A nurse handed him a document, and he responded with a quick nod of gratitude, ignoring Anna.

She waited, her skirt brushing the shelves of supplies, resenting her undisguised need to see him and the pleading expression on her face that anger struggled to replace.

After the nurse closed the door behind her, Kazanjian's demeanor became gentler as he noticed that Anna's clothing was stained with clay, for she had forgotten to remove her smock.

'Something has disturbed you.'

'I have received an official notice.'

Kazanjian reached out and held her hands between his. 'Come and sit with me, Anna. I will prepare a place for you.'

The floor shifted strangely under her clumsy feet as he led her to the Juliet window with a view of the lake. Her body stiffly bent itself into position on the bench. They sat side by side like two pylons at opposite ends of a bridge, an ominous span of water between them. Anna

346

sensed that if he were to touch her, she would shake with relief.

He slipped the letter from her pocket. 'May I open it?'

She numbly agreed.

The letter seemed solid as a tablet in his hand as he read it, then softly said the words her husband had died. Enemy fire. There were official regrets, and exact details were omitted. Volunteers had provided the white wooden cross that marked his presence in a foreign field.

Sorrow was a cold, empty sharpness, then enormously full, and Anna embraced it with a bitter cry that threw her against Kazanjian's shoulder.

In the days that followed the news of her husband's death, Anna shut herself in the studio, refusing to see anyone. An orderly brought fresh water, food, a bromide in a brown bottle. Catherine left an offering of flowers in a bucket, and a bottle of wine was anonymously left on the doorstep.

Anna turned Kazanjian away. He allowed her to do this. He left her candles and an enamel mug he'd taken from the mess at the base hospital, a memento of their time together. When he could steal away from the wards, he stood outside the studio, listening to Anna pacing, never disturbing her.

One afternoon, Anna finally opened the door and admitted Kazanjian.

She was wan, thinner, and there were circles

under her eyes. Despite her time alone in the studio, everything had been neglected. Clay had cracked in containers; paint had dried on brushes and stiffened into irregular smears on the palettes. Dust had collected along the edges of the worktables.

Anna watched without offering to help as Kazanjian silently began to tidy the room. Once she quietly urged him to return to his own work, obviously not expecting an answer. He resealed the jars and tubes of paint, scoured the worktables, rinsed bowls, brushes, and clay tools, emptied dark liquids into the waste vat. He poured turpentine on the palettes and scraped them down. A crimson shape bloomed on the rag in Kazanjian's clenched hand as he carefully wiped paint off a palette. 'You have never allowed me to help you. Even at the base hospital.'

'That was a lifetime ago.'

Imperturbable as the bottles on a shelf behind him, Kazanjian studied her, a solemn appraisal such as he gave patients, although the calculation of the future was veiled. 'I have no defense against you.'

'I cannot.'

He hesitated as if to say something, picked up his notebook, and walked out.

Good-bye, then.

At sunrise, McCleary sat on the edge of his bed, too fatigued to dress. It was extraordinary that he was still animated, could walk and talk, that the flesh hadn't fallen from his body the way snow drops from a branch. His tidily folded clothing, his spectacles, the beaker of water, and the journal on the cast-off velvet chair were strangely unfamiliar, as if they had been left here weeks ago, not the previous evening. Artis. He remembered that the boy was safe and savored a fleeting sensation of accomplishment.

He was deeply tired, his bones too stiff to accept ease. Kazanjian was correct. Bones were secret, unseen, unyielding. The body's ivory treasure. Mast. Pole. Support. Skin was frail, a thin cover for nerves, muscles. A contact and a barrier, transformed by a needle, a splinter, another hand. A cruel word.

A vision came of his own pale fingers in surgery, drawing stitches of catgut with a curved needle, and then the needle multiplied into a forest of green spears – no, it was fine grass growing over the dead. He imagined soldiers rising from the fields where they had fallen or been lovingly interred, and there would be no distinction between the men with whole bodies and the mutilated he had mended. All flesh equal. Bodies with radiant skin.

He remembered a passage: 'I know that my Redeemer liveth, and in the last day I shall rise out of the earth. And I shall be clothed again with my skin, and in my flesh I shall see God.'

Constant in the background, like a current of

suffering, he perceived the faint hiss of air over a moving object, as a bomb neared its target, a life neared its end. He put his fingers to his temples, and the throbbing there was synchronized to this pulse beyond the range of his hearing. Singing, was there singing? As his thought radiated across the fixed net of his body, he sensed it loosen, the veins slipping marvelously free of silken muscles and the anchor of bones as he settled into the cradle of his suspended flesh, conscious of a deep internal vibration that was entirely expected and entirely surprising as it came.

Kazanjian volunteered and was assigned to Base Hospital No. 15, then finally transferred to a casualty clearing station at the front, as he insisted on being close to the battlefield. The conditions were appalling. Month after month, countless numbers of men died around him. After supplies of morphia ran out, he ordered the nurses to inject the most seriously wounded men with sterile water as a placebo. Bombs fell in a field adjoining the hospital tent, and he was unfazed. Kazanjian made his work a trench and buried himself there.

An orderly had been bribed to siphon hoarded petrol into the Wolseley and drive Catherine and Julian into the city. The trip was her gift to Julian, as she anticipated the mask's illusion would be more powerful in an unfamiliar setting.

Julian deftly tucked the blanket around her in the

back of the motorcar, and they exchanged few words during the drive, as the chassis rattled like a cage. The weather had turned chill, the landscape was permanently gray, and a slowly darkening strata of remote, wintry clouds accompanied them along the half-frozen dirt roads.

It was dusk when they arrived, but there was light enough to see that the city had suffered changes. The lake in St James's Park had been drained, and the open acres were occupied by military tents. Protective metal net had been draped over the National Gallery, apparently flung down by a giant. Tanks and immense guns mounted on revolving stands stood in the square before the Museum Library. The war was closer here. The most venerable buildings seemed temporary, artificial, as if broken bricks and debris were the true bones of the city, once hidden but now revealed.

As Catherine and Julian walked under the green awning leading into the Berkeley Hotel, the lamplight struck their faces. Catherine anticipated the doorman's shocked reaction to Julian's bandaged face. She felt her arm tense under Julian's hand.

The gold buttons on the elderly doorman's uniform flashed, his white gloves blurred, and the bored expression on his face didn't change. A bandaged man was not an uncommon sight. Julian swiftly dropped a guinea into his hand.

The hotel clerk was impassive as they signed the registration book. Catherine had remembered to wear her wedding ring, but Julian requested separate suites. Astonished, Catherine accepted his decision without protest and turned to follow a robust young woman in a bellhop's uniform.

The girl easily placed Catherine's hatbox and two heavy leather suitcases in the lift. 'Cold for the month, isn't it, ma'am?' she observed.

Disoriented by Julian's rejection, Catherine didn't reprimand the girl for speaking out of place. 'It seemed warmer in the country.'

'They say it's the bombs that change the weather. Romney Marsh has been invaded by magpies. And there's a plague of antler moths in Westmorland.'

Catherine didn't reply.

Catherine and Julian had dinner sent up to their separate rooms that night. Afterward, she couldn't sleep and stood before the window, cold air radiating through the windowpanes onto her outstretched hands.

A fur cloak draped over her thin gown, she knocked on the door of Julian's room and waited in the enormously wide, chilly corridor. There was no response, his room was quiet, and she returned to her bed alone as if in a dream.

The next morning, Catherine began shopping for Julian at Fribourg and Treyer, relieved that the worn carpeting and dim, smoky interior of the shop were unchanged. She commissioned measures of dry Havana and Latakia tobaccos to be mixed, aged, and hand-rolled into cigarettes. A pair of malacca-handled umbrellas was ordered at Briggs, and a monogrammed silver cigarette box at Asprey. An appointment was made for Julian to be fitted for shirts at Budd. Every shop was busy but understaffed, as only women could be hired as clerks.

Catherine carried her own packages. An armload of offerings. She turned a corner, and the entire street before her sparkled with broken glass, fine as frost in sunshine, and smoke lifted from a building, or what was left of it. Here was rubble to bruise a body, dust to blind. A familiar wave of panic swept over her, and she scanned the empty sky.

Julian gently touched her shoulder, picked up the scattered packages, and guided her into the Berkeley Hotel. He had been following her.

With unsettling solemnity, the maître d'hôtel ushered Catherine through the Savoy, past the immense potted palms, Meyer van Praag's dark-suited orchestra, the chef moving among gleaming copper pots in the windowed kitchen. The rigid smile she offered the maître d', the clumsy flourish of her fan, too tightly gripped, revealed her nervousness.

Julian was late, and she waited, the round diamond on her finger hardening under light from the lamp. She nervously studied the objects arranged on the table like markers on the face of a clock, the tines of the fork, the vertical knives and spoons. Everything seemed significant, signs portending their happiness, Julian's arrival.

Across the room, the maître d' slowly approached Catherine's table, his face bearing an expression of compressed tension as he bowed slightly and stepped aside for a tall man in an impeccable suit. Charles. His face momentarily faded, then reformed as if a wave had covered him, distorting her vision. Julian behind Charles's mask.

'I feel as if I am intruding.' Julian's voice was slightly muffled behind the mask's mouth slit.

'Not at all.' The illusion that he was Charles held if he didn't speak. Instead of the fractional happiness Catherine had anticipated, a stone pressure weighed on her heart.

The black figure of a waiter materialized. 'Madame, monsieur? Will it please you to order?' The *crème de laitues, pilaf de volaille à la* Turque were excellent.

She wished to spare Julian the awkwardness of making his impaired speech understood and quickly whispered they would both order the chef's recommendations.

Julian positioned himself in shadow, offering her only a glimpse of his face. When his eye was turned away and he was silent, he was completely un-readable, a cipher, a man encased in the armor of Charles's face. He moved closer; the candle-light from the table lamp caught his face, and like corrosive salt, it destroyed the illusion of flesh. Catherine interpreted his distress, wordlessly communicated by the strained angle of his neck and shoulders.

The pressure of the cold circle of jewels around her neck, the angle of her heeled shoes, the point of the starched napkin in her lap, unbalanced her. Surely he read her face, knew she had something to confess? The bluntness of skin that cannot lie. With difficulty, she stopped from clutching Julian's jacket in panic.

Julian reached across the table, and at the kind, familiar touch of his hand, Catherine's eyes expanded into tears.

She would beg him to remove the mask.

'Monsieur?'

As dishes were expertly placed on the table, Catherine's smile was directed at the waiter in an effort to blind him to the appearance of the man next to her. The food was exquisite. The mask allowed Julian to sip liquids but not to eat. Catherine silently drank wine, as the pale soup in her bowl cooled, untasted.

The sommelier solicitously interrupted, leaned discreetly over the table to enquire about their lack of appetite, and noticing the eerie immobility of Julian's face, he stiffened, then recovered, motioning that the waiter should attend to their wineglasses.

She was stung with pity, Julian intercepted her look, and in that instant sorrow flickered across his good eye. A splinter formed between them.

Julian abruptly stood up, and the woman at the

next table followed the direction of her husband's astonished glance – unerring as a pencil line on a page – to stare at the strange man. The diners observing Catherine and Julian leave the room sensed something was wrong between them. A lover's quarrel. It was always about the war.

In the motorcar, Julian sat upright against the seat, refusing to touch her. She attempted to speak, but he lifted his hand to stop her words, insisting on silence as they drove to Cranbourne Street. Was he angry? Sorrowful? She interpreted his every action as an accusation against her. The mask was temporary. It could be removed and forgotten. A transgression followed by forgiveness. Like sin. There was a line, a crack between the painted mask and Julian's flesh. She would seek him there.

The bustling crowd in the Drury Lane Theatre ignored Julian, as the chandelier in the lobby gave little light and his mask was scarcely noticeable under his hat. He directed Catherine to their seats in the first tier, explaining he would join her momentarily.

Catherine's nerves were set on edge by the sharp, papery rustle spreading across the theater as programs were opened and examined. She studied the audience below, the men's thick, stern foreheads, the women's bare shoulders rising from the rounded curves of the seats, emanating an air of wholeness. She was repulsed by their confidence, their certainty that they were inviolable.

Her anger dissolved into an unexpected longing for the ill, their hesitant frailty, their gratitude when granted respite from pain. The truth of their bony, suffering figures.

The curtain rose on a performance of meaningless activity. Her fingers curled into claws; her fan dropped into her lap. At this moment – when every face was turned to the stage – she knew Julian was present in the audience. She scanned the aisles and tiers, the rows of seats between the tall columns. She would divine Julian in this place, force him to reveal himself.

The audience applauded, and the movement of their white gesturing hands, strangely shapeless from this angle, seemed marooned in darkness. In the opposite box seat, a lone figure leisurely turned toward Catherine, and in the twilight created by the stage, a spell was cast and Charles was brought back to life.

Catherine stared, then looked away from Charles and back again; each glance struck a shock of recognition followed by the slow waver of disbelief into joy. If her body had been glass, the shift of the emotions that possessed her would have been visible as color. But as the mask became familiar, the illusion faded, and Charles's beloved face became stiff, unmoving, a portrait of a dead man. There was no resurrection. She couldn't fix or save him.

Wild applause signaled the end of the performance, and in the moment she was distracted, Julian vanished. Catherine ran down the stairs.

357

The ceiling settled its elaborate gilt calm over the throng of people in the lobby, chattering, tugging on their coats. A man searched for a dropped glove on the floor. Faint laughter drifted from the aisles. Catherine frantically pushed her way toward a bearded stranger wearing a top hat, who angrily turned around when she mistakenly seized his arm.

Outside, the street was a blank darkness, as every window had been blacked out, the shape of buildings muted against the equally dark sky. An insistent noise in the distance heightened to a siren's shriek, and instantly the invisible current that had held the city in check was broken, and people rushed into the theater, into any open doorway. The globe lamps on the facade of the theater dimmed.

Catherine searched everyone who jostled past, fear seeping into her from their expressions.

'Ma'am, you'd best go back inside,' scolded an elderly man. 'That's a warning siren. Air raid.' When she didn't respond, he shrugged and ducked into the theater.

The siren's wails became more urgent, seeming to transform the sky by sound alone, as it became dirty gray, frayed near the horizon. Thin threads of light stitched the clouds. Searchlights. Another siren repeated, much closer.

'Catherine.'

Julian took her arm, only his eye betraying concern in the expressionless mask, and propelled her into the lobby. They quickly moved with the others down the aisles to the stage, where a distinguished man in a tailcoat shoved aside the heavy curtains.

'Ladies and gentlemen, I can offer you a fine seat below stage,' he boomed.

'Will the price of the seats be lower?' a man called out.

A woman giggled nervously. 'Imagine the orchestra conductor leading an evacuation.'

Holding Catherine's cloak, Julian helped her over the ropes coiled on the floor backstage, then down several flights of steep steps. At that point, most of the group refused to go any farther, preferring to risk remaining where they were. The conductor hastily bid them adieu and guided Catherine, Julian, and a stout, wheezing businessman in a shaky descent down rickety iron stairs. With a flourish, he opened the door into a brick cellar, the shy light of the bare bulbs futile against the cavernous arched space.

Jovial as if guiding a tour, the conductor dusted his hands on the tails of his evening jacket. 'We'll wait out the storm together in this ship. I apologize for the lack of heat.' He shook hands with Julian and Catherine, shivering in velvet. 'But we're completely safe here.'

The conductor and the stout man gallantly pulled boxes and trunks into a clear space so everyone could sit down.

'This is the subcellar storage room where backdrops are stored between productions.' The conductor gestured grandly at a huge canvas flat painted with gray crags and a fiery sunset, and other stacks of flats leaned against the walls. 'I can see the mountains from *Tannhäuser* from here. Although that opera has been removed from the repertoire.'

'Hello? Hello? Is there room for us?' A middle-aged woman and her daughter, a young woman in her twenties with curly dark hair, eased down the rattling stairs, gingerly clutching the rail. Another dilapidated trunk was found to accommodate them, as the jittery young woman refused the conductor's offer to give up his seat.

Catherine clung to Julian as they stood silently in shadow away from the others. She was waiting for the moment to correct the deceit that she had put in motion.

'Please, let's go back upstairs. Take our chances.' The hiss of her whisper vibrated.

Julian woodenly shook his head, and she couldn't tell if he refused her request because of concern or fright.

Everyone but Catherine had previously suffered through a bombardment, and their initial giddy relief at finding shelter soon faded into dull, resentful silence. Time passed. The conductor wished loudly for a deck of cards or a music score to study. No one answered.

'I'm going to amuse myself if the rest of you can't stir yourselves,' the curly-haired young woman announced. As she spontaneously pirouetted before the painted backdrop, the fitful illumination had the effect of obscuring her limbs beneath the weight of her skirt. Glad for a diversion, even a wobbly, eerie parody of a dance performance, the group heartily applauded. As she made exaggerated bows, lights along the walls began to wink erratically.

Catherine fixated on color, her thoughts fiercely burning yellow and orange, praying this would preserve the light. She made cold judgments against herself, swearing to keep certain promises in exchange for escaping this place.

Suddenly, blackness washed over them, absolute as a silent lake. The young woman sank to the floor, whimpering with fright.

'Blast,' a man swore loudly.

'It was her dancing that extinguished the light,' joked the conductor, although there was no amusement in his voice.

'Don't think the authorities could have objected. The girl has talent.'

'It's no comfort, all those bricks above our heads. Ready to bury us.'

'What are you going to do? Well?'

'There's a lantern in my office. I'll fetch it.' The conductor slowly banged his way up the staircase, noisy as a wounded animal. Curses, fumbling, and finally a door squeaked open, admitting a wire-thin line of light.

Darkness magnified sound. Catherine was able to identify everyone by the distinct pattern of his or her breathing, which commanded more space than their invisible bodies. She grew increasingly tense, aware that breath would cease when the air was thick with flying plaster and dust, powdered brick, glass.

The floor vibrated, and a deep rumbling stretched out time, one, two, three breaths.

Fear transformed Catherine, forced her hands, arms, legs, into trembling, clumsy weightlessness. Julian's fingers gently threaded through her hair, caressed her neck. The touch of his hands expanded, became a shield, a raft away from darkness. She pressed herself against him, and locked in an embrace, she wondered if they would perish together. Perhaps in the midst of destruction all around them, they could both be transformed to pillars of stone or salt and be saved.

A droning intensified, moving closer.

'Are we going to die down here?' The young woman wept.

The sound became a shaking that possessed the ground, propelled through Catherine's thin satin shoes, up her legs into the core of her body.

'Never let me go,' Catherine cried against this force, not caring if the others heard her.

A huge crash shook the walls, and their shouts were overwhelmed as the floor tilted free of gravity, and dust and invisible objects rained down in the pitch dark.

Silence. Then coughing, and the middle-aged woman began to moan.

Gasping, Catherine raised her head, spitting out

the rough, bitter grit filming her mouth. 'Julian? Julian?' She inched forward on the floor, grabbed an arm still warm in its sleeve, relieved when his hand responded with a firm clasp. 'Thank God. Thank God. I must tell you—'

'Everyone has last words and regrets,' the stout man interrupted, invisible but nearby. 'Heard the same talk when my boat foundered near Islay. Let's get on with it.'

'That was close.'

Faint movement at the top of the stairs announced the conductor's return, followed by the glowing cylinder of a lantern, clanking and swaying in his hand, his steps blocked by debris.

The lantern was set down in their midst, its light softened by a nimbus of circulating gray powder. Their voices rose, loud with relief, filling the space as they shook the dust from their clothing.

The conductor and the stout businessman crouched together, making bold talk against the powerless indignity of waiting, agreeing that the zeppelins were unable to fly backward or navigate in a gale.

'Trust the enemy to design a machine with a basic flaw. Shows you how shortsighted they are.' The conductor folded his arms with satisfaction.

'We'll knock 'em from the bloody sky.'

'Let us pray the zeppelins have passed and our troubles are over.' The middle-aged woman tugged her shawl closer, and her daughter leaned into the lantern light, her profile in bold relief, staring at Julian.

Catherine squeezed Julian's hand, signaling that he should step away from the lantern light. 'It's all clear now. Let's leave this place,' she pleaded, pulling his arm.

But the young woman wasn't satisfied. 'Wait,' she said. 'Wait. There's something wrong with that man.'

The conductor peered closely at Julian, then looked away. 'The sky is falling, and we all need a bit of luck. Leave him be.'

Catherine sensed her skin contracting, as if fear had diminished her. *Save yourself, Julian*, she thought.

Julian waited, motionless as a statue, as the young woman tipped the lantern, directing its full glare at his face.

'My God, look at him.'

Catherine moved to protect Julian, but he swept her aside. The mask made a deep shadow along his jaw, and only his eye was alive in his uncannily smooth face. With great delicacy, he unhooked the spectacles from his ears, and the entire mask slipped off into his hands, a gesture as simple as drinking from a cup.

The young woman shrieked, and the others instantly recoiled as if they were one body. The lantern fell over; its light ricocheted into huge, exaggerated shapes on the walls, broken by their alarmed shadows. Julian was feared more than the darkness.

'Where is he? Is he gone?'

The two men searched the room, holding the lantern between the flats of scenery, expecting Julian would be crouching there, hiding.

'He has gone.'

The men swung the lantern at Catherine, bleaching her skin and dress white in its glare.

'Who was he?'

'A monster?'

'I don't know,' Catherine whispered. 'I didn't see him. He was standing behind me.'

Not satisfied with her answer, they surrounded Catherine, and her breath hardened in her chest. For a fraction of a second, she was prepared to let the incident pass, to make a joke. To dismiss Julian.

She pushed the conductor aside and stumbled to the stairs, toward the light around the door. Loud footsteps followed her.

'Let her go.'

'For pity's sake, hold the lantern so she can see.'

Catherine's skirt tore on the stair rail and ripped again as she jerked it free, so great was her hurry to reach Julian.

There was slightly more light upstairs, and by the hollow impact of her running feet, Catherine guessed she was back-stage. *If Julian had left the theater, she would never find him. She would be lost.*

Her flailing hands struck a heavy thickness, curtains, and she struggled to find a way around. The curtains admitted a slice of cold air as she slipped through and stood still, darkness blocking any recognition of her surroundings. Her awareness extended into a sense of height, an open space.

'Julian?'

The theater lights slowly returned, everything reestablishing itself in place – the rows of seats, the chandeliers, the length of patterned carpet – before her eyes, and she found herself standing at the edge of the stage. Dizzied, she quickly stepped back.

A man waited in the center of the theater.

'Julian?'

He didn't acknowledge her.

'Julian, forgive me.'

He walked down the aisle, holding his mask in one hand like a shield, stopping in front of the stage.

He was silent for so long, she finally cried, 'What do you want? Tell me. I will do it. I meant—' The pulse of her heart swelled up, filling her throat, choking her.

'One day you'll wish me gone. You can't even recognize it.'

She fell to her knees, her skirt billowing as she held out her arms beseechingly.

A minute passed, then another. The lights that had held steady quickly bled into gray as his tall figure turned and walked swiftly up the aisle.

'Don't leave,' she whispered, then slammed her hand against the floor of the stage.

In the distance, a siren pitched itself higher and higher, soaring in advance of a pounding vibration nearing the theater.

EPILOGUE

At a reception held in the elaborate hall of a civic building, Anna was honored for her wartime work. A prominent Boston socialite had arranged the event, and Anna sat onstage holding an ugly bouquet of carnations, enduring a tedious program of praise for 'Mrs Coleman.' As a girl began to sing, Anna's eyes wandered, and the staring faces in the audience blurred and wavered around Kazanjian, standing in the back of the room. In an agony of impatience, unable to leave the stage, Anna waited through the song and the speeches that followed.

Anna shook hands, bolted from the stage, and, her face stiff with anxiety, forced her way through the crowd, pushing aside a matron attempting to congratulate her.

The double bronze doors at the end of the hall were shut. Kazanjian had disappeared. She stepped outside and found him leaning against a balustrade at the farthest side of the vestibule. He was thinner, more careworn.

'Dr Kazanjian . . . ,' Anna began, then corrected herself at his gesture. 'Yes, Varaztad.'

He returned Anna's smile.

Later, Dr Kazanjian came to the studio behind Anna Coleman's house and walked solemnly around the easels, the modeling stands supporting half-finished busts of a child and a young man. He studied the brushes, paints, chalks, containers of water, cans of turpentine, boxes of plaster and clay, reacquainting himself with her in this way.

'The familiar objects make me feel welcome,' he said softly.

'As you are welcome.'

They spoke of many things that afternoon. He was now teaching at Harvard. He had heard the news about Dr McCleary.

Anna explained she'd stayed at the estate for a time after he'd left for the front. The surgeons had made huge advances, and masks were no longer necessary for the wounded. But the most disfigured patients had remained, waiting for new treatments, for miracles, some men enduring more than forty operations on their faces. Many were still being cared for at the estate.

He received this information like a man hearing news of a foundering ship, miraculously righted, on which he had once booked passage.

'I've had some news of the others,' she said.

'Please tell me.'

'Catherine lived out the war at the estate, volunteering as a nursing aid. She even worked through

370

the influenza epidemic. So many patients died, some in a matter of hours. The medical staff wore masks over their mouths and noses to protect themselves from infection. It seemed the buildings were haunted, as everyone was bandaged or veiled and afraid. The entire estate was in quarantine. It was terrible. Julian had found work as a moving-picture operator in the village cinema. His damaged face was no hindrance in the dark projection room, and it was soundproofed, the walls lined with asbestos because of the highly combustible film. He was one of the lucky few. His relationship with Catherine was entirely unsuspected by anyone else. Until she fell ill and he cared for her.'

So they arrived at what was unspoken between them.

He studied her for a moment. 'Dr McCleary once quoted a Sanskrit proverb to me: "Before you cut, turn the knife seven times in your hand."'

'My dear Varaztad, may we at last abandon such caution?'

He made her wait so long for his answer that the sun through the window became uncomfortable on her shoulder, her body suspended from the ache of her neck.

'I rejoice at your question,' he said finally.

AUTHOR'S NOTE

*T*he Crimson Portrait is a work of fiction. It was inspired in part by two historical figures, Anna Coleman Ladd and Varaztad Kazanjian, and recounts an imagined fragment of their lives. Other characters, names, and incidents are used for the purpose of fiction and are not intended to disparage any actual person, company, or institution.

Memoirs from the Edwardian period as well as World War I were valuable sources for this book. *Memories and Base Details* by Lady Angela Forbes, *Ourselves*, 1900–1930 by Irene Clephane, *Discretions* by Countess Frances Evelyn Greville, and *Turn of the World* by Baroness Elizabeth Wharton Decies evoked the frivolous pleasures of that time. *Bright Armour* by Monica Grenfell Salmond and Lady Diana Cooper's *The Rainbow Comes and Goes* were two young aristocrats' memoirs of their volunteer work in a hospital.

Unknown Warriors by K. E. Luard, *The American Red Cross in the Great War* by Henry P. Davison, and *Observations of an Orderly* by Ward Muir described wartime medical care. Numerous journals provided the history of plastic surgery and details of surgical practice, including *La Revue Maxillo-Facial*, *Journal of the American Medical Association*, *British Medical Journal*, *Proceedings of the Royal Society of Medicine*, and *The Lancet*. Other notable books include *Le Colonel Picot et les Gueules Cassées* by Noele Roubaud and R. N. Brehamet, *Gillies: Surgeon Extraordinary* by Reginald Pound, *The Birth of the Clinic* by Michel Foucault, and *Skin* by Claudia Benthien, translated by Thomas Dunlap. John Marquis Converse's 'The Extraordinary Career of Doctor Varaztad Hovhannes Kazanjian,' published in *Plastic and Reconstructive Surgery*, and *History of the Harvard Dental School* by Richard Locke Hapgood were invaluable in shaping the doctor's character.

I would like to acknowledge the generous contribution of my editor, Terry Adams. For kind permission to research in the Gillies Archives at Queen Mary's Hospital Sidcup, I would like to thank Dr Andrew Bamji, Curator. I also wish to thank the Imperial War Museum, the Armed Forces Institute of Pathology, the Wellcome Institute, and the New York Academy of Medicine.